# THOSE WHO SEEK

ALSO BY TIM STAFFORD

FICTION

*A Thorn in the Heart*
*The Stamp of Glory*
*Sisters*
*The Law of Love*
*Birmingham*
*Those Who Hope*
*Those Who Dream*

NON-FICTION

*Love, Sex and the Whole Person*
*The Friendship Gap*
*The Student Bible*
*Knowing the Face of God*
*As Our Years Increase*
*That's Not What I Meant*
*Never Mind the Joneses*
*Shaking the System*
*Surprised by Jesus*
*Personal God*
*Miracles*
*The Adam Quest*

# THOSE WHO SEEK

A NOVEL

BY TIM STAFFORD

Franklin Park Press




ISBN 978-1-67636-014-8
Visit the author's website at timstafford.wordpress.com

*May those who hope in you not be disgraced because of me;*
*God of Israel, may those who seek you not be put to shame*
*because of me.*

— Psalm 69:6

for Ian

# 1 AT THE MEMORIAL

Elvis Sebastiano paused at the Ft. Bragg Baptist entrance to remove his sunglasses and consider his reflection in the full-length glass door. On his feet were worn, stitched cowboy boots to go with the western-style, sky-blue shirt with pearl snaps. He adjusted his favorite lid, a khaki-colored Aussie-style hat with one brim rolled up and a faux leopard-skin band. His jeans were bright orange. He grinned at himself, thinking he might pass for a minor celebrity.

Would his mother approve? Hard to say. He had seen her so few times in recent years.

Elvis wondered whether he belonged at this service. Would Ray, his mother's new husband, make him welcome? Would Ray's children? You couldn't skip your own mother's memorial, but he felt a little bit like a ghost as he stepped inside the doors.

The church looked like a conference center, with an open vestibule wrapped around a semicircle of theater chairs. He couldn't see a single holy thing about it. The upholstery was teal, with matching carpet down the central aisle. Elvis paused to sign a guest book at a table attended by a grandmotherly figure. He had never gone to this church. His family didn't really go to church much when he was growing up. Part of him felt like he should be welcomed like the Prodigal Son, but he knew that wasn't going to happen. This wasn't really home.

A scattering of people was already seated, mostly gray-headed. Near the front, he saw his brother, Tom, in a black suit. He had hoped for a few other relatives—Aunt Carol and maybe his cousin Rafe or his uncle Noonan—but he didn't see them, and all the other faces were strange. Tom and Francine might be the only people he knew. They gave him the heebie-jeebies. Tom was so square and so judgmental. Still, you had to sit by family at your mother's service.

Aunt Carol's absence disappointed him the most. She was his father's sister, and she lived like a recluse in Garberville. He always liked her, though it had been years. She didn't drive, and they said she only came out after dark. Of course she hadn't come; how would she get here? He could have picked her up if he'd thought of it. Aunt Carol could always make him laugh. She had a tongue on her that could take the skin off a buffalo. His father used to say that, he remembered.

After a moment's hesitation, Elvis went to the front. Rather than sliding past Tom, who was seated on the aisle, he circled around and came into the row from the left side. He nodded to Tom, who looked him up and down as though he had stepped in dog poop.

Somebody had handed Elvis a bulletin with his mother's face on the front. It wasn't a good picture. She looked old, in a way that punched his stomach. What had she been, sixty? Ray turned slightly from the row in front and nodded. He was in a black suit, too. Elvis had only met him once or twice.

Elvis suddenly realized that he had a death grip on the chair in front of him. A sense of overwhelming claustrophobia engulfed him.

He took a deep breath and let it out. He counted to ten. He closed his eyes and tried to remember one of his Bible verses from the New Life program. One blew into his memory, and he grasped at it: "Come unto me, all you who are weary and heavily burdened, and I will give you rest. Take my yoke upon you..." That was as far as he remembered. The rest flew away.

Sometimes he thought that New Life had really changed him. He looked at life with a sharper focus, and everything—his choices, his relationships—seemed to make more sense. Other times, he wasn't sure. Everything got fuzzy. You were supposed to call your sponsor when you felt things crumbling, but how could you make a phone call from your mother's memorial service? That wasn't realistic.

When he opened his eyes again, the band had come on stage. They didn't look like much: a guitar player with gray hair tied in a ponytail, a dumpy bass player, a woman on keyboard who could be somebody's aunt. Only the drummer held Elvis's interest. She looked to be about fourteen, with her hair shaved on the sides of her head. She wore a baggy pair of pink overalls. Thick eye makeup clotted her eyes into dark smudges.

The band started a song that Elvis had learned at the mission three years ago or more: "Lord, I Lift Your Name on High." Apart from the drummer, the band wasn't radical or loud. Elvis went to a church named Breathe. People threw themselves into it at Breathe, and you couldn't predict anything. He had come to today's service hoping for that kind of catharsis and cleansing, and now he sank into the realization that it probably wasn't going to happen. This band was too tame.

When they finished singing, the pastor bounded up on stage with a microphone perched on his face like a fly and his hands stuck in the pockets of his skinny jeans. He was about Elvis's age—forty, maybe—and had shaved his head. "Welcome, everybody," he said. "Welcome to the celebration of the life of Mavis Johnson." The name startled Elvis. It did not seem possible that his mother had become a Johnson. When he looked again at the bulletin, however, he saw that she was indeed Mavis Johnson. No mention of Sebastiano, not anywhere.

"Ray," the pastor said, looking down at Elvis's stepfather, "we really want to strengthen and support you in this time. You and all the family—we want to encourage you that Mavis is with the Lord and is at rest. There's a big hole where she was, and so it's okay to shed a few tears. But it's also okay to say *Hallelujah* for all the beautiful things that we've experienced through Mavis, and an even bigger *Hallelujah* as we celebrate our Lord and Savior Jesus Christ and think what it's like for Mavis to be with him. We want everybody to know that's the beautiful future Christ offers, and it can be theirs, too."

The pastor threw his hands out wide and said a prayer. He then gave a brief eulogy. He admitted that he hadn't gotten to know Mavis in the short time he'd been at Ft. Bragg Baptist, but he knew from talking to Ray and the family she had put her faith in the Lord and lived as a God-fearing Christian. He went on in more generic terms to describe what a godly life looked like and the great results a person could expect. Elvis tuned out when he realized that he knew what the man would say before he said it.

Elvis liked pastors who said surprising things and did surprising things on stage. This wasn't that kind of church.

When the pastor was done, Ray climbed up on stage. He stood with a cordless microphone in one hand, his Adam's apple bobbing. A tall, thin man with a face full of his tragic circumstances, Ray at first couldn't make words come out. His mouth opened slightly, but no sound followed. Ray's grief caught Elvis. He had no feelings for the man—they were barely acquainted—but he wished he could experience the kind of emotions that Ray displayed.

"Mavis and I were married," Ray said and then stopped, unable to continue. He cleared his throat noisily and got control of himself. "For twenty-two years. She was a beautiful woman, inside and out." Ray stopped short again, apologized, and stood silently with his head lowered. The pastor brought him a plastic water bottle and he drank, then stood with his head still down. "I don't know how I'm going to go on without her," he croaked. "She was too young."

*Twenty-two years*? Elvis thought of Ray as his mom's new, short-term husband. Had she been married to Ray longer than to Willard T? Tom was three years older than Elvis, so 13 when their father died, and so maybe Willard T's marriage to their mom had lasted 15 or 16 years. But yeah, surely Ray and his mom had been together longer. That was a surprise.

Ray's voice grew stronger as he talked. He was actually pretty likable, if you gave him a chance. When he was done, two of his kids got up—Shari, who was 14, and Ricky, who was older but still in high school. Ricky was pretty cute. He was a skinny, dweeby kid, but he had a jokey side that reminded Elvis of his mom. He told a story about her obsession with chocolate. The story wasn't really funny, but everybody in the church made a comfortable laughing sound. Elvis was struck by the fact that he didn't know anything about his mother's chocolate obsession. She had been mostly MIA when he was a kid, which he couldn't blame her for. She had lost her husband. By the time she woke up and wanted to be in his life, Elvis was in prison.

After the two kids, the pastor opened it up for other memories. Several people spoke, but nobody even mentioned him or Tom or the fact that his mother had another marriage and another life. It wasn't right, Elvis thought, and the more he thought it, the more offended he became. Twenty-two years was a lot, but it didn't wipe out everything else.

Elvis tried to get Tom's attention, but whether intentionally or not, Tom wasn't hearing. He had his face set in a frown, which could be what he thought you should wear to a funeral, or it could be annoyance. Tom always looked annoyed to Elvis. He leaned across Francine to poke Tom's shoulder.

"You going to say anything?" Elvis asked in a low voice. Tom shook his head. "C'mon, it's like we don't exist." Tom shrugged and turned away.

Elvis raised his hand, signaling to the pastor that he wanted to speak. He wasn't seen at first—he thought he was deliberately ignored—but eventually got the mike.

People had been standing at their seats to talk into the cordless mike, but Elvis decided to go up on the stage, where he could be seen. After he hopped up the stairs, he scanned the auditorium. It was more people than he had realized. He wasn't used to speaking to large groups.

"I just wanted to say a word for me and Tom, my brother. I'm Elvis. Tom is the oldest of all my mom's children. He's married to Francine. Hey, you two wave so people can see you."

Tom gave the slightest shoulder-high wave, scowling.

"The name is Sebastiano," Elvis said. "My mom was Mavis Sebastiano long before she was Johnson. No offense. I just don't think you can leave out that part of her life."

Elvis was of medium height, with shaggy dirty-blond hair that stuck out from under his hat. He was ruggedly built, sturdy and muscular, with tattoos running all up his arms and around his neck. He had an attractive way of grinning when he didn't know what to say.

"I realize a lot of you people don't even know that we exist. You're probably pretty surprised to see me and realize there's a whole story about Mavis that you never knew. See, my father, Willard T. Sebastiano, was a fisherman. He had his own boat, the Bonnie Belle, right here in Ft. Bragg. And one day when I was ten and Tom was about thirteen, he went out and he didn't come back. I don't think there was even a storm. He just disappeared in the big old Pacific Ocean and was never seen again. Lost at sea.

"My mother was a total case after that. I was just a kid, but I can tell you, she was crying all the time. The truth is, she wasn't much of a mother from then on. I'm not blaming her or anybody, but it's true. I mean, Tom and me, if we wanted anything, we had to get it for ourselves. Even food. She never cooked. Tom handled it all fine, and he turned out great. I mean, you may not know this, but he played in the NFL for two or three years. For the Bengals. Made some money and saved it like everybody says you should and nobody does, and came back to Ft. Bragg to raise his family. He's a real Ft. Bragg fan. Go Timberwolves! But me, I started drinking by the time I was twelve, and then I did drugs and I cut school. I was in juvenile hall, and when I got to eighteen, I graduated to jail time. Then prison. And more drugs, which were the cause of all those problems, if you want to get it down to basics. If I hadn't done any drugs, I wouldn't have gotten in trouble. At least I don't think so."

Elvis stopped and scanned the congregation. They weren't smiling, but they weren't scowling, either. Even Tom looked like he had gotten over whatever ruler was up his butt.

"I'm clean and sober now, and I wish my mom had lived to see it. She tried, but life was just too hard for her a few years there."

Elvis realized he had gotten carried away and forgotten what the service was for.

"Somewhere in there, my mom stopped crying and started a new life, but I was already gone. Tom was gone, too, for college. He played at USC. Pretty good, from what I heard. Right, Tom?" Elvis winked at Tom just to tweak him. Tom would hate it. He never talked to anybody about his football career.

"That's when my mom met Ray, and the rest is history. I wasn't even invited to their wedding. That wasn't their fault. I was in San Quentin. I couldn't have come even if they had thought to invite me. But I wasn't really part of Mom's life, and she wasn't part of mine.

"So, now you know." Elvis shrugged and gave a charming smile. The scar that ran down his left cheek didn't keep him from being a handsome man. "The untold story of Mavis Sebastiano. Mom, wherever you are, if you can hear me, I hope you know that you aren't forgotten, and we love you. You did the best that you could. I know that you loved Willard T and all the rest of us. Just wanted everybody to know."

As he hopped off the stage, Elvis heard a sound from the back of the auditorium and looked up to see someone exiting the main door. Whoever it was disappeared before he could make out anything. Maybe somebody was offended. Maybe somebody just needed to go to the bathroom.

The band came back and they all sang the Lord's Prayer together. The pastor paused by Ray's row and ushered him and his wife and children solemnly down the central aisle, all eyes on them. Then it was Tom's turn, and Elvis followed him and Francine out.

* * *

At the graveside, Ray came up and shook his hand. "I'm sorry you got left out of the service," Ray said. "We didn't know how to contact you."

"That's okay," Elvis said. "I got to say my piece. You couldn't reach Tom, either? He's in the phone book."

Ray stared at him as though he had temporarily contracted Alzheimer's. The pastor rescued him. "Take it from me," he said, "when people are grieving, they don't always remember everything. I'm sure it wasn't deliberate."

"Yeah, I'm sure," Elvis said. "No problem. Tom and I are only her oldest kids."

Ray stared at him stonily. "I guess she probably remembered you. I'm not a hundred percent sure. It would have been easier to tell if you'd come around once every ten years or so."

Elvis was not the kind to take offense. He grinned. "Yeah, you're right. Life."

"Yeah, life," Ray said.

"But don't talk that way to Tom," Elvis added. "He wouldn't appreciate it."

Only a handful of people had made the trek from the church, and their little huddle of three was the only one that seemed to be talking. Elvis looked around, surprised that he didn't recognize anybody. He was a friendly guy, Ft. Bragg was a small town, and usually he couldn't go anywhere without somebody coming up and reminding him that they had sat next to each other in eighth grade Spanish. He liked that. It was one of the few things he liked about Ft. Bragg.

The sky was overcast, and you could feel the chill coming in off the ocean, so fat with moisture that it could turn into fog in an instant. Nobody wanted to linger. The funeral director herded them into two rows of green-covered chairs set under a white canopy, and they got to stare at the casket for a few minutes while the pastor and the funeral director whispered together. It didn't look like the pastor had done this very often.

It was an old cemetery, set near the creek on the north side of town, with statues of angels and a variety of headstones. Old, shaggy trees. Elvis tried to think whether he had ever been up here before, but he couldn't remember. He must have been here for his dad. Of course, they never found the body. Maybe they never had a service. He could ask Tom.

Elvis thought that he did remember going with his mom to visit his father's grave. Was it here? He vaguely remembered that the cemetery was old, and how many old cemeteries could there be in Ft. Bragg? He ought to find out where that grave was. He knew he wouldn't, though. He didn't want to spend a day in Ft. Bragg that he didn't have to.

The pastor read a series of verses from the Bible. He said a prayer and announced that Ray had invited everybody to his house. They didn't even lower the casket into the ground. Elvis had expected to throw a handful of dirt on it, like in the movies, but when everybody stood up and started shaking hands, he saw that wasn't going to happen.

He stood for a while trying to gather in the moment, to feel the solemnity of burying his mother, but nothing happened. Nobody approached him. He had driven up from Santa Rosa this morning, and he thought that he might as well drive back down. There was nothing to stay for.

He was just about to go when he felt a hand on his elbow. He turned to see a round-faced man about his own age. "Elvis?" the man asked. "It's Marvin."

"Hey, Marvin," Elvis answered. He had no memory of this rosy face, an orb fringed with hair.

"It's been too long," Marvin said.

"Yeah, it has. Hey, remind me of how I know you. I can't quite place it."

A little jet of hurt pinched Marvin's face. "That's okay," he said. "I've changed a lot. I've lost a lot of weight."

"I bet you have," Elvis said. "Good for you."

"The Rockies?" Marvin said.

"The Rockies?" Elvis repeated. He could not close the loop. Then, something in the experience of forming the words in his mouth brought it home. "Oh, the Rockies!"

"You got it!" Marvin said, delighted. "You remember that play at third?"

Marvin was emerging from the clouds. Little League. The Rockies were his team. Had Marvin been that fat kid who always sat on the bench?

"You had the candy bars!" Elvis said.

"Snickers!" Marvin replied with glee. "You remember the play at third?"

He didn't. "Yeah, kinda. Remind me."

"You have got to remember that. It was the White Sox. Seventh inning, and if we won, we would go to the championship round. We were ahead by two runs, and Stevie Farris hit a single to right field, right to me."

Of course he would be playing in right field; where else? "And you threw him out?" Elvis was guessing. He couldn't remember a play from Little League when he was twelve years old.

"No, no, no! Well, kinda. I threw to second, but it was so high it went over everything and hit the pitcher's slab. Crazy! It bounced back right to you at short, and you made this dive and tagged Stevie out just before he got to third. So we won."

"So we won! Man, I'd forgotten. What a play, right?"

"Yeah," Marvin said. "I could never forget that."

"So what are you up to these days?" Elvis asked. They had started walking away from the grave, toward the parking lot. Elvis was glad to have connected with somebody.

"Oh, not too much. I work the night shift at Me'n'Eds."

"Meanheads?" He was puzzled.

"Oh come on," Marvin said. "Now you're really pulling my leg. I'm sure you remember Me'n'Eds. Man, it's been here for forty years."

"My memory is terrible."

"Me'n'Eds Pizza?"

"Oh, yeah!" He didn't really remember. "So, you knew my mom?"

"No, not really. I mean, I probably saw her when we were playing Little League. But I didn't really know her. I saw her obituary and I thought I might see you."

"Man, that was nice of you."

"Not really," Marvin said, filled with sincerity. "Your brother is like the most famous person to ever come out of Ft. Bragg. And then you."

"Me?"

"What you did in the fires down there. It was all written up in the paper. I still have a copy of that."

It was not easy to embarrass Elvis, but this did slightly. In the firestorm that had devastated Santa Rosa two years ago, he had rescued a lady in a wheelchair. He got his fifteen minutes of fame from it.

"They kinda exaggerated that," he said. "It happened by accident." Then, without premeditation, he wrapped his arms around Marvin and planted a big, fat kiss on his forehead.

When Marvin extricated himself, he had turned a delicate shade of cherry. "Why'd you do that?" he asked.

"That's what famous people do," Elvis replied. "They're always kissing people, didn't you know?" He gave a hoot of a laugh. "Nah, I don't know; it's just nice of you to be so nice."

That shut Marvin up. He kept silent as they walked down the path toward Elvis's pickup. Ordinarily, Elvis enjoyed talking, but he was glad for the quiet. It was a lot of trouble to regather childhood memories.

Tom was waiting for him by the cars, glowering as though they had an appointment for a fight. "Why don't you come by the house?" Tom said. "You can eat dinner with us and stay the night."

* * *

They didn't even offer wine. Tom and Francine both drank, so they must have agreed to skip the alcohol because they thought he couldn't handle it. Elvis wished he had stopped for a beer on the way to their house; he could use something to take the edge off the agitation he felt whenever he was around Tom.

Elvis hadn't been to the house since before Grams died. He missed her. She would have had something to say to that asshole Ray. When his daughter, Amber, was living here, Grams had followed her from room to room, trying to talk to her. Amber had hated that and begged him to take her back to Santa Rosa. He had tried and failed to explain to Amber that Grams was just lonely.

"You got a beer?" Elvis asked. He wanted to stir things up. They were in the kitchen, trying to make talk. Elvis sat at the counter, but Tom couldn't even sit. He paced, and when he paced, you noticed it, because he was the size of a forklift.

Tom glanced at Francine. For sure they had talked about this. He looked back to Elvis with that maddening *I'm-your-daddy* face. "I thought that you had gone clean and sober."

"Well, yeah, I am, but a beer isn't going to hurt me."

"I thought you couldn't touch anything."

"Fine, Dr. Sebastiano; if you don't want to give me a beer, that's okay."

"I didn't say that."

"It's fine; never mind."

In truth, Elvis knew he shouldn't drink. Alcohol had never been his drug of choice, but it had a lot of associations with things that were. He knew what his sponsor would say. It was exactly the same thing Tom would say. When Tom said it, though, Elvis always felt the contempt in his voice. He remembered one particular time Tom had driven to Santa Rosa just to lecture him about drugs, as though he didn't already know what was bad for him.

Elvis told himself he needed to let that go. "Let me ask you," he said, "I couldn't remember a service for Dad. They must have had one, didn't they?"

"I don't think so," Tom said.

"Where is he buried?"

Tom blew air out of his mouth. "He was lost at sea."

"But I remember going with Mom to his grave. I'm almost sure."

Tom shook his head. "When was this?"

"When I was just a little kid. I remember Mom putting some wildflowers on the grass and telling me that Dad was in heaven."

Tom shook his head. "I have no idea what that was. Maybe you dreamed it. They never found him, so I don't see how he could have a grave."

"Don't they sometimes just pretend there's a body and put up a headstone?"

Tom shook his head as though out of pity. He didn't even bother to answer.

"How long till dinner?" Elvis asked Francine. "I want a smoke." She had been a looker in high school, and today she had dressed up and worked on herself, so she looked great. She was doing something with chicken, slapping around big, slippery slabs in a sauce.

"Outside," Tom said. "We don't allow smoking in the house."

"Yeah, I get it. How long before we eat?"

"Half an hour," Francine said. "Don't go far."

Darkness had fallen, but in the gray twilight, he could make out rough grasslands and a gleam of silvery pink in the west. Tom and Francine's house was a California-ranch-style on the headlands south of the Noyo River bridge. Elvis envied them the open land. He told Tom every time he visited that there was plenty of room for a horse, which Tom ignored. It was just as well. A horse would need a fence. Right now, Elvis was glad for no fences to block a dirt path running down to the sea cliffs. He lit a cigarette and sucked a deep breath. Better than a beer, really, for calming his nerves. He walked out to the road and thought about going for a stroll. There was no traffic; the road dead-ended a half mile west, accessing only six or eight houses. People lived out here if they didn't want neighbors. Some of them were drug dealers, and others were like Tom, just antisocial. Funny how everybody coped differently. Elvis had become fast and funny, a good-time Charlie always looking for a laugh or a fight. He knew this about himself. Tom had retreated into moods.

Elvis walked toward the ocean, his eyes adjusting to the darkness. He passed an old car parked halfway on the road and caught a whiff of whiskey: somebody in there, doing something that Elvis didn't want to know about. When he was just past, the car door opened; Elvis heard it and turned quickly, ready to fight.

"Hey," a man's voice said.

"Hey," Elvis answered. "What's up?"

"Are you Elvis?"

"Yeah. Who are you?"

The man chortled. "You ever heard of somebody named Willard T?"

For once, Elvis didn't know what to say.

"Speak up!" the man said. "You know anybody of that name?"

"My dad was named Willard T."

Elvis could see a dark shape but no face, no clothes. He felt the warmth of his cigarette in his hand and lifted it to his mouth, taking a long draw.

The man chortled again. "Yeah, that's right. We're talking about me. I'm your dad."

"My dad died thirty years ago."

"So they told you. Did you ever see his body?"

"He was lost at sea."

"So they told you. Ever think what an easy alibi that is? A man disappears without a shred of evidence except the Pacific Ocean. Very hard to disprove unless you find the man walking around somewhere."

Elvis thought the man was pulling his leg for no obvious reason. It annoyed him, but he played along. He was a kidder himself. "Okay," Elvis said, "if you're my dad, prove it."

"Like how?"

"I don't know; that's for you to figure out."

"Okay, ask me something that only Willard T would know."

"Like what?"

"Like the name of your Pop Warner team."

Elvis snorted. "There you go. You already blew it. I never played Pop Warner. I was too young."

"You did too. I remember. You were the Broncos."

Elvis snorted again and almost laughed. "Tom was a Bronco. I'm Elvis. If you're going to pretend you're my father, you gotta learn to keep us straight."

To Elvis's surprise, the man seemed delighted by this comment. The dark silhouette of his body bent over in laughter, like a cartoon character. The man laughed with a rough, herky-jerky sound. Then he said, "You're right—I never did learn how to remember which of you was which. I would go through everybody's name, including the dog. Whose name was Traveler. Did I get that right?"

Elvis said nothing in reply. There had been a dog named Traveler. Lots of people might know that—the neighbors, for example—but not some random stranger.

"Who are you?" Elvis asked.

"I told you. I'm Willard T. Ask me something else. Go ahead."

"I don't get your game. I just buried my mother today, and I'm not really in a cheerful mood." He felt, as a matter of fact, just a little spooked. When your mother dies, you think about the world beyond, and you don't like to meet people who claim to have come back from the dead.

"Yeah, I was at the service. Can't a father talk to his son? Does that have to be a game?"

"You weren't at the service. I would have seen you."

"I left early."

"Did you hear me talk?"

"Of course I heard you. That's why I'm here. You made the old man proud. Good for you, standing up for the Sebastiano name."

A little pause came, as though shyness had overcome them both. The man asked, "Do you believe me now?"

"Hell no! Why should I believe you? What do you want out of me? This is a pretty weird sales pitch for whatever you're selling."

"Sheesh, can't a father come and talk to his son? Does there have to be an angle?"

"If you've been gone for thirty years, you better have a freaking angle."

The voice grew low and kittenish. "I just might have an explanation for that, if you talk nice."

In the sky above them, the fog ripped open momentarily and revealed a jagged strip of stars. Elvis looked up, disoriented, as though he were floating in space. The dark around him seemed very black, and he was suddenly cold.

"Could we go somewhere to carry on this conversation?" he asked. "You want to come inside the house and talk to Tom?"

The man chuckled. "Is Tom still chewing on a pickle?"

Elvis laughed. He was beginning to wonder if it was true, if this really could be his father. "Yeah."

"Then let's go somewhere else. Let's go to a bar."

"I don't drink," Elvis said automatically. "I'm in recovery."

"You and half the universe. I think they still sell Cokes in bars, don't they?"

* * *

They drove into town in the man's big Buick, neither one saying a word. Several times Elvis started to talk, but he came up short, not knowing how to begin. Elvis regretted not driving himself. He didn't know what he was getting into here. Halfway up Main Street, he tried to point them to the North Coast Brewing Company, but the man waved him off and cruised to a dive on Franklin.

It was an old-fashioned bar, dark and snug. They found an empty booth, and for the first time, Elvis was able to look closely at the man's face. It was an ordinary white-bread face, without beard or mustache, without tattoos or other decoration. It needed a shave. The man stared back at Elvis with whimsical amusement on his lips. He seemed to be enjoying himself, which irritated Elvis until he caught himself. *Come on, why get so prickly? This should be a lark.*

"I can't see myself in you at all," he said to the man.

"That's funny. I always thought you were the spitting image."

"You got any ID?" Elvis asked.

The man pulled a wallet out of his hip pocket and tossed a license across the table.

The picture could have been anybody, or a toad. In a broad bubble of face, you could make out a nose and two buggy eyes. "Willard Trevor Sebastiano," Elvis read. "Trevor?"

"I go by that now," the man said. "People call me Trev."

"I liked Willard T better."

"You can use that if you want. Or you can call me Dad." For some reason, that tickled his funny bone, and he bubbled and fizzed before giving up on keeping it down and breaking out a serious belly laugh. It froze Elvis. It wasn't how he remembered his father, who was strong and tough and strict. His father was tall. You didn't cross him. If this really was his father, he wasn't the man of Elvis's memories.

The waitress brought their drinks—a Coke and a beer with a whiskey chaser. "Bottoms up," the man said cheerfully and took a long, deep swallow.

"Okay, explain," Elvis said. "You weren't lost at sea, but you disappeared. You got a story? What happened?"

The man took another deep swallow. Elvis noticed that he had a bald spot at the crown of his head. "It's not a story. You want to know what happened—it's simple. I got in the boat and I didn't come back. Your mom, God rest her soul, made up all that lost-at-sea crap."

"Let me tell you something," Elvis said with a touch of heat. "I was just ten, but I swear, she cried for days. Weeks. Months, probably. Tom and me, we had to get our own meals. God, I hate peanut butter to this day. We had to get ourselves to school. I think Tom paid the electricity bill because she couldn't get her act together to do it."

"I know. I heard you in the service."

"So she must have believed that lost-at-sea crap."

The man looked like he was trying to make up his mind whether to laugh again. It exasperated Elvis. "What do you think is so funny?"

"What are you, almost forty? And you don't know that there are lots of things a woman can cry over besides 'lost at sea'?"

"Then what was she crying for? Because I experienced it. She wasn't faking anything."

"Women might cry if their husband leaves them for another woman. Don't you think?"

Elvis had seen a lot of the world in his 38 years, but he was not prepared to flip his entire life story on its head. Without realizing it, however, he had stopped doubting whether Willard T was telling the truth. He knew, somehow, that he was getting a mouthful of truth, but it was too much to swallow in one bite.

Could his mother have kept up the lie for all these years? As soon as he thought the question, Elvis realized that he hadn't seen his mother more than a half a dozen times since he was 16. She didn't have to be a good liar. Also, it was a good bet nobody pushed her very hard; you don't question "lost at sea." Willard T was right—it was a good alibi.

"She knew where you were?"

He waved his hand at the barmaid, indicating that he wanted another. "Ah, no. I just left. Maybe she really did think I was out there under six hundred feet of cold water. I doubt it, though. She'd screamed at me enough to have a pretty good idea what I thought about her. I assume that she collected from my insurance. Did she?"

"How would I know? I was ten." Elvis tried to think whether there were major purchases in that period. He couldn't remember any.

Willard T was going at his second beer like a man who has worked a long shift in the hot sun. He wiped his mouth with the back of his hand. "So now you believe me? I haven't seen you in what, twenty-eight years? But I kept up with you and Tom. Read all about you in the papers."

"You mean for football?"

"That, and when you got old enough to get your name in the paper for other stuff." Elvis didn't have to ask what he meant. It was amazing how many people read those police reports.

"Yeah, well, you probably haven't seen my name in quite a while, because I've quit using."

"Good for you. Twelve steps?"

"Sure. I got into this New Life program at the Sonoma Gospel Mission, and it turned me around."

"Is that a religious program?"

"It is," Elvis said.

"Good for you," his father said.

Truthfully, it had taken some time to really get sober. He had come out from New Life feeling strong, but then he'd had several slip-ups. It wasn't until the fires that he had been able to put everything together and keep it together.

He was still clean, but as of today, he felt shaky. He hadn't been to a meeting in months. He hadn't been to church, either. He wanted to sleep through everything he knew he needed, and he couldn't explain why. He just wasn't motivated. For that very reason, he had wanted a Spirit-filled service today. He needed something to pick him up.

And now, this stranger was turning his life story upside down. His life made sense if you accepted that he was victimized by an accident. If his father hadn't drowned, his mother wouldn't have fallen apart, and he wouldn't have run wild and begun experimenting with drugs. One thing led to another, but it wasn't anybody's fault. Accidents happen. If it was true what this man said, though, he wasn't so much a victim of circumstances as of abandonment. Not only that—he had been lied to for decades. You could say that the end result was the same, but it put his life on a more squalid level. It wasn't fate. It wasn't the wheel of fortune. It was crappy choices by crappy people.

He had to swim his way through it before he got his head to the surface.

"So tell me," Elvis asked. "Where did you go? Do you still have the boat? You still fish?"

"Oh yeah," Willard T said. "Once you get seawater in your blood."

"Where do you dock?" There weren't many options near Ft. Bragg.

"Oh, it's a big ocean. I've been all over. Best place for fishing is Alaska these days."

"You took it all the way up there?" Elvis was surprised. He wasn't even sure it was possible to take a small boat that far.

Willard T didn't seem to hear him. He was flagging down the barmaid for another drink.

"You better take it easy on that stuff," Elvis said.

"I'm just getting started." Willard T looked at him and grinned. "I know, you don't drink. I do."

* * *

Willard T drove wildly, recklessly, back to Tom's house. It didn't worry Elvis too deeply. He had taken more than his share of drunken midnight rides in his lifetime. If it was your time, it was your time, he figured.

Actually, he took some giddy pleasure from the ride. They streamed through the darkness like a flaming chariot. This really was his father. When you grow up wild, and teachers and cops and even grocery checkers ask you why you act so crazy, why you can't take an easier pathway, why you have to be such an asshole, you begin to think there isn't any explanation other than that you're just a mutant, a two-headed calf. Watching his father's drinking, his driving, his way of behaving, his talking, his animation, Elvis could see where he got his personality. It was fun, it was partly attractive, it was largely annoying...and Elvis knew that was just what he was. He liked being what he was.

They pulled up to the house, which was a blackened box against the lighter sky. Not a single window shone with light; Elvis hoped they hadn't locked him out.

"I was going to ask you in to see Tom, but it looks like they have all gone to bed."

"Yeah," Willard T said. "No point spoiling a beautiful day."

It came back to Elvis then that he had buried his mother today. He hadn't thought of it all evening, nor had they really mentioned it. Maybe it was too awkward.

"Why did you come to Mom's service?" he asked. "After all these years?"

"She was a good woman. And I was hoping I could see you."

"Me? Why me?"

"Are you a father? If you were, you would understand."

Elvis remembered that he was a father, and that he had not even considered asking Amber along with him on this trip. He felt guilty for that, now that he thought of it. They had buried her grandmother, after all, even if she had barely even met her.

"Okay, you're right; I get it. I'm still getting used to you being alive."

"Okay, kid. Get used to it, and see you later."

"Wait," Elvis said. "You never told me where you live."

"And I'm not going to tell you. I don't want you to think you can just show up any old time."

Elvis opened the door and began to get out of the car. "I wouldn't just show up. You don't know much about me if you think I would do that."

"Not taking any chances." Elvis was half in, half out of the car. "Give me your phone number," Willard said. "I'll call you and we can get together."

Elvis stopped exiting and lowered his head to look in at Willard. "You give me yours," he said.

There was a pause in which Elvis wondered what kind of expression was riding Willard T's face. The car light wasn't enough for him to see.

"Okay," his father said. "I'll shoot you a text. What's your number?"

"Do it now," Elvis said. "Before I go inside."

* * *

Elvis found a note on his bed, telling him to lock up. He sat looking at his phone, at his father's number. He was tempted to call him now, but he didn't. He didn't want to seem weird. He had a feeling that if he acted too anxious, Willard would just disappear. He was like an animal that didn't want to let anybody get too close.

When he got in bed, Elvis lay awake thinking of the day. He could barely believe that he had met his father. He wanted to ask his mother why she had lied to him all these years. Was it the insurance money? He didn't think so. It came to him that his father still had his driver's license, and the boat—assuming he wasn't lying—had to keep its registry. He must have been hiding in plain sight. Had anyone reported his disappearance to the police? To the Coast Guard? Maybe not. What had been in the newspaper, if anything?

He guessed you could look up some of that, but he knew he wasn't going to. It wasn't like him. Then Elvis chortled. Yeah, he was like Willard T. Just do it half-ass. Elvis fell asleep thinking about that.

In the morning, he dragged himself out of bed before anybody else and sat in the kitchen. He didn't know how to work the coffee maker. If he tried and screwed something up, Tom would be all over him. Wishing for some company, Elvis wanted to go and wake up one of them. He couldn't believe what had happened to him, and he wondered what they would think.

After what seemed to be an hour of sitting helplessly restless and bored, Elvis slipped out the door and drove into town. He felt horribly achy and doped, and that was without a hangover. Maybe he had soaked in some of the old man's booze. There had certainly been enough of it.

He found a local version of Starbucks on Main Street and plunged down in a sagging armchair with a large paper cup of black coffee. The barista was a young, skinny thing with spiky hair. She looked worse than he felt. Elvis tried to get something going with her, but she didn't even look at him, let alone answer in a full sentence.

"Come on," he said from his seat. "You're not going to talk to me?"

That at least got her to look up. She yawned deeply, showing her fillings without even covering her mouth, and then went back to fiddling behind the counter. After a few minutes sipping joe, Elvis got up and went to his truck, thinking he would sit somewhere off the highway looking at the waves. When he started the pickup, however, he thought of the cemetery.

That was one piece of the puzzle that wouldn't fit. Everything about his father's death was fogged in his memory, but pictures of the grave were brilliant and clear. He was sure that his mother had taken him to put flowers on it. Was that possible? Had they actually gone to the trouble of faking a grave? How weird was that? His father wouldn't necessarily know about it; his brother apparently didn't; and everybody else was dead.

The cemetery was located along Pudding Creek, just a couple of blocks off Main. The newer section had flat headstones, ground-level granite squares you couldn't see unless you were standing right on top of them. Nobody in their right mind would want to be buried that way. You might as well plant your loved ones in the middle of a football field.

The old section, with its tall, drooping trees and its varied monuments, almost defeated him. He realized he would have to look at hundreds of headstones. Maybe thousands. It wasn't in Elvis's character to search systematically. He wandered through the grounds, sipping at his coffee and feeling revived just from being out in the air. The inscriptions were interesting. Some of the old headstones had what amounted to a mini-sermon. *Blessed are those who rest in the Lord. Too well loved to ever be forgotten.* It was like the old folks wanted to get in one last word.

It made Elvis wonder what he would say. He knew some guys at the mission who had a life verse they were always pulling out. He had nothing like that.

On the far edge of the cemetery, bordered by bushes, he saw a backhoe and a flatbed truck. Elvis walked over and found three men standing around the equipment, one of them enormously fat with wide jowls. The other two reminded Elvis of ferrets. He couldn't see that they were doing anything.

"Hey guys," Elvis said. "You digging a grave?"

They just stared, as though he had addressed them in a foreign language.

Elvis noticed a rolled-up carpet of turf. "How do you do it? You roll up the grass before you start digging with the backhoe?"

They still stared at him. Maybe they didn't speak English, Elvis thought.

"How do you get the corners square using a backhoe? Do you have to get in there with a shovel to finish?" Elvis was beginning to feel tickled by the one-way nature of the conversation. It was funny, if you thought about it. "Let me take a look." He stood on the edge of the hole, where the backhoe's teeth had carved two straight cliffs in the reddish clay. It was deep and dark enough that he couldn't really see the bottom. "I'm going to get in there and have a look-see." Elvis bent over, put one hand on the edge of the grave, and jumped in.

He wasn't really prepared to fall six feet. The landing jolted him right to his teeth. It was darker inside than he had expected, too. He was staring at four walls and the light was over his head, as though he were staring up from a shallow well. "Can't see a thing in here!" Elvis shouted. "Throw me a shovel and I'll see if I can square the corners!"

Nobody answered. He couldn't really see the corners, anyway. Elvis stuck his back into one wall and his feet on the opposite wall, working his way to the top of the hole. The three men were still standing, staring. "Give me a hand?" he said and stuck out a paw. Nobody moved to help, so he flipped himself over and clawed his way out. He stood up, panting and dusting himself.

"Do any of you speak English?" he asked.

"Yeah, we speak," the enormous one answered. "Are you okay?"

"Sure; fantastic. I'm fine. Hey, you don't know how I can find out where my dad is buried, do you?"

But the little window of communication had closed. They stared at him, uncomprehending.

"Okay," Elvis said. "I'll just be going along. The name is Elvis Sebastiano. You seen any headstones with Sebastiano? No? No comprende? That's okay."

He wandered until purely by chance, he found what he was looking for. It was a beautiful old slab of marble with stylized letters cut deep into its slick surface. Willard T Sebastiano. So they actually did it. What did one of these things cost? It raised the further question, why had they gone to so much trouble and expense? Surely not to fool a ten-year-old boy. Maybe there had been insurance money after all.

He stared at the thing for several minutes before realizing the dates were wrong. They were off by forty years. *What the*? This was making him crazy. He should have paid more attention in school; he would be able to think about stuff like this. His mind worked like a chipper, grinding and churning. Then like a flash it came to him: this must be his grandfather's grave. Or if not his grandfather, then some other relative.

Okay, but how strange was that? Why would his mother bring flowers for his father's father? He wasn't her blood. It only made sense if she intended to trick Elvis. A ten-year-old boy can read his dad's name on the stone, but she must have bet he wouldn't notice the dates. Which he didn't.

It seemed to Elvis that it was the saddest revelation of his life. His father had deserted. His own mother had pulled the wool over his eyes. He had truly been abandoned—not just by one of them, but by both.

Impulsively, he pulled out his phone to call his father. Maybe he could shed some light on it. After all, he had come back into Elvis's life, even if 30 years too late. When he called his father's number, however, a recorded message said that the mailbox was full.

* * *

Some deeper instinct made Elvis want to tell his brother. They had grown up apart, but they had been deceived together. At least, Elvis assumed so. He wasn't absolutely sure what they had told Tom.

He drove his old, dented, blue Toyota pickup by Tom's lumber yard, thinking that he might see his truck. Tom was part owner and made sure you knew it. He knew practically nothing about the lumber business, but he did like to go in during office hours to demonstrate that he was a jerk. Tom's truck wasn't there, so Elvis proceeded south over the bridge.

He found Tom at home in the kitchen, eating a bowl of Cheerios and scowling. He didn't look up until Elvis said, "Hey."

"You been out?"

"Yeah, I went to get some coffee."

"There's coffee here."

"Yeah, but I don't know how your machine works. I probably would have electrocuted myself."

"No doubt."

Elvis pulled up a stool to sit opposite his brother at the counter. He very strongly wished for a connection. "Tom, last night, when I was out taking a walk, I saw Dad."

Tom raised his head. "How did he look?"

Elvis was surprised and gratified by the response until he realized that Tom was being sarcastic.

"I mean really. Tom, he's alive. Did you know it? I drove into town with him."

Tom finally looked at him with a bored, deadpan expression. "So that's where you disappeared to. Did you check his ID?"

"I did, as a matter of fact. It's really him. He didn't die. He left. He took the boat somewhere. I don't actually know whether Mom thought he was dead or whether she was in on the game. She might have collected some insurance. Do you know anything?"

Francine came into the kitchen at that moment, still in a worn terrycloth bathrobe, her hair straggling down around her ears. "Good morning," she said. "You boys catching up?"

Tom forced a laugh. "Yeah. I just learned that Elvis saw a ghost last night. He thinks he saw my dad."

"Wow." Francine poured herself some coffee.

"I'm serious," Elvis said. "All these years he's been..." He stopped mid-sentence because he did not know where his father had been or what he had been doing.

"Did you get a picture?" Tom asked.

"No, but I got his phone number."

Tom shook his head as though in pity.

"What?

"When you went outside, what were you smoking?"

"I told you yesterday, I'm not using."

Tom raised his eyebrows.

Elvis was hot in an instant. "You think I'm using? Look at me; don't give me that. What makes you think you know anything? I'm clean. I saw Dad."

"So where is he?"

"I don't know. But I know I saw him. We went to a bar and talked."

"You just said you were clean."

"I drank a Coke. Look at me."

"You two stop," Francine said.

"I *am* looking at you. You can't even dress like a normal person. Do you have any idea what people see when you walk down the street in those clown clothes? And then you want me to buy your opioid dreams about Dad."

Elvis went for him, lunging across the counter and grabbing him by the throat. Tom was bigger; he outweighed Elvis by 40 pounds, and the unbudging force of entropy helped him stay upright and force Elvis back. They strained against each other, grunting, grimacing, until Tom threw Elvis off and they both stood at opposite ends of the counter, red-faced and panting hard.

"I've never done opioids, you asshole," Elvis said.

Elvis had done heroin a few times, but it didn't give him the rush of meth. Methamphetamines were like flute music, high and fast and elegant. He thought of heroin as common. His feelings got hurt when Tom didn't see that he was a better class of addict.

"Do I care what drugs you take? Just keep them out of my house."

"I'm not using. I told you."

"Yeah, and you had a beer with Dad last night."

"I had a Coke. You think you're so smart, but you don't even know. Dad was there. He's alive. Don't you even want to know?" Elvis's voice was breaking. He felt close to tears. It was shameful. Tom always had it together, and he never did. His emotions always undid him.

"Shit, if he's alive, then I say to hell with him. He left us. He's an asshole. But that's just crazy. He's been dead for thirty years, and that's okay with me. Do you think you're going to feel any better, raising him from the dead? What would make you feel better is to get off that stuff." Tom shook his head in disgust. "You're weak."

* * *

Francine came back to his room while he was throwing clothes into his duffle bag. Tom's personality was so strong that she hardly featured, and as far as Elvis could tell, she liked it that way. She had hung in with Tom since high school.

Elvis liked the way she looked: wispy, pliable, quiet as a river pool. She never said much or smiled much. Elvis couldn't prove it, but he thought she had a mind of her own—couldn't prove it because she didn't talk, but he also didn't see her swaying in the wind of Tom's bluster.

"I don't like that you and Tom always fight." She didn't look at him, but at the bed.

"Yeah, well, who does."

"I know you have to go, but I want you to know that Tom feels like a brother to you. He's just frustrated."

"I noticed. I'm frustrated with him."

She looked up, a glimmer of surprise shooting through her eyes. "No, I mean because of your drugs. He wants to help you, but he knows he can't."

"Francine, I'm not using. I told you. I've been clean for almost two years. I'm not going to do that stuff anymore."

"Tom thought you were doing it last night. He was sure of it."

"Well, I wasn't. He's not as big an expert as he thinks."

She nodded to herself. "Okay, well, I hope you keep it together. I mean it."

They had reached a border where words became noise, and he had to get out. Nevertheless, he found it hard to extricate himself from the house. Elvis didn't like to just disappear. When he felt trouble, he wanted to settle it, and despite a lifetime of lessons with Tom, he couldn't see sneaking out.

Elvis took his time, looking around as he went through the living room, half hoping Tom would appear. He got out the door, threw his stuff in the back of his truck, and peeled out like a teenage kid showing off.

He felt better right away, released from the tyranny of that house where he was always under suspicion. Turning right at the highway, he decided spontaneously to go south through Mendocino, then track 128 all the way to Cloverdale.

The two-lane highway followed the coast, flying over gorges that cut through the headlands on their way to the ocean. Water glinted on his right, the color of steel knives. This was the life. In the past 24 hours he had attended a funeral, had twice visited a cemetery, had talked to his long-lost dad, and then to his horrible brother. Tom was like a volcano: mostly old, crusted stone, but with pools of hot lava.

He was done with all that. He was flying down the road as the sun found its sweet way over his head.

So long as he was in the car, on a journey, he could not suffer temptation. Staying clean was a job. The monster hung out just over your left shoulder, and even if you forgot about it for a while, you never really forgot. You had to throw off those thoughts of getting high, just stick them in a hole and hope they didn't come out. But they would. When you were talking to your friends, you would wonder whether they would offer you some and what you would say. Would you get high? Maybe you would. You hoped you wouldn't. You hoped you would.

Here and now, in this car on a rural highway, he was free of that battle. The monster might be near, but it was powerless. The drive would take at least two hours. It was freedom for his mind.

Thirty minutes south along the coast, he descended in fast, winding curves to the Navarro River where it emptied into the Pacific: a wide, blue spot where the sun seemed warmer. Across the inlet, he could see surf crashing into brown-gray cliffs. Soon, he was shooting up the river and into the redwoods. He threw his sunglasses on the passenger seat, letting the strips of shade and sun batter his face, gold-black-gold-black-gold-black.

He remembered Coffey Park.

* * *

Something had awakened him. He struggled toward consciousness, swimming out of the fog of deep sleep. It was inexplicably, unnervingly dark. His clock radio had gone invisible. He saw no glow of streetlights in the window.

Elvis buried his head in the pillow and tried to go back to sleep. Dim, distant shouting caught his attention. When he lifted his head to listen, he heard a hum he could not identify.

Elvis came fully awake. He stepped into some Crocs and felt his way down the corridor to the front door.

He had never seen it so dark: black as a cave. Usually, they left a light on in the living room, but now there was only a faint, pinkish glow coming from the window, too dim for him to see anything in the room. He heard a high screeching noise far in the distance, like metal being torn apart. The front door had three locks, which he had opened a hundred times, but doing it by feel alone was trickier. It took him some time.

When he stepped out the door, Elvis did not immediately understand what he was seeing. Red-black-red-black, the utter darkness of the subdivision stripped of electric lights, with a vast undefined orange-red sky to the east and streaks of light flying in the wind overhead like unguided missiles. A gusting wind bit into his face, hot and full of smoke. He could taste it on his tongue, and little fragments hit his face. Elvis put up a finger to wipe it away and felt oily grit.

The dark outlines of the houses fell into place, and he made out shadowy movement that he recognized as people. To his right, at the end of the cul-de-sac, poles of yellow light appeared, a car's headlights tunneling into the smoke. Elvis could barely make out the shadow of the car behind the headlights. It drove slowly down the street, its headlights blinding him, until it swung in a loop in front of him and stopped.

"You need to get the hell out of here," a voice shouted huskily. "The fire has jumped the freeway, and it's coming. Get out now!"

The vehicle screeched away and then threw on the brakes. "Is everybody out of these houses?"

Elvis was stupefied, boggled. "I don't know. I just woke up."

"Go pound on their doors!" the voice shouted and peeled out again, leaning on the horn all the way to the corner.

Darkness re-took the street. Elvis peered into oblivion. The shadowy figures he had seen were gone.

He was dressed in gym shorts and a T-shirt; his Crocs belonged to somebody else and were too big. All of a sudden, he felt afraid. Fear was an unusual emotion for Elvis; usually in bar fights or other dangerous commotions, he felt exhilarated, almost hilarious.

It was the unknown, the unseen. He had no one to fight. Red covered the sky; heat and ash permeated the air. He saw no flames. The fire had jumped the freeway? What were they talking about?

He started back into the house to get his shoes on and discovered that the door had blown shut. His keys were inside, with his wallet. He yelled, pounded the door. No answer. He did it again, and again. Finally, he heard someone answering. "What the fuck? It's two a.m.! Can you stop banging on the door?"

"It's me," he shouted back. "Is that Hubie?"

"Who are you?"

"It's me! Open the door! You need to get out!"

"Who the heck are you?"

"It's Elvis. The guy in the back room. Open up; it's important."

Elvis heard rather than saw the door open, and he could not see who stood before him, Hubie or another resident.

"We need to get everybody out. It's an emergency."

"Calm down! What are you talking about?"

"Is it Hubie? Are you Hubie?"

"What difference does that make? What's going on?"

"It's a fire, Hubie. They said to get everybody out. Can't you smell the smoke?"

"There's no smoke in the house. It's all out here." Hubie sounded extremely confused.

"Look at the sky, Hubie. This isn't some house fire; this is something crazy." He pushed past Hubie into the living room, stumbling over something—a chair or a sofa. He almost fell, losing his orientation. He had to turn to find the dim outline of the door. "You get your stuff, Hubie. I'll wake everybody else, and we'll get out of here in five minutes."

A silhouette appeared at the doorway. "It's nuts out there." The voice was Hubie's, but it had risen into a boy's timbre.

Hubie had been outside, Elvis realized. "Did you hear what I said?" he asked. "Get your stuff. We have five minutes."

"Really?" Hubie's voice was almost a squeak.

Elvis was living in an SLE—Sober Living Environment—where, at the moment, he had a room to himself. He felt his way back there and found his jeans, with his wallet and phone and keys. He pulled them on.

He couldn't find his shoes. He reached his hand under the bed in a sweeping motion; he raked his fingers over the closet floor. Had he thrown them in the corner? Near the end of the bed, he found one shoe against the wall, but try as he might, he couldn't find the other. It was hard to know how much time was passing. A blaring car horn ran by nearby. *Screw it.* He would wear the Crocs. It was time to get out.

First, he had to get everybody else out. The SLE was a rambling ranch with five bedrooms. Elvis knew the layout, and he barged into each room without knocking, giving loud orders to get up and get out of the house. "Get dressed, grab your wallet, and get out on the street. You have five minutes, max." In the dark, he got confused responses. They were slow to wake, and they didn't immediately understand who he was or what he was saying. Whether they actually moved, he could not see. He had to keep going, whether they responded or not.

Feeling his way down the hallway and through the living room, he paused to shout. "It's time! Let's get out of here! Right now!" He didn't hear any answer. Had some of them already gone? Had all of them? He should make another run through the house, but he was increasingly fearful.

When he reached the front porch, the wind was a shock, hot and urgent. He thought there was more light. What time was it? He heard voices and realized he could see dim figures standing in the cul-de-sac.

"Hey!" he shouted. "What's going on?" He missed a step down from the porch and almost fell but hustled down the sidewalk to approach the shadows. "What's going on?" Elvis repeated. He thought there were three of them. Male or female, he couldn't tell.

"We don't know," a male voice said. "Phones aren't working. We're thinking that we need to evacuate."

"Definitely," a husky female voice drawled.

"Right now?" Elvis said. "I can't see any fire. How close do you think it is?"

Nobody answered. Overhead, sparks were speeding by in a continuous, mesmerizing stream. Not just sparks, either: it was difficult to judge size, but some looked more like missiles.

"Oh my God!" A flaming branch had come from out of the sky, thumping down in the street and scattering embers. Elvis jumped. Several voices yelped. The branch was still flaring, its flames licking sideways in the fierce, hot wind.

"There's your fire," the male voice said. "Time to go." In an instant, everyone had vanished, scattered like leaves. Elvis couldn't say where they went. He heard a car engine starting, cranking and cranking and finally catching. Headlights came down the street. Then another car followed the first one. Elvis kicked the flaming wood into the gutter, and in the process, his Croc came flying off. He had to hop on one foot to get it; fortunately, he had seen exactly where it landed.

Where were the men from his SLE? Elvis went back up the sidewalk and leaned his head in the door. "Anybody home? It's time to leave. Now!" He didn't get any answer. "If you're here, give me a shout, would you?"

Stymied and unsure, he automatically pulled his phone out of his pocket. It came on, its bright screen as welcome as a candle in a dark room. Why hadn't he thought of using it before? He could have found his shoes with its light. But when he tried to make a connection, he got nothing. He had no bars.

In the few moments of talking with neighbors, Elvis had felt the warmth of collaboration. It was almost community. Now, he was cut off. Darkness, no phone, no housemates, no neighbors. He knew he should leave, but where could he go? Maybe the mission. They didn't accept guests after eight o'clock, but he was a graduate; they might make an exception and let him in.

Irrationally, he hesitated to leave. He looked into the sky again, to take in the fireworks streaking through the air above, to see the angry, unnatural orange. He took in a deep breath and then fell into a fit of coughing. The air was foul.

* * *

Elvis left the reverie, returning to his body and his rattling pickup truck following the Navarro River. Stripes of yellow light still broke through the redwood canopy.

That night. Every moment had been concentrated, thick as honey. He had been afraid, but he had also felt full, focused. The thought had come to him that he would never use drugs again. He didn't need them. He didn't want them. Life was bigger than that.

For a long time, he held on to that certainty—for two years, almost. He squeezed it tight whenever he felt a doubt. It was gone now, though. He could feel that he was drifting down, that his thoughts were wrong.

Funny how bad juju slipped in. You thought you were waterproof, but it leaked in from the bottom. The first thing you knew, you were sunk.

No, that was the wrong way to think. He had a disease, but he could choose to overcome. One day at a time. Elvis was choosing today to be clean and sober. He was due to get his two-year chip. He needed to remember to tell the meeting.

What about his father?

The road had straightened coming out of the redwood forest, and Elvis picked up speed through pasture and oak woodlands. The pickup was really rattling.

His father, dead for how many years, alive all this time. He couldn't say why it meant so much to him, or even what it meant. It was immense. In those few minutes in the bar, he had seen enough to sense that his father was untrustworthy, slippery, and crude. Yet he wanted more of him. He wanted it like crazy.

The lies were the worst. Including his mother, crying and coming apart, but lying to him. He had been just a kid. All these years he had lived with a lie.

But really, what difference did it make? If you want to cry about it, you'll be crying all the time. Elvis wasn't the type.

He was proud that he had saved that woman. Wilma. They had written about it in the paper. Somebody at the mission told him. Guys cheered him when he came into the chapel, like he was a hero. Some of them thought it was a big joke, of course. Not all of them, though.

* * *

When Elvis got to Cloverdale, he pulled over and called his sponsor. He and Bill had first connected just after the fire, when Elvis was newly dedicated to sobriety and talking to anybody who would listen about his new life. Bill was a longshoreman who worked on the docks in Oakland, and he wasn't always easy to reach. But he picked up.

"Hey, where ya been?" he asked.

Elvis was naturally expansive; he expected his good feelings to spread through everybody. As soon as he heard Bill's skeptical tone, however, his exhilaration turned to guilt. He had missed a lot of meetings. Appointments with Bill had come and gone without him even bothering to cancel, especially in the last six months. He had claimed—and believed—that he had come so far he didn't need the meetings anymore. They say that once an addict, always an addict, but no addict believes it when he is doing well.

"I'm just coming home from my mother's funeral," Elvis said. "It kinda shook me up. I was thinking maybe we could get together. Maybe go to a meeting."

For a long moment, Bill was silent. "Tonight?"

Elvis was not quite ready for that specific a response. He had intended to have a general feel-good talk.

"Yeah, sure," Elvis said.

"We could go to the Franklin Park meeting," Bill said. "I'll pick you up at six thirty. Where are you staying these days?"

It was the same place he had been in since the firestorm, a room he rented near Coddingtown Mall. Bill signed off as soon as he told him that, though Elvis would have liked to keep talking. He thought Bill was a pretty good sponsor—one of the best he'd had in years of flirting with the twelve steps. The meeting scared him a little. Of course you could go and just listen, but that wasn't Elvis's style. He was bound to talk if he got a platform, and then he said things that opened him up to scrutiny.

Continuing on the road, he stuck his phone in his pocket. He wanted to go to church, too, another place where he had been AWOL. Months ago, he had signed up to usher, and he recognized that the brethren might not be too happy with him for not showing up. He was going to get on board again, however. He had to do it.

Would he tell Bill about his father? Bill liked to stick to business. He didn't like it when Elvis went off on a rabbit trail. Elvis turned that over in his mind as he carried on south. The road was a four-lane highway now, and the country had opened up to fields of grapes and sweeping hills of oak and grasslands. If he was going to do the twelve steps, his father would certainly figure in them somewhere. Not directly. The idea of the twelve steps was that you had to face up to what you had done to others and try to make it right. He had not harmed his father, and he had nothing to make amends for. You could make a better case that his father had harmed him and had plenty to amend.

He wondered whether his father had ever been in AA. He certainly liked to drink. From what Elvis could remember of his childhood, there had been plenty of drinking and fighting before his father disappeared. No drugs, at least that he knew of. In the past, he had wondered whether his father had been lost at sea because he was drunk. Now he knew that wasn't the case, but perhaps alcohol had made Willard T sneak out on the family.

Life was full of grim disappointments, but Elvis couldn't help hoping that his father's return might start something great for him. How, he had no idea, but sometimes great events launched great changes. Who would have predicted that the firestorm would help him?

Otherwise, he could feel that sobriety was slipping away. He was putting off a relapse through sheer willpower, but that wasn't going to work indefinitely. He knew from past experience how it went. First, you started thinking about it a little. Then you couldn't think about anything else.

# 2 THE MEETING

At the clubhouse, an assemblage of addicts and alcoholics was already loitering in the parking lot, like shoppers expecting stores to open on Black Friday. All of them were smoking. Two middle-aged men with full spades of beard stood by their motorcycles, wordlessly radiating apathy. A woman who might be a teenager was dressed in Goth. Her shoulders drooped and her dyed-black hair hung in her eyes. A man in a business suit was puffing away. None of them greeted Bill or Elvis. At one time, Elvis had come to this meeting often, but it had been a while. He didn't see anybody he recognized.

Inside the clubhouse was a familiar semicircle of folding chairs surrounding a card table and a dining room chair. Several people came over to welcome Bill and Elvis when they took seats. A middle-aged woman named Sharon apparently knew Bill, as they exchanged fist bumps and stood together talking in low tones. Sharon wore jeans and Keds and a scooped orange blouse that showed cleavage. She was too heavy to be of interest to Elvis, who couldn't help himself; he always looked at the girls. At one time, this meeting had a couple of women he liked to look at, which Angel would always point out to him drily in the days when she still accompanied him. Angel didn't consider herself an addict and thought AA was more talk than sobriety. She thought nobody would come if not for possible hookups.

Elvis could see the point of her criticisms, but he had found AA very strengthening, especially when he was going good. He looked around brightly at the people beginning to find seats. Church had many of the same qualities as AA, but the scraggly, low-down quality of AA, its least-common-denominator ethos of sarcasm and dark humor, had its appeal. Elvis could relax at AA meetings because hope was doled out one day at a time. Church was salvation with no limit; AA was sobriety for today.

A thin, middle-aged man with a scraggly goatee took a seat at the center table, and as though by signal, everybody quickly found a seat. "Hi; I'm Enos, and I'm an alcoholic."

"Hi, Enos," they said in chorus.

Enos asked if there was anybody new to the meeting who would like to introduce himself. Elvis saw a teenage girl raise her hand about as high as her heart. Enos didn't see her and was about to go on when Elvis interrupted. "Hey, Enos, excuse me; that girl over there put her hand up."

Enos made a hand gesture inviting her to speak. Without raising her eyes from her lap, she said, "I'm Gail Hernandez."

"Hi, Gail!"

Enos asked if she wanted to say anything about herself. Gail shook her head. "Well, welcome; we're glad you are here. You're welcome to say whatever you feel led to say, and you're also welcome to just listen. I hope you'll get some benefit out of our meeting. Everybody is here to help each other, so if you need anything, just ask. And by the way, just FYI, this is Alcoholics *Anonymous*. Just your first name is enough."

She didn't react but kept her head buried. Enos launched into the standard readings. He rattled off the preamble himself and then invited a black man named Ramon to read "How It Works." Ramon introduced himself—"Hi, Ramon!"—and fumbled his way to the correct page in the Big Book. Reading was a chore for Ramon. He got mixed up, jumping paragraphs in the twelve steps. Elvis's mind wandered away for most of it, with the exception of the paragraph that said,

> Remember that you are dealing with alcohol – cunning, baffling, powerful! Without help, it is too much for you. But there is One who has all power – That One is God. You must find Him now!

For some reason, that always sent prickles up his neck. AA actually didn't feature a lot of spiritual talk, but something would sneak in and surprise you.

A woman named Kitty—"Hi, Kitty!"—read the Twelve Traditions. Elvis's mind again drifted off topic. Kitty was young and perky and while she stood in front with the Big Book blocking his view of her breasts, Elvis still looked her over. If Angel were here, she would nudge him.

Enos announced that this was a Step meeting. They had been going over one step a week, and tonight they would do Step Eight: "Made a list of all persons we had harmed, and became willing to make amends to them all." Enos read the relevant chapter from the Big Book.

Elvis had never actually done the eighth step, but it wasn't hard to think of people he had hurt. First on the list was Angel, and then his daughter, Amber, mostly because his addictions had kept him from being a decent partner or father. He could also think of high school friends and fellow addicts he had stolen from, including some business partners when he was selling. Actually, the topic of theft was a big one, because when he was on a tear, he would do anything to get meth, and his conscience—if he even had one under those conditions—got left behind. There were also landlords and housemates he had stiffed, and people he knew from church he had disappointed when they tried to help him. Just in the short time it took to read the chapter out loud, enough damaged relationships came to Elvis's mind to assure him that if he ever got to Step Eight, he was going to have a very long list. Then months or maybe years would be involved in locating people and figuring out how to make amends. In principle, Elvis believed in the Twelve Steps, that this process would help to heal him from his addictions. At the moment, he found it hard to imagine going through it all the way.

The chapter discussed the difficulty of asking forgiveness of people who should be asking you for forgiveness—people who had actually harmed you. "Defective relations with other human beings have nearly always been the immediate cause of our woes, including our alcoholism," Enos read, his flat, Midwestern voice accentuating the quaint language of the Big Book. Elvis thought of his father. Their relationship was completely defective. His father had abandoned him and lied to him. If the point of the eighth step was to untangle defective relations, to gain self-understanding, and therefore to become sane and sober, Elvis would have to settle with his father. He didn't know how he could do that. He didn't know that he exactly wanted to do that. He thought that on some level, he probably hated his father.

Tonight, when Enos opened the discussion, Elvis stood up almost immediately. "Hi; my name is Elvis, and I'm an alcoholic." In the open section of meetings, Elvis often shared his experiences. He liked to talk.

"Hi, Elvis!"

Elvis looked around the semicircle with a shy, impish smile. "You talk about defective relationships," he said. "I don't know if I have any other kind. This week, my father—who I thought was dead, 'lost at sea' on a fishing boat since I was ten years old—showed up at my mother's funeral service. Turns out he abandoned me and his whole family and then arranged to fake a boating accident. Now he shows up thirty years later. I was the only one who saw him. My brother thinks I was hallucinating, high on drugs, but I not only saw my dad, I went with him to a bar and had a long talk. I drank a Coke, by the way, and today I'm celebrating two years clean and sober."

Elvis paused to wait for the applause, which came after a delay of several seconds. Some people hooted and shouted, while Elvis grinned. "Yeah, you see? If I can do it, you can, too.

"So anyway, defective relationships. I got a lot of them, and most of them are my fault. I keep thinking that this with my dad is the worst, because I was only ten years old, and I don't have anything to make amends for that I can see. So how can I get it right? My dad should make amends to me, is what I think. I know alcoholics and addicts always want to blame other people for their problems, but really, a ten-year-old boy? Isn't that a little young?

"I just think it's all God. The answer is God. Your Higher Power. That's been my story. I'm a firestorm survivor. I got caught in Coffey Park. I woke up in the middle of the night with everything on fire. I was helping out this disabled woman, Wilma. I kept her safe, and somehow we survived. We were trapped, but we made it. I didn't think we could. It was all God. He told me it would be all right. Not in words. I didn't actually hear him say anything out loud. The fire was too loud, anyway; it was just roaring. It would drown out even God. You never heard such a sound. It still scares me. Sometimes I dream about it. But I heard God in my Spirit: *It will be all right*. I told that to Wilma, and I don't know whether she believed me at the time, but that's exactly how it worked out. And here's the thing: I haven't had a drink or a hit since. I've been clean and sober since that day, two years ago, and I thank God for it. I couldn't do it on my own power, but I surrendered to a Higher Power and he did it."

Elvis sat down with a proud grin on his face. It always comforted him to talk. The words seemed to activate a different reality. He had heard a sermon on that once: the Word of Power, the minister had called it.

Whereas when he had nobody to talk to, his addictions grew like mushrooms.

A man was talking from across the circle. He didn't even stand up; he had his head pointed into his lap, and you couldn't really hear him.

"Stand up, man!" Elvis encouraged. "We want to hear you!"

The man seemed taken aback, but he did stand, looking around him in surprise.

"What's your name?" Elvis asked loudly.

"I'm Peter," he said.

"Hi, Peter!"

"Are you an alcoholic?" Elvis asked and gave a guffaw. Peter didn't answer.

He told his story, softly at first, but building up steam. He had been married for twenty years, but his wife died. It was his fault. He took responsibility. She needed to go to Tijuana to get her toxins cleansed, but he drank up all the money and the disease got worse and worse. Then their oldest daughter died. She rolled her car into a ditch on Highway 29, and she drowned. She wasn't even hurt, but she was pinned with her face in the water and she sucked in the water. After that, his wife gave up and withered away. He couldn't get her to eat. It seemed like she literally starved herself to death.

Peter began to weep. "I can write their names on a list, but I can't make amends. They're gone. There's nothing I can do. I've asked God for forgiveness, but I don't get any response. I'm just lost."

For a full minute, they listened in silence, waiting for Peter to say more. He sat down. They were all still holding their breath.

The Goth girl began speaking. "What's your name?" Elvis shouted.

"I'm Ruby," she said, blinking her heavily made-up eyes. She searched for something in her memory and then visibly found it. "I'm an alcoholic." It seemed to relieve her that she had found the formula.

"Hi, Ruby!"

"Is it Peter? Peter, you shouldn't think that way. God took them. He had a plan. You have to believe in that, or you'll go crazy."

"Cross talk!" somebody shouted.

Ruby didn't understand. She stared at the rest of them, mystified.

Enos let her down gently. "Ruby, in AA we don't tell each other what to do. We call that cross talk. Everybody in AA can have their own opinion.

Right or wrong, we don't try to straighten them out. We support each other. I'd encourage you to talk about your own experiences."

"Well, screw that," Ruby said, her face turning into a stone wall. "My whole family died in a bus accident when I was a baby, and I've been living with death all my life. It's God. Or you can call it what you like. Your Higher Power. Whatever the fuck that means. Don't tell me that's an opinion. God is not an opinion."

She flounced into her seat. Enos stayed very calm. "Ruby, you are very welcome to talk. If you read the Big Book, which I would encourage, you'll get an explanation of why we ask everybody to stick to their own experience. Now, do you want to talk? We are glad if you do."

Ruby had her arms crossed in front of her, and she didn't.

Herbie did, and then Ron, and then Elsbeth. They were all alcoholics who had stories about how they found peace with their families and friends and bosses once they stopped trying to be right all the time and took responsibility for whatever they had done. Ruby kept her arms crossed and held onto her mad, and Peter never raised his head—his whole body was a portrait of despair—but everybody left them alone. It was a good meeting, Elvis thought. It went fast, too. He was surprised when Enos said their time was up.

"Are there any anniversaries?" Enos asked. He handed out two silver chips to twin brothers who said they had made a decision to quit drinking yesterday. There were three red chips for 30 days, one purple for four months, one gold for ten months, and a bronze for Elvis's two years. Each person who collected a chip was clapped for and congratulated. At the last moment, after a pause, Ruby said she had made it two months. The expression on her face softened slightly when people applauded and she was given a gold chip.

They all stood and held hands in a circle, saying the Serenity prayer together. It was a nice moment.

* * *

Bill and Elvis went for coffee at the Peets on Mendocino. It was cold and windy outside, but they took their cups onto the patio anyway. They wanted privacy from others and enough noise from passing cars to disguise their conversation if anybody happened by. Elvis thought that

Bill looked very sinister in the dim light. He had only a couple of tattoos and no jewelry, but he looked like he had been in a bar fight or two. A couple of his front teeth were missing.

Elvis was still feeling excited by the meeting. Several people had talked to him afterward about his experience in the firestorm. One of them, the good-looking woman who had read at the beginning—Kitty—remembered reading about him in the newspaper.

"Why didn't you say something tonight?" Elvis asked Bill. "I was waiting for you to talk."

Bill hardly acknowledged the question. He was all business. "Elvis," he said, "I want to know if you're really serious about working the steps."

"Yeah, I am. That's why I called you."

"If I'm going to be your sponsor, I need to know that you're really going to do this. I don't want to be calling you up and nagging your butt just so you can blow me off."

Elvis was almost offended. "I'm serious."

"Why now and not before?"

Elvis thought about continuing his line of BS, but in a moment of inspiration, he decided to open up. "You heard me say that my dad appeared?" Bill nodded slowly. "It shook me up. I really don't know what's up and what's down. My brother thought I was hallucinating. He accused me of using again. I think that's what set me off. I got shaky. I swear, if I'd had some stuff available, I would probably have crashed. So I made up my mind to call you, and to get serious, and to go to church, and get straightened out."

"What's got you so confused?"

"I told you. My dad."

They talked it up one side and down the other. Bill didn't really understand why his dad mattered after being gone for 28 years.

"Okay," Bill said at last. "If you're serious, I'm going to expect you to work. I want you to start Step Four. You're going to need a workbook."

"Okay." Elvis shrank from it. Schoolwork had always been painful to him, like a choke collar.

"Some people use ready-made worksheets," Bill said. "I think it's better if you do everything yourself in a notebook. It's got to be really yours, or there's no point.

"What you need to do is make three charts. One is for resentments, one is for fears, and one is for sex conduct and other moral abuse. Each one, you list *what* you did, or resent, or fear, *why* you do it, *who* beside yourself is affected, what the impact was on you and that other person. Resentment, fear, and sex. Can you remember those three? And what, why, who. You get a notebook and start making lists. Next week, we'll go over what you have, and I'll help you do it. The main thing is to go as deep as you can."

He looked at Elvis sideways, his heavy face and dark stubble seeming to belong to a wild creature, bear or raccoon or bigfoot. "You got it? If you want to get serious, you have to do this."

* * *

Monday, Elvis went to work, organizing trucks for Jackson Roofing. That meant getting material and tools on the right truck and then responding when something went missing. Today, work felt like a five-day headache. Elvis didn't want to be at the warehouse. That wasn't really an option, though. He had already missed work twice this month, calling in sick. He couldn't afford to get fired.

His spirits revived as he did the work. He liked moving around. He liked kidding with the men, which verged on the abusive but kept you on your toes. Laughing was a defense as well as a pleasure.

During his lunch break, Elvis called Angel, who was also on her lunch break. Elvis admired her more than any woman he knew. They had met almost 15 years ago and had been together ever since, on and off. It was more off than on right now. After the fire, she had let him come back, and they had cozied up together. Right now, though, he had a room in a lady's house.

"Whatcha doing?" he asked, and they made small talk. It was comforting. Sometimes Elvis thought it comforted Angel, too, though she got impatient with him. He wasn't sure what it was she wanted. Part of her liked the anarchy in his life, and part of her wanted him to start acting like a responsible adult. It had occurred to Elvis that he shared the same opinion about himself.

"You want me to come over and make dinner tonight?" he asked. Elvis was a decent cook and Angel wasn't, though she liked food. Cooking dinner was often part of a bargain: dinner, then sex. They both liked food and they both liked sex, and it seemed as though they should make it into a permanent agreement. At times during their fifteen years, they had. However, at the moment, Angel was skittish. He couldn't predict what she would say.

"I have to work tonight," she said.

"What's that about?"

"I don't know. Doctor Baird asked me to stay late, and I said yes. I need the money."

"Okay," Elvis said cheerfully, though he was vexed.

In his heart, he knew it was for the best. Angel wasn't really good for him right now. Six months ago, she had been in a car accident and hurt her back. The doctor prescribed oxycontin, and she had gotten hooked into using. Lately she was doing heroin, which was cheaper than pills. She smoked the stuff; she didn't like needles. So far, it hadn't affected Elvis. She hadn't offered any to him, and he wasn't an opioid user anyway. However, he knew perfectly well—and she did too—that when you are around users, it matters. It's something about the atmosphere.

She hadn't been a user when he first met her. That was one reason he liked her. They had met at a friend's party, and she was drinking water. She didn't seem to mind being the only one there who didn't have a buzz. She liked partying and didn't need substances.

"Well, maybe we can get together tomorrow," Angel said. She had a deep, scratchy voice that Elvis found very sexy.

"I think I'm going to a meeting," Elvis said. "I told my sponsor I would. You could come along."

"That's okay," she said. "You can call me when you're done."

Elvis went back to work but thought about Angel all afternoon. Most of that time, he was on his own, making up lists and driving his truck to suppliers to get nails or glue or tin. He also bent metal for a job that had five skylights and would need a lot of flashing. Did Angel regret not having children, he wondered? She was probably too old to start now. Maybe she didn't want kids or maybe she couldn't have them. He had never felt right asking her, and she never volunteered. At one point, he had thought it would probably happen. Now he realized it probably would not. That made him feel sad, as though his life was flimsy as a moth, a creature of time. He knew he shouldn't be thinking like that.

He was on his own tonight, and he didn't know what he was going to do. It was difficult to entertain yourself when you weren't drinking. Keeping busy was important. He could watch a movie or Monday night football.

Elvis loved Angel because she was a strong woman, no-nonsense. You knew where you were with her, even though she wasn't the type to talk about love. Years ago, she had taken in his daughter—just gone to get her at his brother Tom's, without asking anybody. Elvis had come home to find Amber sitting in the kitchen, watching as Angel made cookies, which she evidently thought you should do to calm kids down. Angel made the ugliest mess of cookies anybody ever saw. He made a joke of that for months, but she had done what she thought needed doing.

Honestly, he wished she would take him in hand like that. If he was going to stay clean, he needed her help. The first time he went to the mission, it was because she called them and told them to send somebody to come get him. It was Knox who had come, acting just like he was there to pick up a package.

Everything was messed up now. She was using; he was clean. She couldn't kick him out because he was already living elsewhere. They were sliding along on parallel tracks, sometimes making sparks when they touched, sometimes missing each other. *The trouble is*, Elvis thought, *we don't belong to each other. We're just independent.*

* * *

Bill picked him up for the Tuesday night meeting. Dogs on the Roof met in a small Baptist church on Sonoma Avenue. It was a Speaker meeting, with a man who worked in the wine industry talking about how to stay sober when alcohol is all around you. Elvis listened skeptically. He thought the man should find another job.

Afterward, they went to Aker Coffee. Elvis had actually bought a spiral-bound notebook at CVS and begun making the Step Four lists. He forgot the different categories, however, so he ended up scribbling about the worst episodes of his addiction. It became a free-association essay, which he knew wasn't right. It went on for three pages. Elvis couldn't remember ever writing anything that long, even in school, so he handed it to Bill with a certain pride and watched while Bill read.

"Tom is your brother?" Bill wanted to know.

"Yeah. He lives in Fort Bragg."

"This seems to be all about Tom."

"I guess I got a little stuck on that. I've got a lot of problems with Tom."

Bill lowered his head and stared at Elvis through the tops of his eyes. "Yeah, well, the idea is more to be thorough. To cover everything. So this is probably great with Tom, but it leaves everybody else out. I'm sure you've had some other problems with people."

Elvis wasn't going to disagree with that.

"It's what drunks and addicts do. We get all wound up on one thing and we forget everything else. When you do Step Four work, you want to look at the totality."

Elvis would have made a joke of it if he could think of anything funny to say. Bill didn't seem to be in the mood for humor. He did, however, show Elvis how to draw the charts and put in all the categories. He made Elvis fill in a few lines for each chart so he would get the idea. Tom fit under the resentment category. Plenty came to mind for sex conduct and other moral abuse. Elvis was stumped by the question of what he feared, however.

"I'm really not afraid of anybody," he told Bill. "It's gotten me in a lot of trouble, really. I get in fights with guys that are a lot bigger than me or who are holding a knife."

"Everybody is afraid of something," Bill growled. "Maybe not a person. Like, are you afraid of being laughed at? That's a big one."

"Angel would say I'm afraid of not being laughed at," Elvis said. "She thinks I'm a clown. She says I can't be serious."

"What do you think?" Bill asked. His face was so serious, like he was a doctor telling somebody he had three days to live.

"Yeah, well, maybe. I like everybody to be happy."

"Write that down," Bill said.

Elvis began to do so and then stopped, unsure of what to write. "Write down what?" he asked.

"Write that you're afraid you can't make everybody happy."

It took Elvis a minute to do that. His handwriting was hopeless, so he printed. He was very slow at it.

"I think I'm really afraid of being forgotten," he said, looking up.

"What do you mean?"

"I mean, if I died today, would anybody really care? I'm just a piece of fluff that can blow away with the wind."

* * *

That thought plagued him the rest of the night. He had a daughter, Amber, whom he hadn't seen in a year. She was his one slim claim on infinity, and he hadn't even made the time to call her. He hadn't remembered her birthday, either. How long had it been? When she was a kid, he had at least tried, though he was never very good at understanding what she might like. Once he had bought her an Xbox only to find out that she hated games. Another time, when the Giants won the World Series, he had given her a video of the championship year. She hated baseball.

She lived in Ukiah now, and he rarely went that way. She was drifting out of his life, whereas when she was a teenager, she had lived with him and Angel, and he had understood everything about her because she reminded him of himself.

His brother at least had his football career. He had played in the NFL, and a hundred years from now, his name would still be listed somewhere. You could look him up and read his stats. Whereas Elvis you couldn't even look up in the telephone book. They didn't make telephone books anymore.

Lying in bed, missing the consolation of meth, knowing that he was feeling sorry for himself and teetering closer to the edge of relapse, he thought again of his conversation with Bill. After he made up the charts that he was going to fill with all his faults and fears, Elvis asked Bill what the point was. What would they do with the chart? Bill had a copy of the Twelve Steps, and he showed him how it progressed step-by-step. The searching moral inventory of Step Four led to Step Eight's list of people we had harmed and Step Nine's making direct amends.

"You mean like my daughter?" Elvis asked.

"Sure. Or Tom."

"Tom? What's it got to do with him?"

"Only all that stuff you wrote down."

"I never hurt him. He's doing fine. I wish I could say I was doing that well."

"It's not about him; it's about you. You said yourself that you resent him. If you resent somebody, you are going to do him harm. When you get to Step Eight, you will need to figure out what you did and make amends."

Elvis wasn't the type to hold on to grudges, but he knew he resented Tom. Was it really true that he had harmed him? How? Everything went Tom's way.

*Maybe*, Elvis thought, *I am making it too complicated*. He hadn't been a good brother to Tom. Maybe you could see that as harming him. He'd taken away his brotherhood, the kind of close relationship brothers were supposed to have. It was pretty strange that they had both lost their dad when they were kids but never really leaned on each other. They never even talked about it that Elvis could remember.

Elvis fell asleep with that thought on his mind. It was still there when he awoke early, and he could feel that it wasn't going to go anywhere until he did something with it. Not wanting to have it hanging on him all day at work, he decided to call Tom. His brother was an early riser.

Tom answered with a single syllable, "Yeah." It was almost a grunt. That made it hard to get started in a friendly way.

"Hey, Tom; it's Elvis. How are you doing today?"

There was a substantial pause before Tom said, "I'm fine."

Elvis thought to himself that he was going to have to dive in. "Tom, I called to say that I'm sorry for not being a good brother to you and ask for your forgiveness."

After another pause, "What is this about?"

"Heck, Tom, you know we haven't seen eye to eye on a lot of things, and that's not how it's supposed to be. You deserve to have a brother who cares about you. That's what brothers are for, right?" Elvis felt overwhelmingly nervous as he said these words. "I just haven't been there for you. I've been in jail, and I've been messed up, and I'm sure I've said some things. I'm really sorry about that, and I want to ask your forgiveness."

Tom didn't say anything.

"Tom?" Elvis asked. "You there?"

"What's your angle?"

"I don't have an angle, Tom. This is part of my recovery, to accept my faults and make amends to those I've harmed."

"You didn't harm me. There's nothing you could do to harm me."

"I'm glad you don't feel that I harmed you, but what I'm talking about is, I didn't act like a brother, and we haven't been close, and I want to make that up to you."

Another pause before Tom said, "Make it up how?"

"You know, a new beginning, a fresh start. I want to apologize for my part in everything and ask your forgiveness."

"Elvis, you're acting pretty weird."

"Yeah, well, it feels pretty weird. This is new territory for me. Look, can you just say you forgive me?"

"There's nothing to forgive."

"You're saying I've never done anything to hurt you or offend you? I don't think so."

"How about something to annoy me. Like right now."

"Yeah, okay, something to annoy you. I'm sorry. I'm sorry for whatever I have done. Can you just forgive me?"

Tom made no reply, and the silence from his end of the line went on interminably. Elvis wanted to give Tom time, but eventually he had to say something.

"God, Tom, you're making this so hard. Can you just tell me that you forgive me, and then we'll move on?"

"There's nothing to forgive. I already told you that."

"You said that I annoy you."

"Look, Elvis, I can't forgive you for being an annoying SOB. You can't help it. You were born that way. There's nothing to forgive."

"Damn it! You are driving me crazy." Elvis hung up.

How was he supposed to do these steps? The frustration boiled up in his breast. What an asshole his brother was.

But then he deflated. That wasn't going to work. He grabbed his phone and dialed Tom again, but this time Tom didn't pick up.

"Pick up, pick up, you asshole," Elvis chanted, but Tom didn't hear him. The call went into his voicemail.

"Tom, I'm sorry I hung up on you. This is part of getting clean and sober, and I'm trying. I'm just trying, brother. I hope you can forgive me and we can make a fresh start. That's all. Call me if you want to talk about it."

* * *

Every twelve-step group Elvis had been to, people gave these little formulas for success, things like "Fake it until you make it," or "It works if you work it." He must have heard dozens of those. In essence, sobriety was simple. Anybody could grasp it, even a brain-dead addict who never got his GED. It was simple but not easy, obvious but elusive. You had to get your mind around it.

The twelve-step mindset was not so different from the faith he had learned at the mission, where (he got the impression) you had to get the right mixture of humility and childlike belief, which was what they called faith. It would transform your life. At times during chapel he had thought he got it, but then it always disappeared, so he knew he had not done it quite right.

There was a pathway to follow. When he found it, he would do or think the right thing and the gate would magically click open like a good lock and set him free. It would all make perfect sense, he felt sure, when he found it. He was trying.

The subject preoccupied him, especially at work when he was doing something mindless, or at night when he was ready to sleep but sleep wouldn't come. He thought about Tom, and he thought about Angel: somehow they were part of the mixture. Since his mother's service, he thought of his dad, whose sudden and unnerving appearance was like a supernatural visitation. It had to mean something. He didn't know what.

He had his father's phone number, but he hesitated to call it again. What did he have to say? His father was like a deep well; he might toss something in and hear it splash, but it was another thing to get water out.

Wednesday night, he talked about it with Angel. It was the first time he had seen her since his mother's memorial, and he was surprised how comforting he found the sight of her. He went to her house, which used to be his house. Angel had light red-blond hair that fell to her shoulders, and she wore a deep tan that had creased her face with a thousand tiny cracks. It was a no-nonsense face that suited her temperament. He gave her a huge squeeze, and she gave it back, putting all her back and shoulders into it, so it almost hurt. God, it felt good. He put his lips gently on hers and let them soak there a while. They were gummy and soft and unbelievably sweet.

"I have to tell you," he said. "I saw my father at the service. Or actually, that night. He was at the service, but he left early."

"What?"

He explained the whole thing while they sat together on the sofa with their legs stretched out on the coffee table. Angel didn't say a word, she just listened. He wasn't sure how she reacted, but it felt great to talk with an audience that didn't doubt his truthfulness.

"I don't know," he said. "I'm thinking there's something more to this that I need to find out."

"Like what?"

"I don't know," he said again. "Like maybe if I really got to know him, I wouldn't be so messed up. Maybe I'd be able to stay off meth."

"You aren't using, are you?"

"No, not right now, but I don't know how long I'm going to last. I feel like I'm slipping."

It was the first time he had let her in on those doubts. He ragged on her for using but let her think that he was doing great. Truthfully, until this last weekend, he actually thought he was doing great. When thoughts of meth came into his mind, he was able to move them over to the side, like a box that somebody left in the hallway. It seemed easy. He hadn't realized until just this week how nervous he was, nor how often his thoughts jumped the tracks and leaned over the side. It was getting worse, but only gradually, and anyway, denial is what addicts do. He was good at denial. He liked to look at the bright side.

"Hell, you've been lecturing me, and now who's talking?" Angel said.

"I'm not lecturing you. You're not helping me, though. And you know damn well it's not good for you."

"I'm glad you're not lecturing, because otherwise I might have thought that you were."

In the stiff silence that followed, he got up and carried his sack of groceries into the kitchen to begin dinner. Angel never kept food in the house except frozen pizza, canned chili, and microwave popcorn, so whenever he came, he brought food. She liked it when he cooked for her, and the rhythm of assembling a meal often calmed him after they quarreled. Slicing potatoes and carrots, dicing onions and garlic, rinsing big bundles of muddy spinach kept him from thinking too much about the future of their relationship. She didn't come into the kitchen to watch, and for once, he was just as glad.

He was an idiot for coming around when she was using, but he just couldn't stop it. They had been together for so many years, through so many ups and downs. Watching his hands automatically wield the knife, he got caught up in memories of good times. Once they had borrowed a sailboat from a friend at Bodega Bay, both of them thinking the other knew more about sailing than they did. Before they knew what was up, currents carried them far up the coast. They had to tack back up into the wind and against the current, inching south far after sunset and into the night. Thank God for a moon that let them see the silvery crouching coast and keep their bearings.

Transfixed by the memory, he poked his head into the living room to say something about it and caught her lighting a little glass pipe. She pretended not to notice him, and he turned quickly back into the kitchen.

It would never work. He knew that. He shouldn't even be here.

Elvis sautéed the onions and seared two fat, glistening pork chops. Smothering them in the vegetables, he threw in a little stock and then covered the pan to let it all cook on a low heat. The kitchen now had a brown, homey scent, an invisible perfume of comfort and stability. Elvis took it in with satisfaction and forgot again why it was a mistake to be with Angel. Sauntering into the living room, pleased with what he had made, he found her without her pipe, reading *People*. She did not look up or welcome him, but he threw himself next to her on the sofa, took her head in his hands, and began kissing her. In a moment, she kissed back, and in no time at all they were back into old ways, hard up against each other, stripping off clothes and appropriating every inch of skin, wrestling their way to the logical end, panting with exertion.

Elvis lay slack on the floor, naked except for one leg of his pants that had stayed bunched around his left ankle. "Don't get old, do it?" he said.

She had already begun re-dressing, but Elvis lay limp with his head jammed against one sofa leg until he smelled his dinner. He leapt to his feet, tripped on the trousers and almost fell, then hopped on one leg into the kitchen. The scent of home had been replaced by the sharp smell of burned food. Elvis ripped the top off the skillet, pulled it off the heat, and grabbed a spoon to stir the contents.

"I think it's okay," he shouted to the door. "I think I can salvage it." Breathing hard, his heart racing, he saw that only a thin layer had carbonized, that most of the food was delectable. For just that moment, all his worries flew off. He was in the one spot in all creation where he most belonged, and he was very happy.

# 3 EXPLORING NORTH

After spending Wednesday night with Angel, Elvis felt energized and euphoric. He still believed, however, that he was heading for a relapse. The worry gnawed at him when he was up on the roof with a nail gun, placing shingles. He didn't need to think about what he was doing, so his mind wandered freely. He could conjure up Angel as such a physical presence that he got an erection, imagining her thick reddish-blond hair and her white skin. She was using, and he would too.

Desperately he grasped at an idea: somehow his father would provide the escape he needed from himself.

Angel dismissed the idea when he brought it up. "The man sounds like a dick to me," she said. "He's never done a thing for you in his life."

"Yeah," he said reluctantly. He didn't want to believe it.

Elvis really knew nothing about the man, even from when he was a kid, because what kid thinks to accumulate that kind of knowledge? Your father is just a fact.

He called him. He didn't know why it took an act of such courage to make a simple phone call, but he felt his hand trembling while he waited for the man to pick up, half hoping that he would be thrown into a voicemail. His dad answered with a raspy, "Hey!"

"It's Elvis," he said, trying to keep it bright. He couldn't bring himself to call this stranger "Dad," but he thought it. It seemed extremely weird.

"I know; I can read."

"Have you got a minute?"

"That depends. If you need money, I've got no time. If you found money, I've got all the time in the world."

It occurred to Elvis that a phone call wouldn't get him far with his father. "I was thinking that I might come to see you," Elvis said.

"Why?"

Elvis was surprised by that; he had assumed his dad would be happy. "Hell, I don't know why. You're my father. Why did you want to see me after Mom's service? I think it's natural, don't you?"

"Let me ask you this: if I didn't come see you for thirty years, was that unnatural?"

"But you said you kept track of us. You read about us in the paper."

"Correct. And never showed up. Think about it."

Elvis thought about it. "Okay, fine," he said. "Can I come see you?"

"When?"

"After work on Friday, I could drive up to wherever the hell you are. Where are you, anyway?"

"I'm a lot of places. Why don't we meet in Willits? You know Willits? There's a bar there; what's it called? Hanleys. Meet me at Hanleys."

"Wait," Elvis said. "I told my daughter I'd see her on Friday night. In Ukiah. How about we meet on Saturday morning? Is there a breakfast place?" He hadn't actually talked to Amber, but he shied away from meeting his father in a bar. That was a bad recipe.

"What's her name?" his father asked.

"Who?"

"Your daughter."

"Amber. She's your granddaughter."

* * *

On Friday, Elvis took off directly from work. He was covered with grit but figured he would shower at his daughter's place, where he planned to spend the night.

Amber was 18—or was she 19 now? He had missed her birthday again. That was bad. What a mess their family was, like a pack of strangers. Her one living grandfather didn't even know her name.

Maybe that was the secret to his problems. At one time, he had thought that Angel would pull them together, being so practical-minded. She had taken Amber in hand, doing the girl thing with her, talking to her about clothes and makeup and God-knows-what, after she drove up to get her from Tom's when he threw all her meds in the trash. Elvis still wasn't over that. The doctors had given her those pills for her ADD, and without asking anybody, Tom just tossed them. He didn't believe in mind-altering pills, he said. What an idiot.

Elvis had thought that they would all settle down as one happy family after he graduated from the New Life program, but it hadn't worked out exactly that way. Angel had seemed to lose interest in being cozy, probably in response to his continuing problems. Amber had drifted off in her own teenage direction, sometimes disappearing for days at a time with some scuzzy boyfriend. They had given up even trying to stay in touch with Tom, and as much as Elvis had loved his Grams, that sharp-tongued realist, they weren't ever going to connect as long as she lived with Tom. As she had, right to the end. When he got word that Grams had passed, he was so messed up with meth that he missed her service.

And his mom, his poor, dead mom—she was living her life with Ray and never showed much interest in him or Amber or Tom either, as far as he knew. It was like she started a new book without bothering to finish the old one.

At least Amber finished at the alternative school, Elvis thought as the road flattened out through vineyards along the wide river valley. The sun was just dipping over the hills, brushing the vines with a soft light. Elvis was a town person. He never wanted to live out in the country the way Tom did, but he did like to drive through it in his truck.

He scanned the rim of hills, trying to see where the fire had burned. This wasn't the same fire that had roared into Santa Rosa. This one had covered more territory, but they just didn't have that many people up here. Vast ranges of country didn't even have a road. Nobody could get to the fire to stop it.

He was proud of what he had done in the Santa Rosa fire, saving that woman. He'd gotten a lot of credit for that. What nobody ever mentioned—and he didn't bring up—was the people he'd left behind. The other men in the SLE. He'd woken them up, but he had no idea, even now, if they had gotten out. He didn't know their names, so he couldn't check the lists. That was the thing about disasters: some people made it out, some were left behind. He felt guilty for not making sure.

Amber had never said why she was moving to Ukiah, and he didn't ask because he thought it might be to get away from him. He didn't need that. Now that she was here, he was glad, because he could place her definitely on a map and come through this country every so often to visit her.

Amber had said to come to the restaurant, a place called Rosie's. He found it on State Street, arriving while there was still enough light to stand across the street and check it out. The building was square and white, with those wedding-cake decorations at the top indicating it was old. From looking at the building, he thought it might be a classy place, which he wasn't dressed for. Every town had to have one nice place where you could take somebody. Steaks and baked potatoes, he guessed.

Inside the front door, he saw that he was wrong. A drinks menu was chalked on a blackboard; the floor was wood, with an old-timey western feel to it. His eyes followed a woman in high heels who was popping out of her blouse. She had on the kind of tiny shorts you might see at a beach resort. Elvis realized that he was looking at his daughter.

Rosie's was a Hooters-type restaurant, selling beer and hamburgers and tits.

By the time he got his bearings, Amber had seen him. She threw her arms around him, which also startled him because he couldn't remember the last time she had shown more familiarity than a coyote. "You actually came!" she said so loudly that people looked around, and then she introduced him to the hostess and another waitress who was scooting past, and then the busboy, who was probably 15.

Amber had grown, and he found it confusing. She seated him at the bar and asked him what he wanted. When he said a Coke, she looked at him with a crooked smile and asked, "Are you sure?"

"Yeah, I'm sure."

"I'll come back," she said. "I gotta check on my customers." He watched her go with the guilty bewilderment of a parent seeing his little girl dressed as a sex object.

The room was a swirl of noise and movement, replete with big-screen TVs and hopping with girls dressed like his daughter. It looked to be a hard-drinking place. By reputation, Ukiah was a tough town, so that fit. When Amber came back, she asked him what he wanted to eat. "I get half off," she said.

He knew he would never relax in this environment. "Nothing," he said. "I'm okay. What time do you get off?"

She gave a frowning pout. "I have to work pretty late," she said. "We close at midnight, and then we have to clean up and set up for tomorrow."

She could see that he wasn't happy. "We can talk during my break," she said with a shrug.

"How long is that?"

"Fifteen minutes." She put her hands on her hips. "Look, if you'd given me some warning..."

He told her he needed to clean up. "Can I get into your place and just wait for you?"

Her pout grew, taking over her whole face. "My roommate might be there."

"I won't bite her. Hell, I'll find a meeting to go to. I need to do that anyway. Just if I can clean up. I'm straight from work because I wanted to see you."

* * *

The apartment building was one of those Hawaii-style arrangements popular years ago, with tropic gardens set in and around the units. It had a swimming pool in the middle, just about bathtub size, surrounded by a wrought-iron fence. The plantings were lush, with big, glossy leaves. Elvis let himself into Amber's apartment and was relieved to find it unoccupied. It was just a normal place; the tropical flourishes stayed outside, and the interior was neat, uncluttered, spare as a demo. Where did that come from? Amber had been a typical teenage mess when she lived with him. The refrigerator shelves had signs indicating which belonged to Amber and which to Mandy; Amber's had practically nothing except yoghurt and baby carrots. She must eat at the restaurant. He grabbed a handful of the carrots.

He hadn't thought about it when he saw her, but she did look skinny. When she lived with him as a 13- and 14-year-old, she had been pudgy. He wouldn't have been surprised to find her soft as buttered toast.

He flicked on the TV and found Trump answering shouted questions as he moved to a black limousine. There was something hypnotic about that guy: the funny hair, the pear shape, the way of walking like a mechanical bear. Elvis was not a political type, but he liked Trump. Watching him move to his car and get in, Elvis tried to think what Trump reminded him of. When it came to him, he laughed. Trump reminded Elvis of himself. Something about wanting to have everybody look at you.

It was a funny thought. Imagine him as President of the United States. What a horrible idea.

After his shower, he got on his phone and found a meeting. This was working out perfectly, he thought. He had noticed an In-n-Out getting off the freeway, so he drove there and ordered a hamburger and fries. It wasn't far from there to the meeting, which was in an Episcopalian church hall. He parked across the street and ate in his car, watching as people arrived. Some of them stayed in their cars, like him. A lady in a priest's getup walked up the sidewalk to the church and unlocked the door. Elvis got out of his car, stretched, and crossed the street.

He didn't much like the meeting. Only eight or nine people attended, and the leader was an old dude with a wobbly head. One woman said that her Higher Power was a Krispy Kreme donut. Elvis started to laugh and then noticed that everybody else took it dead seriously. Elvis felt no motivation to speak, but the Krispy Kreme made him feel responsible to represent.

"I'm Elvis, and I'm an alcoholic."

"Hi, Elvis!"

"I just want to say that I'm struggling right now, but I'm still clean and sober. I got my two-year chip last week. I owe it all to Jesus Christ, who is my Higher Power, and according to me, the only Higher Power who actually cares. Not to criticize anybody, but I don't think a donut is very concerned about you."

He looked around the group to see whether they were tracking. After saying that he was from out of town, visiting his daughter, he sat down. He didn't know any of these people, but it made him nervous not to know what they were thinking. *There I go*, he thought to himself. Just like Bill said, I'm afraid that I won't make everybody happy, even though I will never see them again after tonight.

Then he thought of his other fear—that he would disappear, that his life would be just one big melting marshmallow. This passed through him like an ocean wave. He was visiting his daughter because she was his link with posterity, and there she was popping out of her blouse and putting on a show for any man with five dollars for a beer. Here he was in a meeting in a church hall with people who probably couldn't even remember his name, people he didn't know and didn't want to know. People who thought their Higher Power was a donut.

Impulsively, he got up to leave, but before he had made it halfway to the door, the woman who had testified to the Krispy Kreme got up to follow him. Just outside the door, she touched his arm and asked him if he was all right. In the dim light, it was hard to tell how old she was; she had a pleasant, sweet expression that made him think of the girl in the old Carnation milk commercials. She was looking right up into his eyes.

"I'm fine," he said. Surely she was a nice person and he had been too hard on her. "My daughter is waiting for me."

"The meeting is over at eight," she said. "Can't you stay that long?"

"No, I need to go," he said and walked away. Over his shoulder he said, "Thank you!"

Immediately, he felt like a hole had opened up in his stomach, leaving him empty and weightless. He got in the car, started the engine, and didn't know where to go. It wasn't even eight o'clock, so he had hours to kill. He didn't want to go back to the apartment, where the roommate might come in. She was probably nice, and he would like having somebody to talk to, but he hated to inconvenience her. Also, he might terrify her if he showed up unannounced, assuming that Amber hadn't warned her.

He felt lost and rootless. What did he have? He had a daughter, and he had Angel. But he didn't have either very securely. They weren't tied down.

He had a job. He had a truck. Neither one was great, but they functioned and were a lot more than many people could claim.

It came to him that his father was like a root growing from his past into the present. That was why he needed to see him. Here was half his identity, the only living half, and he didn't know him at all.

* * *

Elvis parked in a dark corner at the Walmart, and his thoughts went back to the fire. Those memories could still take over his mind. It was the biggest thing that had ever happened to him, and remembering it could be comforting, somehow. It could remove him from whatever misery he was going through.

He remembered the strange darkness: absolute except for the orange sky. The man in the car had told him to pound on doors and wake people up. There were six houses on the cul-de-sac. Doorbells didn't ring—there was no power—so he pounded on doors, shouting. At the first house, he raided the landscaping for a rounded river rock the size of his fist. It made a satisfying noise when he pounded the door, a loud, hollow *thunk*.

He gave it twenty knocks per door. Three knocks, a shout, three more knocks, another shout, and so on. By the time he reached fifteen, though, he decided that was enough. He moved on.

At the fourth house, he paused in his knocking after hearing something inside. He knocked again and shouted. "There's a fire! You have to get out!" This time, he heard a definite human voice, though he couldn't make out what it said. After more pounding, he heard fumbling with the lock. The door opened. Elvis couldn't see who was there—only the slightest shadow. "I'm your neighbor. You need to get out now! There's a fire!"

"What?" a woman's voice said.

"I'm your neighbor. You need to get out now! There's a fire!"

"Omigod, what time is it?"

"It's time to get out," Elvis said. "Most of the neighbors are already gone."

"I was so sound asleep," she said. "How long were you knocking? It sounded like you were going to break the door down."

"Lady," he said, "I gotta see about the other neighbors. You need to go."

He was just turning away when he saw a dark blur streak by his feet, an animal. The lady in the doorway let out a shriek. "Martha!" She pushed past Elvis onto the sidewalk. "Martha! Come back! You need to come!"

"That's my cat!" she wailed. "Help me catch her! I can't leave her here; she's an indoor cat!

"Listen," Elvis said, grabbing her arm. "You can't go looking for a cat. You need to go."

"I've got to find her!" she said and walked away from him, calling out the cat's name into the darkness.

"Lady, go! You need to get out of here!"

Elvis went on to the next house, pounding on the door until his hand hurt. Nobody. And so on around the cul-de-sac, his heart racing.

At least he had saved one lady. Unless she chased her cat for too long. Elvis found it strangely satisfying to be helping others in the midst of an inferno.

Was it his imagination that the wind had died a little? The air was not quite so hot. He had time. Apart from that one fiery branch, no flames had yet appeared. Elvis continued around the corner, pounding on more doors.

Maybe it was all unnecessary. Elvis cast his eyes along the street. Dark rectangles stood black against the sky. Smoke softened the lines as he looked down the street, fading into nothing. Maybe the fire would not come.

At that moment, a fierce blast of wind kicked up, blowing embers bright as neon down the street and the sidewalk. He had no time. He had to get out soon.

From somewhere ahead, he caught a glimmer of light. Had a car's headlights reflected in one of the windows? Or was a fire breaking out? The light flickered again and remained, coming from a window in one of the dark houses. Elvis hustled toward it.

He had a good fix on the house. He battered the front door. "Who's in there?" he shouted. "You need to get out!"

Elvis heard a whimper.

"Hello? Are you all right?"

He got no second answer, so he banged on the door again, hard. "If you're in there, open up!"

Maybe he heard an animal, a pet. But that wouldn't explain the light.

"Can you help me?" It was a weak, high ghost's voice.

"You bet!" Elvis shouted. "I'm a neighbor. Can you open the door?"

Now the voice was a wail. "Can you just come in?"

"You have to unlock the door."

"How do I do that?"

Elvis was agitated. "How do I know? It's your door!" While he said it, he jiggled the door handle. The door swung open. "Never mind! I'm here! Where are you?"

"I'm here!" The sound of a woman's voice was near, but in the absolute dark, he could see nothing.

"Wait a minute," he said, grabbing at his phone. "I can't see a thing."

A flashlight came on, dazzling him. "Hey, can you point it at the wall or something? I can't see with that thing in my eyes."

The light zigged away, making a dim streak on a wall across the room. Eventually, he made sense of the shadows: a woman sitting in a wheelchair.

"Oh my God," Elvis said. "Can you walk?"

* * *

Slowly, he drove back to Rosie's, the fire still sticking to his mind. The restaurant was ramping up into a party mood. People stood at the bar shouting from close range, trying to be heard. He grabbed the last seat and sipped a Coke while watching the waitresses come and go in their skimpy costumes. There were four big TV screens behind the bar, each one tuned to a different football game. Ordinarily, Elvis enjoyed watching football, which he had played in high school, but tonight his head wasn't in it. The colorful uniforms made him think of candy, and watching them tumble over each other was like a very primitive version of a computer game. He tried to strike up a conversation with people sitting beside him, but they kept shouting, "What?" until he gave up.

Wilma, the lady in the wheelchair, had needed his help, and he was glad he could give it. What he didn't like thinking about were the other men in the SLE, or the lady with the cat. He didn't know what had happened to them. People had died that night.

After 11, the crowd began to thin. The football games had ended; now there were game highlights repeated again and again and panels of beefy men making large hand gestures while grinning at each other and chortling. Amber, with tired eyes, came over and asked him if he was okay.

"You working tomorrow?" he asked.

"Unfortunately. I'm on for lunch and we open at ten."

"Maybe we can have breakfast together," Elvis said. "I need to be gone by nine."

"Where are you going?"

"Up to Willits."

"What's in Willits?"

He almost told her about finding her grandfather but decided now was not the time and place. "Just somebody I haven't seen in a long time," he said, and then he realized that she wasn't really listening anyway.

By midnight, everybody else had left the bar. Amber said he could put chairs on the tables. All the staff were too tired to chatter, and nobody thanked him for his help. By the time he and Amber were out on the street, shivering in a cold breeze, it was nearly one a.m. "You know where to go?" she asked, and he said he did but followed her anyway.

They whispered entering the apartment to avoid waking her roommate. Amber got a blanket and situated him on the sofa. She looked as though she were asleep on her feet. You forget this about youth, he thought; they need their rest. After she disappeared into her room, he took off his shoes and wrapped the blanket around him. The next thing he knew, he was waking up to daylight.

It was just seven. He thought he might fall asleep again, but in short order, his mind started working its way into the day. He would see his father. Maybe some of the mysteries of his life would be illuminated; maybe he would understand himself in the clear light of disclosure. Maybe his addiction would dry up like a puddle on a hot day. Maybe Santa Claus would declare an early Christmas.

He wanted to tell Amber what was going on. She was an adult now. She should hear it from him. He had always tried to hide his addiction from her, but she wasn't dumb; she had to know most of it already. A lot of friends and relations—not to mention Tom—had surely talked about him.

Elvis got up and put on his shoes. There was only one shared bathroom, and he used it as quietly as he could. Splashing water on his face, borrowing a brush for his hair, he examined himself in the mirror. He had on a green rugby shirt and tight white trousers. His Aussie hat he had left in the truck, along with his Raiders jacket.

They didn't have any coffee. He searched everywhere to no avail, quietly opening drawers and cabinets, even looking in the freezer. All he found was a box of mint tea bags.

He thought he would go out and get some, then come back. But he remembered Amber had the key. If he went out, he would leave the door unlocked with two sleeping girls inside. What kind of a dad would do that? The place was so neat, you couldn't miss a set of keys. There was no clutter of mail that might obscure them; no basket full of junk where she could have tossed them. Amber must have taken the keys into her room.

He listened for any stirring. Cars rushed by on the street, but the apartment offered only the dead silence of sleeping youth on Saturday morning. They had gone to bed after one; what were the odds that his daughter had set an alarm clock?

He decided to go. Only after he was in his car did he think that he ought to leave a note. It was too late. He had locked the door behind him.

By the time he reached Starbucks, he realized he could text. "DECIDED TO GO SO YOU COULD SLEEP," he wrote, and then added separately, "SEE YOU SOON I HOPE." He thought about saying I LOVE YOU, but he had never talked that way with Amber, and he didn't know how it would go over. When he read over the text, he didn't feel good about it, so he deleted the whole thing without sending it. It was stupid to go explaining yourself all the time. He got a large coffee and a muffin and took off for Willits, stuffing the muffin into his mouth with one hand and brushing the crumbs from his chest. He felt great. The short night would catch up with him sometime, but right now, he was energized to be on the road.

* * *

As instructed, Elvis stopped for breakfast at the Lumberjack Inn, a place notable for its gigantic, painted-plastic John Bunyan figure facing Main Street. Willard T had said you couldn't miss it, and he was right. For a Saturday morning, the place was bustling: pale-white people wearing sweatshirts and jeans, with baseball hats on their heads advertising tools and agricultural chemicals in addition to the usual sports teams.

Elvis sat down across from Willard, who was already halfway through a large platter of hotcakes. "How are you?" he said through a mouthful. He had his focus on getting his breakfast down, greeting his long-lost son with about as much interest as he would show for somebody he ran into at a hardware store.

"I'm glad to see you," Elvis said, really feeling it. He almost couldn't believe what was happening. This was his father.

He had plenty of time to study him, because his father barely looked up and made no attempt to talk. He had an old-fashioned haircut, slicked straight back. The longish ends curled up on themselves in the back, and the hair itself, which had started out a deep brown or almost black, was streaked with gray. Willard T had not shaved in some time. His beard was stubbly and gray, and his face a sickly yellow. You couldn't think that it was a handsome face, though perhaps it once had been.

Elvis couldn't see himself in it at all. After his mother's service, he had thought his dad's erratic driving and offbeat, prickly humor proved that he was really his father; but now, he wondered.

Willard T leaned back from his plate, brushed his mouth with a paper napkin, and said, "So, you ready for some adventure?"

"Adventure? I don't know about adventure."

"I told you I would let you in on some secrets. We're going up to Garberville."

"You got a high school reunion?" His father had grown up in Garberville, Elvis knew. His reclusive Aunt Carol lived there still, as far as he knew.

"We're going to visit your Aunt Carol. My sister. I don't know if you even know who she is."

"Yeah, sure," Elvis said. He thought, *Nobody forgets Aunt Carol and her potty mouth.*

"There's something funny going on there, and I want you to help me with it. When did you last see her?"

"Not since I was a kid."

"You got some ID?"

"Yeah. Why?"

"Good, because you might have to convince her who you are. I doubt she would know your face. You look like a goddam clown."

"You don't look so good yourself." Which was true. Willard's face was puffy and worn.

"I mean those stupid clothes." Elvis had to look down to see what he was wearing. He liked bright clothes, something with a little energy. He never understood what people had against it.

Elvis merely shrugged. "What do you want me to do with Aunt Carol?"

At that, his father's face achieved a remarkable, dreamy elation.

"Is this some kind of joke?" Elvis asked.

His father's face turned suddenly grave. "No joke," he said. "I don't joke around."

"Then what?"

A quick shake of the head. "I'll tell you when we get there. Let's get going." He moved as though to rise from his seat.

"I haven't had breakfast yet!"

Willard T was now on his feet. "Too bad. You should have gotten here earlier."

Meekly, Elvis followed. His father didn't hesitate, but walked out and into the parking lot. "Where'd you park?" he asked. Elvis indicated his truck, which was one of eight or nine cars aiming straight at the Lumberjack building.

"You better move it to the back." Willard threw a hand toward the rear margin of the parking lot, where it shaded into a dirt lot covered with dusty weeds. When Elvis hesitated, he explained. "I'm not riding in that bucket of crap. You come with me."

Elvis had already begun moving toward his car when he stopped and asked over his shoulder, "How long are we going to be?"

Willard seemed to think that amusing. He sniffed. "It's not going to take long. Just a day." Then he thought better. "I'd bring all your crap. You never know."

They were on the road in Willard's big Buick when it occurred to Elvis that his father hadn't paid for his breakfast. At least, he hadn't seen him pay.

"You pay back there?" he asked.

His father didn't say anything. He acted like he didn't hear.

In no time, they left the town behind and drove into oaks mixed with pasture. Then, not far on, they entered the redwoods. Elvis had forgotten. In his memory, these redwoods were like those he saw on the highway to Ft. Bragg. Not so. These were a world apart: huge and austere, telling him to shut up and look.

His father talked as though he didn't see anything. He was driving at a reckless speed, squealing through the curves, even though the trees flanking the road would not even feel the bump Willard's car made in killing both him and Elvis.

They passed through a tiny roadside town. An aging motel or two, a café/general store giving off smoke from its stovepipe chimney, a broken-down pickup parked lazily on the rippling asphalt. There were fading signs advertising redwood burl and bigfoot memorabilia—signals of entrepreneurial hope—but this was a zone that commerce and even tourism had passed by. With the summer's end, the towns had emptied out, which seemed to lend even more glory to the unconcerned trees.

"You ever been to that house?" his father was asking him.

"What house?"

"The one that Carol lives in. You ever been there?"

Elvis tried to think. "Where is it?"

"In Garberville. It's the house I grew up in, you know. Should put up a plaque. Or sell tickets. Sebastiano Mystery House. Me and your Aunt Carol. She was the looker; can you believe that? She looks like a pile of dog shit now—at least she did last I saw her. When did you last see her? Did you ever go to the house?"

"I don't think I've seen her since you died." Elvis snuck a smile in, though his father didn't appear to notice. "I remember her, though. I always liked her. She talked to me like I was an adult. Gave me cigarettes, too."

"How old were you?"

"Not too old. You died when I was ten."

"And already smoking." Willard shook his head.

"Well hell, you started giving me beer when I was in kindergarten."

"I never did that."

"Yes, you did."

"So that's how you became an addict? It was my fault?"

"Absolutely," Elvis said. "Beer at five, crack at six, heroin at eight, meth at nine. A life of crime that started right there. All your fault."

His father didn't respond. He was leaning into the steering wheel as though he were nearsighted, trying to guide his way through the trees. Elvis leaned back in his seat and smiled. "Nah, you didn't make me an addict. I didn't start doing drugs until after you died. Mom was nowhere to be found, Tom was a football superstar, and I was a lost puppy. I hung out with the wrong people, and I got hooked."

"So now you're clean?" His father was tight-lipped, grim, driving too fast. With his hair swept back, he looked like he belonged in a black-and-white crime movie from the '40s.

"Yeah, I am." Elvis hesitated before claiming it. He had lately felt so weak.

"And you said it was one of those religious programs. Twelve steps?"

"Yeah. That plus a lot of other stuff."

"Like what?"

"Bible study, prayer, service."

"Service what?"

"We run a shelter for homeless people. Meals, beds, showers; whatever they need, we provide." Elvis was surprised to hear himself talk in the present tense.

"God, sounds horrible."

"You should try it."

"I ain't no addict."

"You aren't?"

"No, I just like to drink."

"Alcohol is a drug, you know."

"So is aspirin."

The high canopy over their heads made the forest a perpetual twilight, especially with the sun so low on the horizon. It hushed their conversation. Elvis wondered what they would do with his Aunt Carol and how long it would take, but for now, he was content to let the road wind ahead of them. He felt like a kid again, riding in his daddy's car.

The long quiet got boring, however. Switching on the radio, he tried to find some music but got nothing but signals full of static. "We're really out here," he said. "Like the wilderness." He kept fiddling with the stations until his father reached across to slap his hand away, then turn off the radio. Elvis did not protest, having seen that there was no music to be had.

"So, bring me up to date," Elvis said. "What have you been doing for thirty years?"

"Where do you want to start?"

"Okay, start by telling me where. You said something about Alaska. Were you there long?"

"Nah, not long. Couple of fishing seasons. I can't stand Alaska."

"Why not?"

"Too cold. Six months of snow. I never got warm the whole time."

"Then where?"

Willard took his time answering. "I've been in California most of the time. In Oregon a little, too. But mainly California."

"Where in California?"

His father shot him a glance. "Anywhere by the water. Figure it out."

Elvis mentally ran through the possibilities. There were 200 miles of coastline north of Ft. Bragg. A bunch of towns around Eureka. Crescent City, way up at the Oregon border. He didn't know all the places you could dock a boat; he had never gone up there.

"I guess it must be Eureka. That's the biggest port up there."

"Guess again. Eureka is a dump."

"Then where?"

"That's for me to know and you to find out."

"Have you been fishing all this time?"

"I'm a man of many talents."

"Meaning what?"

"Meaning you can't make any money fishing these days. The salmon are gone; the government gives you about three days for crab. I'm in business now."

Elvis was tickled. "Shit, you're growing?"

"I didn't say that. I'm not a farmer. Not a pothead either."

"Then what?"

"Then what what?"

"What kind of business you in?"

"Any kind. I look for opportunities."

Elvis shook his head. "You must be missing something if you're looking for opportunities up here. This is more like the land of missed opportunities."

"Yeah, well, not to me."

They were quiet for about five minutes, watching the scenery flow by. Then Willard asked, "How much time have you done?"

"Quite a bit," Elvis said.

"How much?"

He calculated. "About five years. Maybe six."

"You don't even know?"

"I've had quite a few stints in jail. They're hard to keep track of. Four and a half years in prison, all together."

"And when did you get all those tattoos?"

"You like 'em?" Elvis chuckled. He had been with tattoos so long he rarely remembered that he had them. "I got my first one when I was sixteen. Been adding them ever since."

"They look ridiculous. Make you look like something you'd see at the freak show at the county fair."

"You're just jealous, Pops. You wish you could be young again." Elvis laughed. It struck him as funny and a trifle sad. He wished *he* could be young again. Part of his resistance to doing Step Four was the fact that when he reviewed his life, he couldn't see anything worth fighting for. He hadn't accomplished a thing. That was a melancholy fact he didn't want to dwell on, but Step Four made you dwell on it.

* * *

Just off 101, Garberville had a two-block downtown with three cafés, a similar number of bars, one grocery store, and roughly equal numbers of small, quirky shops and vacant storefronts. The town felt as though it had been put up on a temporary basis. It was built on the slope of a hill, but you got no view to speak of; Doug fir or oak covered the sky.

Willard didn't hesitate; he didn't even slow down getting off the highway, but drove at a dangerous rate of speed straight to the Eagle Room, a bar on the north end of the strip. He hooked left, slammed on the brakes, and skidded to a halt in front.

The building might once have been a paint store, with the windows covered over. The parking lot, if you could call it that, wasn't paved. Some gravel had once been thrown down, but that was long ago, and now all you could see was tan dirt rutted from car wheels and pocked with holes that would be puddles when it rained. Hanging at roof level was a neon sign with the silhouette of a resting eagle and two dancing cocktail glasses.

"I'll stay here," Elvis said when he saw what his father planned.

"Suit yourself." Willard hustled inside as though he had to go to the bathroom. Elvis sat in the car wondering what he had gotten himself into. This was not a good environment for staying sober.

After ten minutes of boredom, he got out and wandered the street. There were no curbs and no sidewalk, and even the painted line marking where the parking lot stopped and the street began was wearing down to invisibility. Across the road was a low-slung building with a painted sign, the "Garden of Beadin.'"

Elvis walked past houses and vacant lots to the commercial strip. Feeling hungry, he considered eating in one of the cafés. The trouble was, his father might come looking for him and simply leave if he didn't find him.

Back at the Eagle Room, he decided to go inside. The smell hit him as soon as he opened the door: beer and whiskey and men. He could hardly see in the gloom, though he made out three solitary figures slumped at the bar, which gleamed with the light of a Coors sign on the back wall.

"Hey, Willard," he said, and one of the figures straightened and turned toward him. "How long you gonna stay here?"

"Come and sit down," his father said, not unkindly. "You want a beer?"

Elvis declined. "I'm kinda hungry. I thought if you were planning to stay awhile, I would go get some breakfast."

"You're too late for breakfast," Willard said.

"Lunch, then. Some food."

"Nah, come sit here. I'm just going to finish this one. Let's talk."

Reluctantly, Elvis took the stool next to his father.

"Did I tell you that Carol was a looker? I did? Hard to believe now, she's so fat and old. But no, she was tall and willowy and a lot of fun. Older than me, you know. I always looked up to her. She was wild right from the get-go. Didn't like school. I think she needed glasses and they didn't know it until the sixth grade when one of the teachers figured out she couldn't see the blackboard. They got her glasses, but she wouldn't wear them.

"She had something wrong with her. It wasn't the glasses. She said the letters would jump around when she tried to keep an eye on them. She's smart enough, but she didn't try hard. And she was always getting in trouble. She started smoking when she was in about the fifth grade." Willard gave Elvis a playful punch. "Just like you!"

"What about you? What were you like?"

"Oh, I was the golden boy. I could see my sister wasn't getting anywhere, so I acted different. I kissed up. Everybody loved me. I was an athlete, you know. That's where you and your brother got it. We had a pretty good football team."

"What position did you play?"

"Oh, hell, we had such a little-bitty team, I played everything. Tackle, mostly, but halfback, and even quarterback. Up here in the woods, we were just glad to have enough people to make a team. Course, in those days, what with the lumber industry going strong, there were some tough dudes around."

"So what are we going to see Aunt Carol about?"

His father looked at him sharply. "*We* aren't going. *You* are going. She doesn't need to know I'm around."

"Whoa. Hold on. You need to explain this to me. What are we doing here?"

"Okay," Willard said. "Here's the deal. You know she's living in the family house. The one I grew up in. She never left. I went into the service, and she never went anywhere. I moved to Ft. Bragg, and she stayed here. Supposedly, she took care of our parents. I think it was more the other way 'round. After they died, she just stayed on. She never goes out anywhere. God knows what that place is like now. She's a total slob. It's probably crawling with vermin. Who cares? That's her problem. I want to know who the house belongs to. I think it's mine."

Elvis was caught short. "I'm not following you," he said.

His father took a long pull on his beer. "She doesn't trust me." Elvis waited for more, and it came after another long swallow. "She'll be glad to see you. When did you last get up here?"

"I've never been up here. I haven't seen Aunt Carol since you died. That reminds me, did they have a service for you? I can't remember one."

"How should I know? I was dead. Well, anyway, I want you to find out where the papers are."

"What papers?"

"What papers? For the house, you ding-dong. She's never changed the title. I went to the courthouse and checked. It's still in Father's name."

"Wait. You're saying Grandpa died what, thirty years ago, and the house is still in his name? How is that possible?"

He shook his head. "She just never reported it. This county wouldn't notice if you jacked up the house and took it away in a truck."

"So she's paying taxes in his name?"

"She has to. If she didn't pay, they would auction it."

"Why would she do that?"

Willard laughed. "Maybe because it's not hers. She can live there on the cheap, as long as nobody knows. The taxes aren't much."

"So you want to throw her out?"

"I don't care. As long as I get what's coming to me."

"And what makes you think you get the house? She's older than you."

"Yeah, but I'm the boy. My father was old school. He wouldn't leave it to a girl. And if there's no will, then I get half."

Elvis was not the most scrupulous person, but the thing gave him the creeps. "Tell me why I want to do this," he asked.

"Cause your old dad, back from the dead, asked you to? I'm letting you in on all the old family secrets here. Wasn't that what you were aiming for?" When Elvis didn't answer, he went on. "I'm just asking you to help me get some information. What I do with it is my business."

"You want me to go up there and talk to her like her long-lost nephew, and meanwhile steal her papers."

"Not steal. Borrow. Or even just find out where she keeps them. If she caught me up there, she would shoot me."

"What did you do to make her so hostile to you?"

"Nothing! She's stiffing me, you know. Naturally, she's not that excited to see me come around."

"Wait a minute," Elvis said. "Doesn't she think you're lost at sea?"

Willard shot him a look. "Hell, no. Nobody thinks that. You're probably the last person."

"Tom does."

"Okay, you and Tom."

"So Aunt Carol knows you're alive. She's seen you since you died."

"Yeah, a few times. We don't see eye to eye."

"But you don't actually know that she's doing anything to cheat you."

"No, I don't actually know. I suspect. That's why I want you to find out."

* * *

As Elvis was going out the door of the Eagle, a woman stopped him. She had the kind of face that looked like somebody sprayed it with lacquer. Too much sun and too much booze, Elvis thought to himself.

He was shocked when she said she had been in elementary school with him, just a grade ahead. Her name snapped into place: Barbara, Barbie, the fastest girl in the school, winning the 50-yard dash going away when he was in fifth grade. He would never have recognized her.

"So what are you doing now?" he asked, genuinely interested.

"I live here. I own the place across the street."

"The Garden of Beadin'? Really? Did you come up with that name?"

"No, I bought the place a few years ago. Awesome name, though, huh?"

Willard, who had been settling his bar bill, came through the door. "This is my father," Elvis said. "We're up here visiting my aunt."

Barbie shook Willard's hand while looking warily at him. "Who's your aunt?" she asked. "If she lives in Garberville, I probably know her."

She didn't, though. "We're a strange family," Willard said by way of explanation. "My sister is a recluse. I'm a dead man."

Elvis laughed. "My father is a little weird. You probably don't remember, but when we were in school, he died. That's what we thought. He's a fisherman, and we thought he was lost at sea. Turns out he really didn't die; he just took off. We are renewing old acquaintance."

"And how is your brother?" Barbie asked, her face still and tight.

"Tom? You remember Tom?"

"I had a crush on him. Like every girl in Ft. Bragg."

Willard excused himself and went outside. Elvis found it easier talking to this woman than following his father, so he lingered. "So, did you ever go out with Tom?"

"Are you kidding? He was so much older. And taken. What was the name of his girlfriend?"

"Francine. He married her."

"I heard. How's he doing?"

"I think he's doing okay. We were just at my mom's memorial a few days ago."

"Oh, I'm sorry for your loss. Where's he living now?"

"He's still in Ft. Bragg. Just south of the bridge."

"God, I'd love to see him. When you see him, tell him to look up Barbie in Garberville."

"Yeah, I'll tell him."

"And take care of yourself," Barbie said, giving his arm a pat.

It was always like that, Elvis thought when he got outside. Tom was a hero. Occasionally, Elvis had tried to draft off that. One time, when Tom was playing in Oakland, he had gone down to see him. That was just after he got out of high school, when he was hopelessly stupid. He thought he could just go up to the gate and ask for him. What had he imagined, that they would usher him into the locker room just because he claimed to be Tom Sebastiano's brother? Instead, he spent the whole game at the gate, listening to the rumble of the public address system and—faintly—the crowd's roar. He spent three hours talking to security people and ticket grifters, letting them know how important he was because his brother was playing inside. He never even saw Tom.

He couldn't blame his brother for that. What he did blame his brother for was the one time he had come down to Santa Rosa. Elvis had been tickled, thinking he just wanted to see him. They sat across from each other in Denny's while Tom lectured him about how much he was screwing up. He poured on the self-righteousness and contempt. Finally, Elvis couldn't take any more, and he just walked out. Tom had never apologized for that.

* * *

They checked in at the King Kwality Inn, a line of rooms built in tan brick with newly painted black doors. The office was the front room of a small house. A buzzer went off when Elvis pushed the door open, but nobody appeared at the desk. Elvis could hear a TV behind the partition. "Hello?" he said. "Anybody here?"

On the desk, a hand-carved wooden sign said "The Patels." A young South Asian woman appeared, holding a hefty toddler and trailed by a fluffy white dog. "Yes," she said. She had dark, sad eyes, as did her child. After he had checked in, Elvis asked Mrs. Patel where the best place to get lunch was. She looked nervous, tightening her lips. "I believe all the restaurants serve lunch," she said.

"Sure, but which one do you recommend?"

"I would not like to recommend one over the others."

Elvis guessed that she had not eaten in any of the restaurants. It would be hard enough to be a Mexican in this town; to be an Asian would be unthinkable.

"Is this your daughter?" Elvis asked, which prompted her to look down at the same moment that a wispy smile crossed her mouth.

"Yes," she said. "We have two girls. The older one is at school just now."

"I bet she's a great student."

"Yes, sir, they do their work."

"I bet they do. That's what I never learned how to do, and look what it got me."

Elvis dumped his suitcase in the room and went to the market. He bought a package of two beef burritos, offered one to his dad—he declined—and heated the other in the room's small microwave. After he had eaten, he said, "I'm ready."

His dad had stretched out on one of the beds. "Ready for what?"

"Ready to go see Aunt Carol."

"So go."

"I don't know where she lives. And I don't have keys to the car."

"You don't need keys; you can walk." He sat up and gave him directions.

He was right—it was not far. The house stood on the edge of town, set back from the road in a copse of conifers. The drive was overgrown with weeds, and trees shrouded the second story so you could barely see it. It was old and needed paint.

He had the right address, assuming he had gotten it correctly from his father, so he mounted the wide cement porch and rang the bell. Moments later, he rang it again and pounded on the screen door.

"Goddammit, stop that!" a voice cried out—a low, smoker's voice. "Come in or go away!"

It was too formidable a voice for him to go right in. "Aunt Carol?" he shouted. "It's me, your nephew, Elvis. Long time, no see. Can I come in?"

"I said come in. What are you, an idiot?"

Elvis eased into a dark room, its windows heavily curtained. Seated in a burgundy vinyl recliner was a heavyset woman wearing striped pajamas and a crocheted cap. She stared silently at him.

"Hey," he said nervously. "I haven't seen you in such a long time. I was hoping to see you at my mom's memorial. Did you get word about it?"

"It's Elvis, is it?" she asked. "Good God, what is that outfit you've got on?"

Elvis had on one of his favorite western-style shirts, satiny scarlet with a cowboy silhouetted against an Arizona mesa painted on the back. He also wore purple jeans, cowboy boots, and his Australian outback hat with the brim rolled up on the side.

"I don't want to look like anybody else, do I?" Elvis grinned.

"You got a great name to keep up."

"It's yours, too," he said.

She shook her head. "I'm not talking about the dago name; I'm talking about the King. I'm a big fan of the King. Just look around."

His eyes had adjusted to the dim light, and he was able to see that there were Elvis Presley memorabilia all through the room: on the walls, on the TV console, and on the end tables. Behind Aunt Carol was a clock made from an Elvis cutout, with the clock face emanating from his swiveling hips. By the sofa was an 18-inch ceramic statue of the King in military fatigues.

"Where do you keep the really tacky stuff?" Elvis asked.

"Where do you think? In my bedroom," Aunt Carol answered. "Why don't you sit down. Let me look at you. You're the short one, aren't you?"

"Shorter than Tom," he said. "Fun size."

"I bet you are. You want anything?"

"No, I'm fine. I just ate."

"This Mary Jane is good. I just got it from a guy I know who grows it in the woods."

Elvis had been too nervous to take in the strong, skunky flavor of the room, but now he instantly recognized the scent, and then noticed a hand-rolled joint in an ashtray on the arm of the recliner. It jolted him; he had never thought of his aunt that way.

"That's okay," he said. "I'm off all substances."

She drew herself up. "Well, aren't you special. What happened, did you get religion?"

"I guess you could say that. I was in a program at the Sonoma Gospel Mission, in Santa Rosa. Twelve steps."

"So you've got a Higher Power."

He couldn't tell whether she was mocking him. "Yeah. It's a Christian program, so we don't really talk about it that way. We talk about God. But I go to AA, so I know what you're saying."

Aunt Carol shook her head, as though trying to loosen something. "You must be the first Sebastiano in history to be clean and sober. Except my grandfather, who was a religious fanatic. You're not like that, are you?"

"I don't think so. Just trying to live by what's right."

She snorted. "So is that why you came to see me after all these years? You come here to convert me?"

Elvis shook his head. "No, Aunt Carol; like I told you, at my mom's service, I was hoping you would come. I saw my brother for the first time in a long time, and I saw my stepfather and his family. Thinking about Mom just made me wish to catch up with family. I've been out of touch for the last few years. Which all ties in to getting sober, because when I'm wasted, I isolate. You know about the fourth step? It makes you think about all the people in your life and setting things right with them."

"Sounds horrible," Aunt Carol said with a grimace.

"Yeah, well, it kinda is. You wouldn't do it if you weren't kinda desperate."

"The one who ought to set things right is your father. My brother."

Elvis stared in alarm. Talking about the 12 steps made him feel like a dog for coming up here to bamboozle his aunt. Willard T said she knew he was alive, but did she know what he was up to? Just what did she know? Elvis chose to play dumb.

"So, what did he do? I was just a kid when he was lost at sea."

Aunt Carol smirked. "Don't want to say anything against the dead. What did he do? What *didn't* he do? He was bad when he was sober and worse when he was drunk, which was most of the time. He owed money to everybody. He stole. He cheated." She picked up her joint and took a long drag, closing her eyes as she held the smoke.

"Aunt Carol, maybe you can tell me something that I've been trying to figure out. Did he have a service? Because I can't remember one. I remember my mom taking me to what I thought was his grave, but now I'm pretty sure that was your father's grave. They had the same name, didn't they?"

She nodded. "They did. They were as different as can be, and they fought like cats. I had to listen to them go at it. But they had the same name.

"I don't know about a service," she added. "I doubt anybody wanted one. What could you possibly say about a man like that?"

"So, what was your father like? You said he was opposite."

Carol took another long toke. "Yeah, but also alike in some ways. Hardheaded and belligerent. He was a Foursquare prophet; did you know that? Preached at us on Sunday and every other day of the week. He thought it would make us Christians, but it just drove us away."

"What's a Foursquare?"

She waved her hand, dismissing it. "Oh, that's a brand of holy rollers."

"I never had any idea," Elvis said. "I thought he was a logger."

"Well, he was. In a little-bitty church up here in the woods, nobody gets paid for preaching. A man of God has to work to support his family. He was a hard worker—I'll give him that. We never did without. He lived for that church, though. He just knew that Jesus was going to come, and we would all be left behind. We heard that all the time, like he looked forward to it. At first it scared me, and then I realized it was a big joke, and he didn't like that."

"He wallop you?"

"No, he was unusual; he didn't believe in hitting. Most of the people around here, it was spare the rod, spoil the child, and he never said anything against that, but he wouldn't hit us. At least he didn't hit me, and I don't think he hit Willard T, either. I never saw it if he did. No, my dad just ran his mouth. He would tell us what we had coming to us, and when we got old enough, we would roll our eyes and make fun of him. Which made him mad. And now look at us. He's gone, Jesus didn't come, and I'm still here."

"This is the house you grew up in, isn't it? Who gets it when you go?" Elvis tried to ask casually, but his heart was pumping. He didn't like this business. Why he was doing it, he couldn't really say. It went against his principles.

She shrugged. "The county will probably end up with it. I don't care. I won't be here to worry about it. Say, did you ever get married?"

It took him a moment to realize that he had been asked a question. "No," Elvis said. "I never did."

"Because I heard that you were shacked up with some woman in Santa Rosa. You still together?"

"Angel, you mean. Who did you hear that from?"

"Through the grapevine," she said.

"I didn't think you kept in touch with any family."

"Look who's talking."

The marijuana seemed to be forgotten, leaking a thin thread of smoke toward the ceiling. Elvis couldn't help feeling its appeal. He needed something to slow himself down.

"What a trailer-trash name that is," Carol said. "So you're still with her but you don't want to marry her? With all this religion, I would think you'd want to make her an honest woman."

He knew she was yanking his chain, but nevertheless, it rankled him. It touched on a sensitive point. How did she know about Angel in the first place?

"It's complicated," he said. "I don't know if she'd want to marry me. And we're not living together now."

"What happened?"

"Nothing happened." Which was true. Elvis couldn't say why they weren't together. It just worked out that way. They got along better when they weren't trying to share the bathroom.

"Hey, I know!" Aunt Carol said suddenly. "Why don't I give you Willard's Bible? Since you're so religious now."

At first Elvis thought she referred to his father. Then he remembered the duplicate names. "You mean my grandfather's Bible? You've got it?"

"Yeah, somewhere. It's a big black thing, all marked up with underlinings and little tiny notes. You should take it."

"Can I see it?" he asked.

Aunt Carol directed him to a big rolltop desk in the dining room. She didn't get up, but took up her joint again, pulling it in and out of her mouth while telling him where to look. The desk was vomiting papers: bills, manila folders, bank statements, checkbooks, yellowing junk mail. She said the Bible was in there somewhere.

Elvis tried to excavate the piles without moving them, but that didn't work; it was like trying to see through mud. In the process of shifting papers out of the way, he came to a thick green folder, like something he could have used in a high school report, if he had ever done a high school report. In black marking pen, it was labeled "Official." Opening the cover, he found it stuffed with an inch-thick stack of papers—what looked like plot maps, incomprehensible legal documents, medical bills, school transcripts, resumes, bank statements. This kind of paperwork made Elvis dizzy; he had a physical reaction to it. He put the folder on top of a stack of other junk—magazines, circulars, more bills—and set them all on the floor. He pulled out more papers, opened drawers, and poked in crannies. Finally, he happened on the Bible, in the bottom of a deep drawer that was meant to hold hanging files.

It was indeed a thick, black Bible, its soft leather cover worn with use. When he turned the pages, he saw that it was more complicated than any Bible he had ever seen. Tiny footnotes covered the bottom of each page, and a one-inch column diving down the middle contained inscrutable numbers and letters. Some pages had maps or illustrations. Drawing his eye above all else was the mark of his grandfather, who had written on almost every page, sometimes in a scrawl so thick and dense that the words overlapped each other or spilled around the bottom corner and up the side of the page.

"I found it," he cried out.

"You want it?" Aunt Carol shouted.

"You don't mind?" he asked.

"Hell no," she said. "You take it. Maybe you'll get some good out of it."

He had taken a seat in the swivel chair. Fascinated by his find—a root extending into his family's past—he twisted the chair back and forth while he paged through the Bible. In the book of Proverbs, he came to emphatic underlinings, pencil marks that dug into the thin Bible paper. There were no added words here, just the insistent marks. The chosen verses had to do with a father's discipline, with wasteful living, with hard work. Elvis's attention was riveted by a verse on drinking: "Look not thou upon the wine when it is red, when it giveth his colour in the cup, when it moveth itself aright. At the last it biteth like a serpent, and stingeth like an adder." Not only had his grandfather underlined this, but he had drawn double lines on all sides to set it in a box.

He came wandering out of the dining room still looking at the open Bible. "Look at this," he said to his aunt. "Have you ever seen all the things he marked up?"

She was still puffing on her weed. "He used to sit with that thing in the kitchen, and you didn't want to get too near, or you'd get a sermon."

"It's almost like I can hear him," Elvis said in wonder.

Walking back to the motel, Elvis marveled at his discovery. Before today, he never knew he had any believers in his family. At the mission, he had stumbled into faith like Columbus bumping into America. Now he knew his grandfather had been a prophet. More than that, he obviously had a thing about alcohol. Was he preaching to himself? Those underlinings came thundering out of the pages. "Like a serpent." That applied to drugs just as well: slithering into your life, sleek and deadly. His grandfather was warning him.

* * *

At dinner in the Blue Rose Café, Elvis tried explaining to Willard T his reaction to finding the Bible. "I came up here hoping that it would help me get started on a different course. All my life, I've been the kid whose father died, so he got in trouble. Now I know you didn't die, but how does that make it any better? You abandoned me. If we could reconnect, though, that would be a different kind of story. I'll be honest; I came looking for that.

"I didn't dream of finding this, though. What this Bible means is something deeper. It means I'm grounded in a man of faith who loved his Bible. I've got a solid past."

Willard sucked down a beer with his burger and ordered another. He seemed bored by Elvis's explanation. "The old man was as stiff as a fireplace poker," he said. "No bend in him at all. He spent all his time preaching at people, and the more he preached, the farther away they went. By that, I mean me."

"And Aunt Carol?" Elvis asked. He was disappointed by the reaction, but it wasn't unexpected.

"Yeah, her too. He never got it."

"Did he drink?" Elvis asked. "He had these underlinings about wine and beer and stuff."

"I don't know that he ever drank. I wish he had."

The café was clean and well-lit, with Formica tabletops in a butcher-block pattern. Each booth had a single artificial flower in a small vase. Elvis had insisted they come here instead of eating in the bar. He didn't want to be around a bunch of booze.

The waitress was a plump type who called everybody "hon." Elvis had already found out that she had six grandchildren, four of whom lived in the area. She showed him pictures on her phone.

"This one looks just like you," he told her.

"God, I hope not," she said.

"C'mon," Elvis said in mock astonishment. "What if they looked like him?" He pointed at Willard.

"That would be okay," she answered sweetly. "So what are you two eating tonight? The chicken is good, if you like chicken."

Now she laid their plates on the table, brought a bottle of catsup, and asked, "Can I do anything else for you?"

"Would you say grace?" Elvis asked.

"No, you should be the one to pray," she said. "Pray that nobody brains you."

Elvis dug into his fries. He had ordered a hamburger, food that he loved but hardly ever made.

"So, what did you find out about the will?" Willard asked. He was cutting into a steak.

Elvis sank. He had forgotten all about the purpose of his mission. "I didn't really find out," he admitted. "I asked, but she didn't really answer. It sounded like there isn't any will. She said the county would get the house."

His father threw his paper napkin at Elvis.

"But I think I know where the papers are," Elvis said, trying to recover. "When I was rooting around in her desk, looking for the Bible, there was this folder that said 'official' and it had all these legal papers in it. If she has your father's will, I bet it's in there."

"Why didn't you look?"

"I didn't think of it. I was looking for the Bible."

Willard scowled. "Where is the folder?"

"It's in the big desk in the dining room. Actually, it's on top, in a big pile of junk."

"I need to see that," Willard said.

"Why don't you just ask her?" Elvis said. "That might be easier."

Willard shook his head. "There's no way she would even talk to me. Hell, I don't think she would tell you anything, either. She's not a fool, you know."

"Then why did you send me up there?"

"You have to start somewhere." Willard said no more, but he ordered a third beer. When it came time to settle up, he asked Elvis if he would cover the bill. "I'm a little short right now."

Elvis was taken aback. He had enough cash for the meal, but his credit card was nearly maxed out. "What are you saying? I don't have enough to pay for our motel room."

His father waved him off. "Don't worry about that."

"What do you mean? You just said you're a little short." He kept his voice down, but there was an urgent tilt to it.

Willard puckered his lips and then gave a big, happy grin. "We'll just owe it to them."

"They're not going to let us do that."

"We're not going to ask. We'll just go."

"Yeah, well, they'll catch up with me. I had to give them a credit card when we registered."

His father seemed to find that amusing. "You've got a job. I'm sure you're good for it." At that, he got to his feet. Elvis thought that he was going to the restroom. He half-watched him because he was thinking madly of the money situation. Only after his father went out the front door did Elvis realize that he was leaving. Elvis got to the door in time to see Willard's back in the parking lot. His father turned expectantly when he called.

"Where are you going?"

"I'm going back to the Eagle," Willard said. "I thought you didn't want to go."

"I thought you said you were a little short."

"I am. I've got enough for a few beers."

Willard waited expectantly for a few moments, then shrugged and turned to be on his way.

From 7:00 to about 9:00, Elvis watched TV in the room. After he got thoroughly bored, he decided to go for a walk. There weren't many cars on the main highway at this time of night, so he could walk on the edge of the road without having to dodge too often. There was a moon.

He was thinking about all that he'd experienced that day. He now knew his father. He knew his aunt. The pieces of his life were more visible—maybe held together with duct tape, but nevertheless finding their places. He really had no urge to join his father in the bar. Temptation seemed to have vanished, and maybe, he thought, it had gone for good. He had found the missing pieces in his life. His grandfather was a man of God. He had his Bible, even now, back at the room.

He got back to the room after midnight. His father was already in bed, breathing heavily, smelling of liquor. He didn't stir when Elvis turned on the light by his side of the bed. Elvis brushed his teeth and started to undress. He wondered what would happen in the morning. If they just left with the bill unpaid, would he be arrested? He had finally gotten off probation, and he wanted desperately to avoid going back. They would put him in prison for practically nothing.

His father's clothes had been dumped in a pile by the side of the bed. Elvis picked them up to put them on a chair and noticed the weight in his father's pants pocket. From curiosity, he pulled out the wallet and unfolded it. Elvis found a wad of cash in the billfold, mostly twenties.

Glancing guiltily at his father to be sure that he was absolutely asleep, Elvis counted out $200 and stuck it in his own pocket. He then folded the wallet and returned it to his dad's pants.

Quietly gathering his stuff from the bathroom, he threw his few things into his suitcase and zipped it shut. As soundlessly as he could, he eased it off its stand and onto the floor, then wheeled it to the door.

Outside, the moon was still shining, gleaming on the colorless cars and the rough, bright surface of the building. Elvis paused to see whether he heard a sound from inside. The quiet remained. As silently as he could, with a cheerful song in his heart, Elvis went to the office and rang the bell for the night service.

Mr. Patel came to the door almost immediately. He must have been awake, reading, or thinking, or maybe praying. He was a small man, balding on top despite his youthful face. He turned on the porch light and asked how he could help.

"I'm in number six," Elvis said. "I'm with my dad, and I just found out tonight that he was planning to skip out without paying. He's sound asleep, and I'd like to leave him that way. If I could, I'd like to pay you for the room in cash and take an Uber."

The light was too dim to see Mr. Patel's color change. For a moment, he did not speak. "All right," he said. "There can't be too much harm in that."

"He might rant in the morning, but you can just tell him I decided to leave early."

"All right. Would you like to come in?"

# 4 USING

The sun had yet to rise over the hills—only a thin wash of light painted the town—when a sleep-deprived Elvis drove his truck into Santa Rosa. His eyes drooped, and his face wanted desperately to cave in to blessed oblivion. At the same time, he felt weirdly exhilarated. He kept rehearsing his conversation with Mr. Patel at the motel, feeling again the excitement of leaving in secret. And then he was thinking about Angel's skin, her soft mouth, the warmth of touching her. It made him shiver and kept him awake. He couldn't wait to get to her.

After only two nights away, his dazed mind took in the town as though for the first time. He had absorbed the north, where trees and rivers dominated, and human construction clung to the earth like limpets. Now he was back in the world of straight lines. Santa Rosa was a medium-sized city, confining nature to backyards and planter boxes. That felt like a relief to him. The city was a comfort. He was uneasy in the woods, he realized.

He got off at the downtown exit, drove past the mission, and parked outside Angel's small redwood-sided home. He had thought briefly of going home to shower, but he didn't want to wait.

Angel's cat came down the sidewalk to greet him. She was one of those very fluffy felines that act as friendly as a dog. Elvis picked her up—it was like lifting a ball of dryer lint—and carried her to the door. He knocked and entered.

Angel was sprawled on the sofa in a loose-fitting robe. Her eyes seemed lost, her long reddish hair was tangled, and he thought she had probably spent the night on the sofa, never moving to go to bed. He could tell she had been using. What momentarily confused him was the smell, vaguely like cleaning fluid.

"Well la-di-da," Elvis said. "Look who's doing meth."

Very slowly, she smiled. "Amazing," she said, as though the word held the moon.

"You've had it before."

"No. I never did. I always stuck to what I knew."

"It's something, isn't it?" Elvis said, feeling the arousal beginning to permeate him.

"You want some?"

He hesitated. "I need to take a shower. Is that okay?"

Angel waved it away.

"You want to join me?"

She didn't seem to register. She waved her hand again, dismissing him.

"If you change your mind," he said, "feel free."

The hot jets of the shower felt wonderful, as they always did, but his mind was on what would happen after. He knew he would smoke with her and immediately they would join together in an explosion. Meth and sex were such a combination. It would be intense enough to destroy them both. Two years of sobriety were passing out of his mind like a melting cloud. He felt regret and some guilt, too, but it was as though he were already long gone. No sense crying over spilled milk. Elvis scrubbed himself conscientiously with soap, washed his hair with some apricot stuff he found, turned off the water, and fumbled for a towel. After combing his hair straight back, he stuck some toothpaste in his mouth with his index finger and swished it around. Angel liked him to smell clean. The mirror revealed a skinny dude with a red-brown face and a torso the color of a fish belly. Not the prettiest sight. *At least I know how to dance*, he thought. Wrapping the towel around his waist, Elvis opened the door to the narrow hallway that led to the main room.

She already had the pipe in her hand. He could smell the match, its wood smoke and sulfur. She turned when he came in and held the pipe his way, offering it. "Let me have some of that," he said, slamming down on the sofa next to her and grabbing it out of her fingers.

* * *

Afterward, he told Angel about Garberville. They lounged on the sofa, his head in her lap, with strong sensations still rippling through him. Elvis described meeting his father and Aunt Carol, trying to explain to

Angel how foundational it felt. He could swear he had stumbled into a place where healing could begin, what was lost could be found, and missing connections would find their mate.

Angel didn't get it. "I really don't understand why you left in the middle of the night. It seems like you ran away."

Angel had always had a family. Her two brothers lived in Sonoma County, and she had cared for her dad in his declining years, right up to his death. She couldn't grasp how Elvis's broken pieces chafed him, nor why meeting a crabby aunt was such a big deal. He tried to explain that he felt connected for the first time in his life. No, not connected, but on the edge of connection. It stretched visibly before him, like a fertile valley. He had the token of it, his grandfather's Bible.

Angel didn't get that, either. He went out to his truck and brought it in to show her. She was polite, handling it like a gun that might go off, but he could see that she didn't understand why it meant something to him. She wasn't, as she told him, a church girl.

Years ago, she had gone to church with him and he thought she was all in. When her father was sick, she stopped going. Elvis thought it was just a matter of scheduling, but she never came back. She said it wasn't her thing. He couldn't get her to explain why.

He could never doubt her. Partying had brought them together, but it was prison that had sealed them with Gorilla Glue. She had visited him after he was put away. He wouldn't tell her what was happening, but she saw his terrified eyes. All on her own, she went to the public-defense lawyer to ask if there was any way out. She was sure he was in danger. The lawyer went back to the judge and got Elvis into the New Life program. Elvis couldn't believe it when they escorted him out of the walls of San Quentin and took him to Santa Rosa. He had thought he would die there. They hauled him into the courtroom, where the judge warned him sternly that if he violated the terms of the program, he would go back to prison, perhaps not fully realizing just how motivated Elvis was.

Elvis pondered it as he lay there, very comfortable and warm. Angel fell asleep, breathing heavily and then beginning to snore. He owed everything to her.

Elvis could see ahead well enough to know that he would surely go back to using daily, and his life would crash. For the moment, though, he was in happy bliss, cuddled next to a sexy woman and feeling the residual buzz from the meth. The dark horrors were somewhere ahead and hard to envisage; today, tonight, was life.

The amazing thing was that it wasn't even a big deal. *This is the real me*, he thought. They said it in AA: once an addict, always an addict. The sober Elvis of the last two years was an aberration. You couldn't bury this; it was bound to surface again. This was real.

He had always traced his addictions to his father's death. Now that story had been knocked sideways, leaving space to think again. Maybe it went even deeper. Maybe addiction had always been his destiny.

He had started smoking before his dad even disappeared, and they said cigarettes are as strong an addiction as any. To Elvis's mind, though, drinking was the true beginning. Eddie Costas, who was two years older, had offered him a beer when he was in sixth grade. It happened at Glass Beach, where kids hung out after school. Eddie was there with two or three other boys, their legs dangling over the edge. He had called Elvis over, wanting to know what had happened to his father. He pulled out a beer can and offered it to Elvis, maybe as a gesture of condolence. As soon as Elvis tasted it, he liked it. There was no grimacing at the taste; it triggered a desire. You couldn't get drunk on one beer, even when you weigh 120 pounds, but Elvis thought his issues had begun that day.

Elvis remembered hearing that Eddie had joined the marines. He might have gotten killed in Afghanistan, for all Elvis knew. God, he might be a drunk in some bar in Ft. Bragg.

What if Eddie turned up at the mission? Would they even recognize each other?

That line of thought made Elvis feel very weak. It pulled him back to those dark years that led to prison and then to the mission, years of feeling wretched and going to jail and sleeping in patches of brush where he would not be seen. That was where he was heading again. He could pull back, in theory, but he knew he wouldn't. He was like a man on roller skates on a steep hill. Once you start going, you are going to go all the way down.

After beer came marijuana, he remembered. When? Probably when he started high school. He couldn't recall the occasion. He remembered that he hadn't liked it at first. In those days, it was serious stuff, legally speaking. Beer was kid stuff, but you could go to jail for Mary Jane. It would give you a scare just to think about it. Beer was more physical, loosening your body; marijuana mostly mental, loosening your mind. It took time before he could enjoy the wide space where his thoughts wandered.

He did remember precisely when he'd first tried meth. It was the summer after he graduated. He was working for May Lindecott's father and hanging out with her. He had known May since elementary school. She had always been wild, and it was no struggle to get into her pants. About the second time they had sex, she pulled out a needle. They were in her bedroom at home, and it freaked him out, watching her plunge that long, sharp steel into her own arm. Elvis was afraid of needles and he was also afraid of her father, who was a mean SOB. But she said it made sex better, and that was enough to get him. She was right. He had never felt anything like it. The euphoria was incredible, and then he had such energy, he didn't need to sleep. Her dad could see Elvis bouncing around the job site, hyperactive, and he knew enough roofers to recognize the signs. He made some reference to it, just slyly to get his point across, that he wasn't fooled. He didn't do anything to try to stop it.

May blew up at him about something, and then her dad fired him, and before Thanksgiving, he was jobless and rootless. Everything in his life changed, but the craving for meth didn't. Apart from the months he had spent in jail and prison, he hadn't been really clean since then.

Except for the last two years. Lying on the sofa, listening to Angel buzz softly, resting a hand on her warm thigh, he grasped the fact that he hadn't been able to keep it together. All that effort, all those prayers to God, all the meetings. This very week, he had gotten his two-year chip. Now he was nothing but an addict again.

* * *

When Angel woke up, Elvis wasn't sure whether she was mad, or miserable, or what. She wasn't really a moody person, but when something was bugging her, watch out and keep your mouth shut. You let her work it out herself.

Elvis went out to buy some food, and he cooked a great dinner. He went all out on some salmon with saffron rice and garlic-sautéed green beans. For dessert, he bought a tiny container of ice cream. He didn't say hardly anything the whole time. Angel took a shower and came back to the sofa, sitting in a stupor. Her hair was running down in ringlets, and she looked rosy wrapped in a towel. He gave her some warning that dinner would be on the table, but she was still sitting there when it was ready. After watching her, perplexed, he went to get her a robe out of her bedroom and led her to the table in silence.

They ate in silence, too. "What are you thinking?" he asked her, but she didn't answer. She seemed to have a healthy appetite, so she wasn't sick.

"You got any more?" he asked her when he brought out the ice cream. That seemed to activate her. She nodded and got up from the table. In a minute, she was back with a pipe and a baggie of powder. They smoked it, taking turns, still not talking. The hit was tremendous; you forgot how good it was. Elvis was soon nuzzling her, wrapping her in his arms. She came awake and he led her into the bedroom. They spent the rest of the night there, smoking meth twice more, having sex three times more, and finally falling asleep at about four in the morning.

Angel was up at seven, getting dressed.

"Where are you going?" he asked.

"Going to work," she said. "You should, too."

He couldn't even think of it. He was wasted. More significantly, nothing meant anything. All he was going to do all day was think about doing more of what they had done all night.

"Why don't you stay home?" he said. "Call in sick."

She ignored him.

"C'mon," he said. "It's just one day."

She walked past without looking at him. "Are you paying my rent?" she asked.

"It's just one day!" he said.

"You should go to work, too."

He rolled over and buried his head. "I can't," he said.

* * *

Elvis did go to work on Tuesday, but he wasn't good for anything. He would stand in one place trying to remember what he was doing until the foreman yelled at him. Then he ran around, going one direction or another, but never arriving where he belonged. As soon as he got up on the roof, he would remember a tool he needed at the bottom of the ladder; when he got down, he would rush up again without remembering the tool. He looked like a fool. He felt like a fool. Everybody could see it.

Already the meth wasn't as good. They said that your receptors got clogged, or something. You had to hit it more often—and harder—to feel half of what you had felt before. There was no bargaining with the stuff; it kept receding, calling you in deeper.

Sometimes Elvis wondered whether it was just tricking his mind. Maybe it wasn't really any less powerful; he just thought it was because the first surprise was ended. Some pleasures were like that. Sex, for example. You would die to get it, but it often disappointed you after you had been with a woman a few times. Or to put it on more childish terms, like a carnival ride that scared the bejabbers out of you the first time, but when you went back, it wasn't quite as frightening. The third time, you got bored and wanted the ride to be over. It was the same ride; what changed?

The drugs, though, had their own chemistry. He thought they probably really weren't as powerful after a while. Somehow, they muddied up something, like a coat of slime, and you lost the feeling.

Even at half strength, though, meth had power over you. You wanted it so much. Elvis knew that even if he could calculate the benefits and the costs of doing drugs, all that thinking would be pointless because he wasn't really under the control of his own will. Even if he saw God himself and God told him to stop, scaring him to death with his glorious holiness, he wouldn't be able to. At least, not for long.

On Wednesday, not wanting to look like a fool again at work, he stayed home. His anxiety ramped higher and higher through the day while he waited for Angel. For dinner, he marinated steaks and cooked broccoli and baked potatoes. By the time she came through the door, he was pacing and sweating.

He loved Angel in her nursing uniform. Somehow, that made it like playing house, a delicious naughtiness. They ate, they smoked, they made love, and they didn't go to sleep until the early hours.

"You okay with this?" Elvis asked after they finally quit and lay still in the dark. He worried that sheer fatigue would undo Angel. You can't party all night and work all day. They weren't so young anymore.

"I'll let you know," Angel said. She had a tough, self-possessed way that both excited him and made him wish he knew how to melt her.

She was watching him, evaluating him, but he couldn't figure out what she was looking for. He even asked her: "What do you want me to do for you?" She brushed it aside. He could feel that he was sinking deeper. The very idea of getting clean seemed far-off, a fantasy.

Elvis wondered why connecting to his father had apparently made him worse, not better. A few times he raised the question with Angel, but she didn't seem to understand. She pointed out that his father had treated him like trash, and not just once. She had no use for the man, and when Elvis thought about it, he had no trouble admitting that she was right. However, there was a pull. It wasn't like meth—there was no pleasure involved—but like meth, it had unexplainable power. Maybe you had to be an orphan to get what he was experiencing.

His life got swallowed up in the binge. Each day fell off the calendar like a leaf dropping from a tree. Elvis never lost track of time, but he submitted to it. Its current carried him along. On Thursday, Angel asked him if he was going to go back to work. "You have to work," she said. "We need the money." He didn't understand how she could do it. To him, it seemed impossible and unnecessary. Meth made him feel like Superman. He didn't worry.

In the intervals, though, while Angel was gone and he waited for her to come home, he worried that she was plotting something to get him back to the mission. He worried that she would stop feeding him drugs.

By Friday, he noticed that he had no appetite. That was a detail he had almost forgotten: you got to be too busy to want to eat. He didn't sleep, either. He could only lie in bed twitching with energy, thinking about the next hit, until he got up in the middle of the night to clean the kitchen. He scrubbed it floor to ceiling and took a toothbrush to the corners.

When Angel got out of bed in the morning, she asked him what he had been doing.

"Cleaning," he said. "I couldn't sleep, so I cleaned the kitchen."

"It's clean," she said. "Leave it alone." But the next night, he was up again, scrubbing. This time it was the bathroom.

Angel was off work over the weekend, which made him happy. He didn't like being left alone all day, but he couldn't go out. Where would he go? The idea of staying snug with Angel, extending the hours together, using, eating (he didn't really want to eat, but he wanted to make meals), watching football, playing with each other, maybe even talking (though

Angel wasn't really a conversationalist—she made her point and listened while you made yours, and then she was done)—he imagined all this when he woke up Saturday morning and realized Angel was still beside him.

He made cheese and bacon omelets for breakfast. Then they had a pipe, and then he carried her into the bedroom, screeching and kicking. He could have continued all day, but Angel wanted to watch football. She kept falling asleep in front of the TV, whereas Elvis got restless. The uniforms still looked like candy to him, just like at Amber's bar in Ukiah. It still looked like a video game, arbitrary and weightless. He couldn't focus on the plays.

While he was thinking that, Amber called, almost like she could read his mind. Amber never called. He picked up.

"Where are you?" she asked, sounding rushed and mad, like he was late for an appointment.

"I'm in Santa Rosa. Where are you?"

"I'm in Ukiah; where do you think?"

"I don't know. Where did you think I was?"

"You just disappeared. We were going to have breakfast, weren't we? You just took off without even leaving a note."

"That's true. I was trying to be quiet so you could sleep, and I forgot about a note until I got out to the truck. Then I couldn't do anything about it. I'd locked the door behind me."

"Well, you could have texted."

Elvis felt a flash of remorse. "Yeah, I'm sorry. I just didn't think of it." He had to admit that he neglected his daughter. He wanted to spend time with her and get to know her. He just forgot. He got his mind on something else until it was too late.

"Can I come and see you today?"

That panicked Elvis, though he didn't know why. "Why? What are you up to?"

"Nothing. I mean, I need to do some shopping, but I thought we could see each other."

"That's really sweet," he said, "but it won't work today. Too much going on."

Angel had woken up and she was looking at him, mouthing, "What? What?"

"Why? What are you doing?"

With a shot of shame, he realized why he had panicked. He didn't want his daughter to see him like this. Left to himself, or left with just Angel, he could believe he was having a wonderful time. But not with his daughter. She had never really seen him when he was using.

"I have to work," he lied. It killed him to say it.

"Then why aren't you there now? Dad, it's late."

"I'm on my way," he lied. "I overslept. The boss already yelled at me on the phone, and he's going to yell at me when I get there." The shame he felt surprised Elvis. He didn't usually lie; he always said he had too much pride for that. If you couldn't take the truth, he didn't care.

After hanging up, he wanted to talk about it with Angel. She had her eyes closed and her mouth open, not the prettiest sight. He nudged her until he got her eyes open. "That was Amber," he said. "She wanted to come see me."

It took Angel some time. She lay without responding, blinking. Finally, she shifted her gaze to him, studying his face. "Is she coming?" Angel asked.

"No, I put her off."

"Why did you do that?"

"I didn't want her to see me like this."

"Like what?"

"Strung out," Elvis answered. "Using."

"You think she would know?"

"Yeah, don't you?"

She took a minute. "Yeah." Then, "Why do you want to hide it from her? She must know."

"Yeah. But it's different for her to see me."

She closed her eyes again. It spooked him. He thought that she was disappearing from him, and he tried to pull her back. "What do you think I should do?" he asked.

Angel opened her eyes. He had never noticed her eyelashes. They were pale, almost white. That must be why she wore that dark makeup. It did help her looks, he could see.

"I don't see why you care so much."

"She's my daughter," he said. "She's all I've got."

* * *

The second week of his binge, Elvis felt his body beginning to shut down. He was high energy when he was awake, but that wore him out, and he slept ten hours a night. When he woke up in the mornings, Angel was gone, already off at work. Somehow, she could do it: party at night, work in the day. Would it get to her? Elvis didn't know. He hadn't seen her falter yet. He was glad for her, but also jealous. What was wrong with him? He felt weak. He felt disgusted with himself.

It was low-level disgust, and he could ignore it and pretend it wasn't there, but like a smell from a leaky toilet, it never left him. He didn't like what he was doing, and he wasn't proud of what he was. He was an addict. He had said it himself a hundred times, but always with the thought that it was an incidental aspect of his life; that his goofy ways, his comedy, his hard-work habits, his friendly nature were what people saw. Now, he suspected that they summed him up more simply: he's an addict. They didn't add those other qualities. More to the point, he suspected that people had forgotten all about him, that he wasn't even worth their notice.

He woke up still exhausted, and usually lay in bed until lunchtime. He had no appetite. Sometimes he made himself a sandwich and then would leave it on the counter with one bite out of the corner. In the afternoon, his anxiety would begin to rise as he anticipated Angel's arrival home. The stuff was in the house somewhere, but as a point of honor, he didn't try searching for it. That was partly because he feared it would set off Angel. If she kicked him out, he had nowhere to go. She was his lifeline.

He knew his job was toast. He couldn't go back there if he wanted to. Same with his room. By now, they would have put his stuff in a cardboard box and given his bed to somebody else. These realities played in the back of his mind, but his attention stayed on the meth like a compass needle. It didn't swing far off true north.

By the time Angel got home on Wednesday, he had gone through three cycles of paranoia. He thought she was plotting against him, that she would call the mission, that she would kick him out and lock the door. When she finally came in, he was like a dog that has been kicked, expecting her to kick him again. Of course, she never did. Angel was a matter-of-fact person, not given to declarations of love. By her actions, she made clear her loyalty. Elvis had lost the ability to see it. Fear had taken control—principally, fear that came in like the tide every afternoon.

Just looking in the mirror, he could see that he had lost weight. The contours of his face were changing, making it more difficult to shave. He missed patches, but when he detected tufts of hair, he did nothing to fix them.

"You look horrible," Angel said when she got home from work on Friday. "You need to eat. And comb your hair."

He pulled a comb from his pocket and ran it through his hair.

"And you've been wearing those clothes all week."

He couldn't think how to answer. He wasn't sure of the state of his clothes. He was only sure that Angel had the meth, and he couldn't lose her. One corner of his mind recognized how pitiable he had become—he, Elvis, the king—but he couldn't hold on to that for more than a few seconds. Paranoia had control.

"Why don't you go get your stuff?" Angel asked. "At least you'll have something to wear."

He set off to do that on Saturday morning—late morning, after another sleep-in. He called first and the landlord said his stuff was on the back porch, in a cardboard box. If he didn't come soon, they would throw it out. The landlord wasn't mean, but he was firm.

He hadn't driven his truck in over a week. The only time he left the house was to buy groceries, which he did on foot, either to the new Aldi on Third Street or at the Wednesday Farmer's Market. He felt strange unlocking the pickup door and climbing into the driver's seat. It might have been years instead of days. He put the key in the ignition like a child working on a jigsaw puzzle. It took three tries to insert the key, and then, when he cranked the engine, it wouldn't catch. He ran it all the way down, pumping the gas and swearing at the engine until it slowed to a stop and began clicking. He kept the key turned until the clicking itself stopped.

He was scared. What if this was Angel's plan—that he couldn't start the truck, that he couldn't get his clothes? What if she locked him out because he didn't have fresh stuff to wear? What if somebody had sabotaged the truck? He got out and stood on the curb, staring at the truck as though it were possessed. He looked furious, but he didn't feel furious; he felt overwhelmed by fear. "I have to get my stuff," he said to himself, talking out loud. "I have to get it. I can walk."

He set off, compelled by panic but moving slowly because he felt so weak. It was a moody day, clouded and chilly with the sky low and dark. Most of the trees had already lost their leaves, and the sidewalk in front of the house was squishy with the macerated mash of dead foliage. Elvis hadn't even known it had rained. He had to get to Coddingtown, which was a long walk. He thought he would go up Wilson and then take Cleveland Avenue. Just in time, he remembered that going up Wilson, he would pass by the mission. He diverted to take a long swing around it using Coulter Street as far as West Ninth. He knew he needed to avoid the mission, though he couldn't explain why.

Elvis's steps were heavy, like Frankenstein's monster. It took hours, seemingly, to get to College Avenue, and when he had crossed it, he did not think he could go any farther. He had begun to tremble. Where the cuffs of his shirt touched his wrists, he itched intolerably. Mostly, he was exhausted.

Cleveland was narrow and busy, with no parking on the street and virtually no shoulder. Cars whizzed by, bewildering Elvis. He needed to sit down. He was standing at a bus stop, where a flimsy tin shelter housed a low, flat, backless bench.

He held back, though. If he sat, he might be trapped. The bench was too easy, too convenient. He must continue. He must get his things; Angel demanded it. He needed a fix and she had the stuff. She was his lady; she said for him to get his things.

Just at that moment, a bus wheezed up to the stop, going north. The door flapped open and the bus exhaled, lowering its step toward the curb. Elvis realized he could take this bus to Coddingtown.

He raised an arm to alert the driver, then began to work his way toward the door. His legs were creaky; his body moved slowly, like the Tin Man. He was ten feet from the door. One step, two steps. He could see the driver's head turned toward him. He was seen; he would not be left. But his legs caught. He was unable to move. He stood stiffly, trying to get his body to comply, rocking slowly back and forth like a chameleon on a tree.

The bus driver waved him up, trying to get him to move. He could not. His arms were itching. He felt like tiny ants ran up and down them. Shaking began in earnest. His legs trembled like a puppy yet would not shift from their position locked to the sidewalk.

The driver came to the bus door and leaned his head out. He had a dark complexion and a short, trim, black mustache. “Are you okay?” he asked.

Elvis tried to wave him off, but his hand would not obey. He tried to say he was okay, that the bus should go on, but the only sound that came out was a mooing sound that might come from a disabled child.

“Do you need something?” the driver asked, coming out of the bus onto the sidewalk. “Should I call nine-eleven?”

Elvis could not answer him.

The bus, fortunately, was completely empty of passengers. The sidewalk was deserted. This part of Cleveland Avenue was a no-man’s-land for anybody on foot. He and the driver must settle this by themselves.

“Mister.” The driver spoke politely, with a delicate foreign accent. “Mister, can you come now? I can’t leave you here.”

Elvis tried to look at him, to make a sign with his eyes that he could go. His head would not cooperate.

“If you cannot come, I have to call nine-one-one.”

He hovered by Elvis, not touching him but willing him to move. “Can you not come? Or tell me what is the matter?”

He left Elvis and walked briskly back to the bus door, reemerging a few minutes later with a phone. After a long look at Elvis, filled with pleading hope, he called 911. Then he approached Elvis again. “Don’t worry; they are sending an ambulance.”

Unfortunately, the police arrived first. The squad car pulled up with its siren calling and its lights flashing, blocking traffic. The officer who got out of the car was a veteran who had arrested Elvis more than a few times.

“Oh God, it’s you,” the officer said. “Elvis? I haven’t seen you in years. What on earth are you doing?”

“He is frozen, sir,” the bus driver said. “He cannot move or speak.”

The officer ignored him. “Elvis, can you tell me what is going on?”

Elvis was mute.

“Elvis, I think you know the drill. I don’t want to take you in, but I can’t leave you like this. Either you have to talk to me, or I’m going to have to take you to the station.”

“Excuse me, sir, he has not done anything.” That was the bus driver again. The cop ignored him.

In no time, the whole universe arrived to stare at Elvis, and even a kid on a trick bike wheeled up and stopped to watch. The ambulance came with its siren and lights, maneuvering slowly through the stopped traffic until it came within forty feet, with cars blocking its further progress. Two workers in blue uniforms got out.

"I got it," the cop said. "I don't think we'll need the ambulance."

"We'll stand by," one of the workers said.

Another squad car pulled up, though it could not make its way through the blocked traffic and settled for parking around the corner on College, blocking a lane of traffic there.

"Okay, Elvis," the first police officer said. "Time to fish or cut bait. I don't want to take you anywhere. You and I know that's not going to do any good. But if you don't move, that's what I'm going to have to do. I can't leave you like this."

Elvis began to hear waves in his ears, like the sound of a washing machine spinning its load. He was trembling uncontrollably. His arms and now his armpits itched outrageously. He could not move or speak. He was stuck.

"Okay. I guess that's enough. I'm going to restrain you before I put you in the car."

As soon as he touched Elvis's arm, pulling it behind him, Elvis was unfrozen. He shook off the hand, and then, when it came back and applied force, he fought against it. Elvis let out a huge bellow.

Instantly, the other officers were on him. Three men wrestled him to the ground, smushing his face against the grit in the sidewalk.

"Get that thing out of here!" one of the officers shouted angrily. The boy on the trick bike had a phone and was taking video. He didn't move away on command; he got closer. Elvis had all his strength now; he struggled valiantly to resist, but they had him on the ground and somebody was sitting on his legs. With almighty power he fought against them, sometimes briefly throwing someone off, though he had no leverage. His arms were pinned behind him and he heard the snapping of the cuffs. He was still a whirling dervish, writhing and twisting—for what end, he had no idea. One of the police swore suddenly; he had taken an elbow to the mouth, which he held while blood seeped out of his fingers.

"Get lost! Now!" another officer yelled at the kid and swiped at him. The kid dodged back while keeping the phone pointed in their direction.

Elvis wasn't enraged. He could no more help fighting than he had been able to prevent freezing up when the bus came. It was all reflex. As they forced him to his feet, one man on each arm, he thrashed at them with his feet and even with his head. Even as he flailed, he could see the scene as clearly as with a movie camera; he observed as it happened to him.

* * *

Elvis was in jail for just two nights. He slept most of the time, covering his head with the stiff gray blanket and pushing himself against the wall next to his bed. He was never hungry, but when he was awake, he craved a fix. The itching on his arms and armpits grew fiercer, and he scratched until he bled. The guards offered Band-Aids, but he waved them off, knowing he would scratch them off, too. Sleep was his only refuge, and fortunately, it came—a dark squall that pulled him down and into the lower night.

On the third day, a guard called his name, unlocked the cell, and said he was free to go. "They dropped the charges," he said as he led Elvis down the corridor.

"What did they charge me for?" he asked.

"Resisting an officer of the law," the guard said.

"That's fair," he said. "Why did they drop it?"

The guard shrugged, hesitating as they stood at the door waiting for the electronic lock to *thunk* them out. "They knew you were bombed out of your mind."

Soon, he was standing in the open air of a late afternoon. The air felt moist, and the sky was dark. They had given him his cell phone back, but when he tried it, he found the battery was dead. For a moment, he considered going back into the jail and asking to use a phone, but the thought of reentering was repugnant.

The itching had stopped, he realized, and he took a deep, air-sucking breath. He should take his arrest as a gift. God didn't want him strung out; he wanted him clean. Today, he could begin anew, clean and sober. He didn't need the stuff. He should stop.

His resolution helped him feel better. But first, he had to get home. He stood on the sidewalk puzzling over that, finally deciding that he could walk.

It was about three miles to Angel's house, which would have been nothing except he was so weak. He followed Mendocino Avenue past the junior college, past the high school, through the old neighborhoods, straight downtown. By the time he reached the mall, he felt wobbly. He found a bench in the bright, hard interior and sat inert for a long time, wondering whether he could make it home. A thin strip of nausea hovered under his shallow breathing, not enough to trip a gag reflex, but very unpleasant. Could he eat anything? He did not think he could keep it down.

*At least I'm not itching*, he thought. And not craving.

Elvis wondered how long it had been since he put food in his stomach. He could not remember eating in the jail. He couldn't remember much about anything for the last two days. He had no idea who he had shared a cell with.

Struggling to his feet, he stood unsteadily, hoping that nobody noticed. Security would call the police on him, he thought. He made himself get out the door, and in the chilly gloom of the parking garage, he felt revived. Cars already had their lights on. It wasn't far to the house now. Half a mile?

He felt very happy when he finally arrived. The lights were on inside, a bloom of warmth spreading from the windows. The door was locked, and Angel took a long time to answer his ring. Elvis was ready to try again when he heard the door rattle and stepped back to let her open it. He had been leaning against the screen, he realized, using it to prop himself up.

"Oh my God," she said. "Get in here." When he came under the lights, the air caught in her throat. "Oh my God," she said again. "Are you all right?"

"Can I sit down?" he asked.

He couldn't lower himself into the armchair. He dropped, dead weight.

"You look like crap," Angel said.

"Thanks," he said.

"Are you all right?" she asked again.

"Yeah," he said.

He did feel better resting in the chair. Angel looked so good to him, he wanted to cry. "Geez, you are so beautiful," he said to her when she brought a glass of water. She only grimaced.

She asked if he wanted to eat. Elvis hesitated. He still felt no hunger, but he knew he needed food. "I can try," he said.

She made a peanut butter sandwich and brought it to him on a plate. He dropped the plate, and it shattered at his feet. Angel helped him pick up the sandwich and make sure no ceramic shards clung to it. When he took a delicate bite, he could feel the intricate texture of the bread on his tongue. It was dry to the touch, and the act of chewing it seemed unfamiliar. He set the sandwich down on a small table, thinking he couldn't swallow any more. However, in a few minutes, he realized he would like more, and he took another little bite. This time, it seemed more normal. One mincing little bite and then another; eventually, he ate the whole sandwich. Then he fell asleep in the chair.

He woke up in the dark, famished. "Angel?" he called quietly. No answer. He began to call again and then thought he didn't need her. He felt more like himself; he thought he could walk.

In the refrigerator, he found half a personal pizza. He didn't bother to warm it up. Cold and slippery, it tasted delicious. He could eat another. He found some peanuts in a can and shoveled those into his mouth. That left him thirsty, so he poured a glass of milk and drank that. He could feel strength flowing into him.

Angel appeared, blinking in the light, dressed in a plaid robe. Elvis was so glad to see her that he choked up and couldn't speak. He gestured for her to take a seat, and she did. The kitchen was small, with a scarred wooden table just big enough for three. Elvis had eaten many meals here, but he had never looked at the room. Had he known it was wallpapered in elephant cartoons?

"Why did they release you?" Angel asked.

"I guess 'cause I didn't really do anything. They said they knew I was just bombed out of my mind."

"Do you have to go to court?"

"I don't think so. They said they dropped the charges."

"Wow," was all she said.

After a long interval of silence, she asked, "What are you going to do?"

That sounded ominous. "What do you mean?"

She was quiet for some time before saying, "If you want to quit, I'll help you."

He knew his answer immediately. "I do. I can't do it with you using, though. If you quit, I can, too."

# 5 THE TURNAROUND

Angel was as good as her word. They didn't smoke that night. They went to bed and slept wrapped together like children. She was gone when Elvis woke in the late morning. Light poured in the bedroom window, making amber squares on the wooden floor. It looked to be a chilly, bright day. Elvis lay under the covers feeling hungry and sleepy and content. The fever had passed. It was like a dream now. He was back to sanity.

Elvis slowly pulled some pants on and went into the kitchen to make coffee. He took his time about it. The coffee machine sputtered and spat, and he sipped his cup. Now that he was sober, he would need to get a job, but he didn't need to do that this morning. He got up to find his phone and plug it in. Then he ate some cereal, savoring its faint sweetness. After rinsing the bowl, he tried his phone, but it was still dead.

He thought of their conversation in the middle of the night, and of Angel's willingness to go clean. It moved him. Even though they had been together for so many years, he never completely believed in Angel's devotion to him. He didn't feel worthy of it. He always wondered whether she pondered the possibility of moving on. Telling him such thoughts would go against her nature; one day, she would just do it. She could certainly get somebody better. She could probably get anybody she wanted. She was good-looking and sexy and she made good money; she didn't need Elvis.

Angel put up with a lot. She didn't yell at him or make demands. And now she would help him pull his life out of the fire.

Elvis thought, *I wonder if she would go back to church with me*. He felt that was what he needed—not merely to go himself, but to have her by his side. Just imagining it made his throat stick.

He wondered idly where she kept the stuff. She must have it here. She wouldn't have taken it to work with her, would she? Unless she had flushed it when she got up this morning, she had a bag of junk here in this little house. Somehow, that made her sacrifice all the more poignant. She was giving it up—and it wasn't simply theoretical, it was physical. She had the stuff.

She kept it in her bedroom, he was sure, but he had never actually seen her take it out. He didn't know whether she hid it in some secret place, or whether she simply put it out of sight. He had always had too much pride to search for it. It could be in a drawer with her socks. It could be tucked under the mattress.

He wasn't going to ask her where she hid it; for somebody who was going sober, that might seem a little questionable. He was curious to know, however. He thought he would look to see whether it was in an obvious place, just to satisfy his curiosity. It would be gone tomorrow.

Elvis went into her bedroom. He had been in and out a million times, but at the moment, it felt strange and naked to enter. He wouldn't want Angel to catch him doing this, even though it was perfectly innocent. He opened the drawer in her bedside table. It was full of junk—makeup and lotion and contact cases—but he didn't find a bag of crystals. He opened all the drawers in her dresser, but likewise found nothing. Now he was more than curious. Elvis ran his hands under her mattress, all the way around the bed. Nothing. He dropped down to the floor and looked under the bed. There was a large plastic container, which made him smile, but when he pulled it out and opened it, he found nothing but photographs. Some of them, he saw, were snapshots of him.

Where had she hidden the stuff? It was in this room, and there weren't that many places to hide it. This search was becoming unhealthy and compulsive, and he knew that he should give it up, but now he was aroused. This would be his only chance to know. Elvis went back to the drawers and searched them more carefully, pulling out clothes and returning them meticulously. Nothing.

He sat down on the bed and took his time looking over every inch of the room. It wasn't a big space, and it wasn't stuffed with furniture. He got up to check the mirror that attached to the chest of drawers. There he found it: one small bag nestled behind the old-fashioned mirror, on a shelf hidden near the bottom. There was a small glass pipe with it. As soon as he pulled it out, he knew he was going to use.

* * *

By the time Angel came home from work, Elvis was lost in methland. That first night, he smoked with her and had sex; but after that, he largely lost interest in sex. He was so far gone, he didn't care whether she joined him in using. He just wanted his next fix.

Elvis went off into the deepest binge he had ever experienced. He spent most of his time sitting in Angel's wine-colored wingback chair, watching TV. He didn't care what he watched; he never switched channels. He began to pick at his arms and his armpits again, scratching them until they bled. Angel got upset with him over that. She said he was making a mess, and it wasn't healthy. He couldn't focus on what she said.

Angel didn't rant and whine at him like some women would do, not that it would ever do any good. He was grateful for that. A couple of times over the years she had told him, just as a matter of fact, that she was done and he had to get out. He had always obeyed, like a gentleman. But she never tried to talk him out of using. That wasn't her.

By the third day, he thought his mother was there and he was talking to her. On Friday, he stopped watching TV and paced the house. He had run out of meth. While Angel was at work, he went through her room looking for more but found nothing. When she came home, he didn't even say hi. He was talking to his mother. Mainly, he told his mother he was sorry, that he didn't want to be like this.

At dinnertime, he slipped out of the house. Angel had cooked some frozen lasagna she got from Trader Joe's, and she even tried to make a salad. He loved lasagna; it smelled delicious, but he knew it was a trap. She was trying to keep him quiet until the police came. He disappeared out the door while she was putting it on the table. When he rang the doorbell close to midnight, he rushed through the opened door without saying anything. He had been in a fight, but he couldn't remember where. A crust of blood leaked from the edge of his mouth, and he had a gruesome bruise on the left side of his forehead, a raw scrape over a soft purple swelling. He walked around the room like a madman, lifting piles of paper and throwing them aside. After minutes of raving, he turned to Angel and demanded to know where the pipe was.

She got it for him and watched him light up and take a puff. His frozen jaw relaxed as the drugs ran through him. He started talking into space again.

Angel came gently up to him and put a hand on his arm. "Why don't you talk to me?" she said.

He thought it was his mother. He shook off her hand. "You disappeared on me," he said. "I couldn't help it."

"What do you mean?" Angel asked. "How did I disappear on you?"

"Dad was gone, and you lied to me, didn't you? You can't tell me that was right."

He strode around the living room and into the kitchen, an angry twitch in his walk. "It's not my fault," he said, almost shouting. "You have to take some responsibility, don't you?" He slapped at a slender vase on the kitchen table; it flew across the room and shattered against the wall. The noise and destruction momentarily caught his attention. "I'm sorry," he said, recognizing Angel and filled with remorse for his behavior. "I didn't mean it." He knelt on the kitchen floor and began picking up pottery shards.

She knelt beside him and took his hands. "You don't need to do that," Angel said. "Why don't you get in bed? Rest."

Suddenly, he felt exhausted. He let her lead him into the bedroom, pull the covers back, and remove his shoes. "Aren't you going to come?" he asked as she tucked him in, but she shook her head, sitting down next to him on the side of the bed.

He woke in the early morning hours, hearing his mother again and trying desperately to correct her. That was his pattern for the next few days: sleep and agitation. When he was conscious, he fumed at material objects like microwaves, doors, walls, and appliances. Sometimes, he was paranoid, accusing Angel of hiding his drugs from him when he could not instantly put his hand on the little bag of crystals that he liked to smell and fondle.

"Elvis, honey, you can't wake me up in the middle of the night. You need to sleep. I need to sleep." He tried to hear her; he knew she meant the best for him, but he couldn't hang on to what she said. He would spring out of bed sweating and shouting, only minimally aware of the world around him. Angel cooked meals for him, but he didn't have an appetite, and what appetite he had was for junk. He bought tortilla chips and other snacks at the local mini-mart with money he took out of her purse.

He feared what she might do to him. She might throw him out, cut him off. Sometimes she looked at him so strangely that he knew he was scary in his mania.

"I want to take you to McFriends," she said on Wednesday.

McFriends was the county detox facility. Elvis had been there several times, as had virtually every addict in Sonoma County. It was a perfectly faceless government building where cops and frustrated family could drop somebody off and expect them to go safely through withdrawal. It had the personality of a tax office. All it offered were walls and clean tile floors and beds and toilets.

Elvis had been striding around the living room, picking madly at his arms, but he stopped cold when she said it. "I hate that place," he said.

"I know you do. But I don't see any alternative. I don't want to call the police."

That was a hard word. She and Elvis had talked about this before: if you call the police on somebody who is acting crazy, they might just shoot him.

Elvis stayed stuck in one position, standing straight, scratching his arms but otherwise not moving. He was thinking.

"You're going to kill yourself," Angel said, "and you'll probably kill me."

He thought about that, too.

Soon, he fell back into his agitation and his paranoia, raking his arms with his fingernails in an orgy of agony. Angel tried to get him to lie down in the bed, but he was sure that somebody wanted to smother him. "Who?" she asked. "Who is trying to kill you?" He didn't answer. She gave up on the bed but got him onto the sofa, propped up by cushions and covered with a sleeping bag. In that way, he sometimes slept, though never for long. When he woke, he was usually in a panic. He imagined that somebody was outside, or that he had been poisoned by the air coming out of the heater vents.

On Friday, out of the blue, he looked at Angel as she tucked the sleeping bag in around his legs and said, "You better take me."

It was the middle of the night. Neither of them had slept. For just a few seconds, Angel stared hard, as though she couldn't trust what he had said. She went into the bedroom—he followed her—and pulled a small suitcase out from the closet. Elvis watched while she packed his clothes. (While he was in jail, she had gone to the trouble of getting his box of things.) In the bathroom, she got his toothbrush, his deodorant, and his razor. Zipping up the bag, she wheeled it out to the living room. Elvis followed. "Okay," Angel said, "let's go."

"Where?" he asked, raising his head.

"McFriends," she said. "Like you said."

He descended into a state of whimpering, but she wouldn't listen. "We have to go," Angel said. "You told me to take you."

He let her lead him outside, one hand on his arm and the other pulling the suitcase, with him whining all the way that he hated that place, they could go in the morning, he was tired and he wanted to sleep. He knew his complaining wouldn't stop her; she had authority. He got into the car. During the short drive, he was almost shouting. Angel didn't answer him, except to say again, "You know you told me to take you there."

Finally, they pulled into the unlit parking lot, set on a back street near a strip mall. McFriends was an innocuous one-story building with plywood siding and a flat roof. It could have been a 1960s-era army barracks or a temporary health clinic on a junior college campus. Past midnight, it seemed to harbor demons. Angel got Elvis out of the car and led him around to a dimly lit ramp. One small sign on the side of the building announced a no-smoking campus, and a larger one on the door said simply, "Detox—Sonoma County."

Elvis pulled back and stopped, rooted as a tree. "What's the matter?" Angel asked.

"They'll hurt me."

She blew out a deep breath. "You told me that they were great," she said. "Very supportive. Didn't preach at you."

"I mean the addicts."

Angel's mouth tightened. "There can't be anybody in there you haven't seen on the streets a hundred times. What are you talking about? You're the man who can take care of himself, aren't you?"

He didn't have an answer, but he stayed stuck. Angel opened the door and tugged on his shirt. "Come on," she said. "You'll be fine." After a moment, he followed.

Just inside the door was a small desk with an unsmiling middle-aged woman. She had long, messy, dirty-blond hair and no makeup. Elvis didn't know who she was, but she wore an expectant look on her face.

"Tell her what you're here for," Angel said.

He was able to focus on the woman's face. "I need to get off the stuff," he told her.

The woman's expression did not change. "This is not a medical program," she said. "It's strictly detox."

"He knows," Angel said. "He's been here before."

"Have you?" the woman asked. "What's your name?"

He knew the answer, of course, but he couldn't say it. He froze.

"He's Elvis Sebastiano," Angel said for him.

The woman's face slowly relaxed into a smile. "Elvis!" she said. "I didn't recognize you! It's been a long time, hasn't it?"

Did they know each other? He looked at the woman again. "Two years," he said. "Three, maybe."

"I remember you," the woman said. "I'm Angie. It was for heroin?"

He quickly shook his head. "Meth."

* * *

While they filled out papers and went over the rules, Elvis tried to remember Angie. He knew her from somewhere, but he couldn't grasp the details, except that it had been in another bleak time. Maybe she had harmed him; he couldn't say. Elvis knew he wasn't thinking straight, but that didn't prevent him from falling into more paranoia. It got worse after Angel left, and he lay in a slender bed covered with an army blanket. He could hear other men breathing. The room was dark, and he stared at the invisible ceiling. He thought that if he didn't move, he couldn't be hurt. Then, he realized that if he could hear their breathing, they could hear his breathing. He tried to barely inhale; he even held his breath to keep utterly silent, but that was foolish. He finally couldn't hold it any longer. He ended up exhaling noisily and waiting for the assault. It didn't come, but that proved nothing. They might be waiting until he fell asleep.

His thoughts spiraled into the dark. He had ruined his life. He was a helpless addict and everybody had deserted him, which he deserved. His mother was dead. His father had died and come back, but only to use him. Tom hated him; he had stolen from Tom and come on to his wife, and Tom knew. Tom wanted to hurt him. Elvis got the image of Tom's brooding, angry face, and he wanted to cry out. He was so, so tired. He wanted a pipe; that was the only way to stop these feelings. He would die for a pipe.

Floodwaters of bad memory washed over him for hours. It was like lying in the light of a video projector, pictures playing over him, except that these images penetrated; they cut into him; they seemed to etch themselves onto his skin. Whenever his mind escaped the bad past, it latched on to the dangers of the moment. The building itself seemed to harbor malice. Finally, just as wan light began to make the room visible, he fell asleep. Worn out from his own fears, he slept deeply through the ordinary noise of ten men getting up and going to breakfast.

At least, some of them got up. When Elvis finally woke, he recognized that some lay in bed sweating or heaving or writhing or shaking. Those were alcohol or opioid issues. Meth was simpler. Elvis mostly slept. On the second morning, his paranoia dissipated, and he was hungry for the first time in weeks. Pancakes and eggs were served for breakfast. He gobbled them up, thinking that they were delicious.

Angie walked through the little dining room and stopped by his table. "Feeling better?" she asked.

"Yeah," he said. "These pancakes are fantastic."

"You like those? I can get you some more." She limped over to the counter and brought back a platter, then sat down at his table. "You doing okay?" she asked.

He shook his head. "Too soon to tell."

She didn't pursue the question, but he told her anyway. He explained about going to his mother's service. "I was two years sober, and it all went out the window." He left out seeing his father; that seemed too complicated to explain.

Angie was a good listener. He asked her if she was an addict—he thought she had that look—but she said no. "Don't worry; I've got my problems," she said, as though to excuse herself. It didn't matter to Elvis. He sometimes heard people at meetings talk like they could only trust other addicts, but he didn't feel that way.

Two other men joined his table. Both of them put their heads down, nibbling at their food. They seemed to be suffering too much to talk. The man across from Elvis had tattoos across his broad, dark face. Elvis asked him how he got them, just trying to make conversation, but the man only stared at him.

The other man was more friendly. He had his eyes closed, but when he heard Elvis's voice, he opened them and said his name was Jeff.

"Pardon me, but my head is about to explode. I can't really talk. It hurts too much," he said.

Looking around, Elvis recognized someone he knew from the mission. What was his name? Ian. Ian looked over and winked. He got out of his seat and came over to shake hands. He used three grips: standard shake, wrist shake, finger snap. "I read about you," Ian said.

"Oh yeah?"

"In the newspaper. How you rescued that woman in the fire. That was something, man. You're a real hero."

"Yeah, well. A lot of people I didn't rescue, too."

"That was a crazy business. You should have seen the stuff that came into the mission that week. Like water bottles, a whole truckload of them. We had to unload them in the yard, and there was no room left anywhere. Then food, clothes, gift cards, boxes of Bibles. We didn't know where to put it all. We were giving it out as fast as it came in, but there wasn't any room. People wanted to help, but they didn't know how, so they brought stuff."

Elvis wandered back to the dorm room and lay down on his bed. He felt very tired again, and almost immediately, he fell asleep. When he woke up, he had no idea what time it was, though there was plenty of sunshine outside the window. He thought it might be afternoon. There was nothing to do but turn over in bed.

What a mess he had made of everything: his family, his life with Angel, his job. Nobody would miss him if he were gone. Previously, he would have imagined Angel missing him, but not now. She had brought him here for a reason. She must be very happy to have the house to herself now.

McFriends was for 72 hours max. He would have to leave by tomorrow. He had no money, no job, no friends. Nobody wanted him. Like a water-logged ship, Elvis sank under the weight of his own life. Maybe he should do what his father was supposed to have done: go into the waves and keep going. Disappear. How long before anyone realized he was gone?

In this sudden depression, Elvis lay on his bed, paralyzed. Then, by the blessings of an exhausted body, he fell asleep again.

* * *

Next time he awoke, the day was almost gone. Out the windows, he could see the wind whipping through the liquidambars that lined the back of the property. Some kind of weather must be coming in. His head hurt. He had slept with his neck crooked, and a pain ran up into his brain.

Tomorrow morning, he would be forced to leave McFriends. He could go to a shelter. He could go back to the mission as a guest. He could even start the New Life program again, beginning at the very beginning. He couldn't imagine that. It involved more humiliation than he could contemplate, for days on end, month after month. Elvis thought of a slogan he had heard at AA. How did it go? "Most things can be preserved in alcohol. Dignity isn't one of them."

He knew perfectly well addicts have to get sick and tired of being sick and tired. Maybe he was one of those people who couldn't.

He thought about the fires. Ian had called him a hero, but he wasn't a hero. He'd helped that lady mostly because he didn't know what else to do. Why, then, had the firestorm kick-started his recovery? Two years he had lasted. It was the longest he'd been off drugs since he was 16.

It was gloomy now in the room. Sunlight was fading and you could hardly see somebody's face. For once, Elvis didn't want to see anybody. He wanted it to stay dark. He hoped they never turned on the light.

He should get up and move around, he knew. His body needed a break from the bed. If he lay here now, he would never get to sleep again; he had done nothing but sleep, and now he would lie awake all night.

But he didn't want to move. He wanted to obliterate the world of sense and sight. He didn't really want to die; he just wanted to stop.

That was death, he realized. It was stopping. Other people would clean up the mess.

And what if he really did go to heaven? Or hell?

He thought he would have to take that risk. *Nobody really knows*, he thought.

What he would do, he decided at last, was get up for dinner and see. If he ate dinner and afterward he still felt this way, he would figure out how to end it.

Having put off the decision, he was able to close his eyes. His mind rested, he almost slept, and his father's face drifted in. They were in a bar. His father was drinking—he could smell the whiskey—and Elvis was trying to tell him to quit. "It's bad stuff," Elvis told his father.

"I'm not an alcoholic," his father said indignantly. Elvis wanted to cry out in despair. They were all caught; it was all hopeless.

Elvis woke up. He had been tapped on his shoulder, and he opened his eyes. Daylight had come, but the room was still too dark to see who looked down on him. It was a woman, but her face lay in shadow. He thought it was Angie and tried to turn away. Why did she have to wake him? He hoped he could find his way back to oblivion.

"Elvis, wake up! It's time to go home!"

He recognized the smoker's voice, rough and coarse: Angel. She looked down on him like a real heavenly being, her hair spread around her head. Flooded with joy, Elvis could not speak. He put up a hand and she took it in hers.

"Come on," Angel said.

"Where?"

"Home," she said. "Angie says you're feeling better."

He didn't answer that. Was he feeling better? He had been thinking of killing himself. He hadn't been able to imagine how he would go on. But now, with Angel, everything looked different.

"You really want me?" he asked.

"Sure. Why not?" she said. It wasn't the most shining response.

Elvis talked nonstop all the way home. He didn't want to let the silence come; he wanted to charm Angel and not let her think about why she didn't want him. He knew perfectly well why she wouldn't. He had acted like a complete asshole, and not just a few times. He had stolen from her. She was supporting him, and he had quit a good job. You could say it wasn't him, it was the drugs, but in his heart he knew he wasn't done with the drugs.

So he told her about Angie and what he remembered of her from previous visits. He told her about the men at McFriends who couldn't really talk. "You know, meth is way easier to kick," he said. "Those heroin addicts, they were getting their butts kicked. I just needed to sleep." He didn't mention the fear or the depression.

He wanted to have sex as soon as they got home. He was already touching her in the car while he talked, with Angel driving and acting like nothing was happening. She looked wonderful. He realized that she had tried to look her best, and that she was rested. She must have slept, just like he had. Sleep was good for everybody.

When they got home, she let him tug her into the bedroom. It was good, but he wasn't sure how good for Angel. She didn't have much to say, which was normal.

"You're scaring me," he said as he put his clothes back on. He was hungry, and he thought he would cook something, but first he needed some sign from Angel. "I don't know how you really feel about me."

She was hooking her bra. Amazing how right after sex, you could see that and feel nothing. "I came and got you, didn't I?"

"Yeah."

"And I'm taking the day off work for you." She looked at him in what he thought was a cold way. "Let's just see how it goes," she said.

He looked away from her, afraid for what his eyes might show. He wondered whether she had any idea how desperate he was.

After taking a shower—he hadn't washed or changed his clothes while he was at McFriends—he took his time getting dressed. His clothes were in the second bedroom, and he was glad to go there and shut the door. He couldn't look at Angel now.

Elvis picked a pair of tight white jeans out of the dresser. For a shirt, he went with a black tee that had an Escher design on the front. Over that, he wrapped a blue-jean Grateful Dead vest edged with black faux fur. Red high-tops with purple laces, and he felt better about himself. Clothes were a comfort to Elvis.

"Enchiladas?" he yelled when he came out of the room.

"What?" Angel was in the bathroom. He went near the door.

"I was thinking chicken enchiladas. Does that sound good?"

He borrowed money from her purse and walked to Aldi. The store was just four blocks away, tucked in a strip mall off Third Street. Elvis enjoyed shopping for groceries, though Aldi had such limited selection it didn't give you much to look at. Perusing the glossy green and red peppers, he realized that his stomach was as big and empty as a basketball. Enchiladas made his mouth water. He wasn't sure he could wait while they cooked. He would have to buy some chips to carry him through.

The second wave of hunger came unexpectedly on top of the first, like a sleeper wave that catches you unawares. He wanted a pipe.

The craving was so huge that it felt like an ocean wave, knocking him sideways.

As soon as it came, he knew he was going to give in. He must have known all along, because the realization seemed natural, almost easy. Elvis hesitated for just a fleeting moment, then left his cart where it was and walked out of the store. Around the corner was an old stucco house, faded orange in color, with a parade of potted succulents on the cement porch. He knocked on the door and waited. Eventually, his friend Wade appeared.

"Hey, man, where ya been?" Wade was very offhand, very cool. A bomb could go off across the street and he wouldn't flinch.

Elvis wagged his head sheepishly, ashamed of himself and yet eager to get his hands on the stuff. "I was in McFriends," he said.

"God," Wade said.

"Can I come in?"

He used right there, in the funky living room dominated by a gigantic screen and a roomy wraparound leather sofa. The stuff was good, or maybe his sensitivity had been restored by not using for a few days. It was the very best feeling, a rush of pleasure so strong he didn't even think about what would happen with Angel.

A short time later, he was on his way home. At every step, his jauntiness faded and dread increased. The meth had blasted through him, but its effect died down. He had a bag in his pocket, which reminded him that only a minute was required to bring back the beautiful feelings. But the money was gone and he had no groceries. He didn't know what Angel would say.

By the time he reached the house, he was very nervous. He could feel his agitation rising. The only cure for that was another pipe, but he wasn't going to do that in full view. He had to get inside. That meant facing Angel. He steeled himself and opened the screen door. The sooner he got through it, the better.

She was standing, waiting, across the room. She knew what had happened instantly. "Shit," she said, and stared at him. Elvis tried to read her expression. What was she signaling, disgust? Dismay? Could he ride this out once again, or was this really his doom?

He could hardly stand the suspense. One part of him was itching to move past her into the bedroom to light up, to bring back a wave of pleasure and of forgetting. Another part hung over the edge of a chasm, filled with self-dismay, dreading his fate at the judgment of this woman whom he loved.

"Shit," she said again, still staring at him. Angel took a deep breath and blew it out again. "Okay, I'm going out to get something to eat." She dropped her eyes and moved toward the door. Her body movements were as tightly angry as a frustrated cat's.

"What about me?" he asked plaintively.

"What about you?" she echoed, pausing.

"What am I supposed to do?"

"You can do whatever you want to do. It's none of my business."

# 6 CHURCH GIRL

Everybody has a limit, and Elvis thought Angel had reached hers. She had almost saved him, but not quite. Elvis expected the cops to come, Angel having called them to get him out of her house. It wasn't the threat of arrest and jail that unsettled him, though. He had been arrested plenty of times and could take it in stride. What distressed him was the death of the only love he had ever experienced. From now on, he would be alone in the world.

Elvis was still awake and pitifully agitated when Angel came home that night, late. He had smoked another pipe as soon as she went out the door, but the effect lasted less than an hour. He watched TV—at least, turned the TV on. He watched a wild animal show that worked like wallpaper in the room of his tumbling mind.

When he heard her car, he opened the door to greet her, eager and nervous as an eight-week-old puppy. She walked right past him without a word. Elvis followed her and watched while she washed her face and brushed her teeth. He turned away when she got out of her clothes. After she was in her flannel pajamas and under the covers, he followed suit as quietly as possible. It wasn't like him not to talk, but he was hoping not to draw attention to himself.

He lay awake next to her, wanting badly to talk or touch but not daring to make the first move. Angel lay perfectly still. He thought she was awake, but he couldn't say for sure.

Then he noticed her changing breathing, growing gradually deeper and longer until there was no doubt: she was actually sleeping. Her mouth made a slight whistling sound with each breath. He reached out to touch Angel's shoulder, and she did not react. Gradually, carefully, he inched closer to her. She was on her back so he could not mold himself to her, but he made himself conform as closely as possible without waking her. This was some comfort.

He did not sleep, while she slept as soundly as a dog. He felt all the questions: could she forgive him, could she help him, did she still love him. He knew he had used up his last chance, and he also knew that he would use again. It made no sense in the world, yet he knew the impulse would come and he would surrender. He didn't understand, but he knew. It was the most awful reality in the world.

He finally relaxed and went to sleep. When he woke up, he was intertwined with Angel, limb on limb. It was light in the room. He lay very still, and the memories came back. He was mortified when he thought what he had done.

The idea of going back to the mission and reentering New Life crossed his mind again. He didn't see how he could. Maybe he would rather die than suffer such humiliation.

He knew he should call his sponsor. That was what AA said. He should have called him before he relapsed. AA seemed too flimsy for the power that afflicted him. It amounted to an addicts' club—and he belonged, certainly, but he couldn't see how it would fix what was wrong with him.

Lying awake, thinking about AA, he remembered what the Twelve Steps said about the Higher Power. The foundation of all the steps was the Higher Power, God as we understand him. When he thought of that, Elvis realized how far from God he had gone. He realized he hadn't been doing the steps at all, not really.

Not so long ago, when he was at the mission, God had been in his heart and on his lips every day. It was always God. No doubt if he walked into the mission today, he would feel the same thing. He wasn't there, however. He was far off from there (even though it was only down the street), and he didn't want to go there, either. He was in a sad place, lost in the woods, and he didn't know how to find his way home.

Angel snorted in her sleep, stirred, and turned over onto her side. He desperately willed her to wake up. He wanted to tell her what he was thinking, to ask for her forgiveness, to ask for her help.

She did finally stir, turn over again, and open her eyes. She was looking right into his. He searched her hazel depths, and she focused and found him. She smiled slightly.

"Angel," he said, "would you go to church with me?"

She didn't answer but kept her eyes focused on his.

"I'm lost," he said. "I need God."

She still said nothing.

"I can't go by myself," Elvis said. All this was coming out of his mouth without a plan. He didn't know what he would say next. "I can't go unless you go with me."

* * *

Breathe met in a converted industrial park off Airport Drive, sharing parking with Live Oak Charter School. Entering the building was difficult for Elvis. Guilt and shame supposedly had no place in a grace-based church, but they weighed heavy on him. Breathe had been like family to him, and he had let them down. He felt like the last bit of toothpaste squeezed out of the tube.

Angel walked beside him, looking like a movie star. She had dressed up in a pleated silk blouse and tight silver-metallic pants, and she wore dark glasses. Without her, he might have driven past the church and gone out for breakfast. They got in the door. Elvis blinked to adjust to the darkness in the small, busy lobby. He felt intensely nervous. Men and women bustled around, none of whom he recognized.

Then he heard a loud "Awwwwwww!" over one shoulder. Just as he turned toward the sound, he found himself tackled by a puffy green coat. "Where have you been?!" a voice shrieked in his ear. "Robby! Robby! Look who's here!"

Elvis extricated himself and put his hat back on. A woman named Sandra had accosted him. Robby was her husband. They were both rotund and blond and very friendly. Robby asked if they wanted a cup of coffee, and Elvis followed him while Sandra chatted with Angel. On the way to the coffee station, Elvis was greeted by two different men whose names he could not remember. He thought he had met them at a Bible study at the pastor's house.

While he waited in line for coffee, he heard the band begin to play, which was a relief. He didn't want to linger in the lobby, forced to explain where he had been. Armed with coffee, he and Angel found their way into the auditorium, which was small with a low ceiling. Lights were dimming already, and the music triggered memories of comfort and release, of mercy so close you could feel it.

He had been saved right here, rescued from himself and his failings, lifted up and introduced to the Spirit of God. His brothers and sisters were all around him now, not looking at each other but standing shoulder to shoulder to look toward God himself. He could hardly stand it, the scene was so majestic.

Someone in front began waving their arms forward and back, bowing down again and again. The whole room joined in, including Elvis, swaying like a tree in a high wind. One song led to another. The band was loud. "We adore you, we adore you, Mighty God, glorious King." Elvis was aware that Angel was standing stiffly by him, not waving, not bending. He wanted terribly for her to join in. She was so tough, so strong; she had come here to stand next to him, and he needed her, but he couldn't make her bend. Only God could do that.

The service was a little wild, with women dancing on stage and waving banners in the aisles. The whole congregation repeated phrases over and over. Elvis threw his arms back and lifted his face to the sky, singing while tears streamed down his cheeks. He could have done it forever.

The pastor spoke. He wasn't a young man, such as you expected in a church like this. He had a balding pate surrounded by tufts of gray hair, like a monk's, and he looked slightly dumpy and very ordinary. For Elvis, though, something about him communicated forgiveness. What he said didn't necessarily stick in Elvis's memory, but there was a sense to it, a tone, that was grace poured over him like honey. It felt like healing oil rubbed into his shoulders. It was a grace massage. He wanted to sink down and listen to this man talk forever.

The band played again, backing up a woman singer with hair sprawling down her back. At the song's break, the pastor began speaking over the music, guitars weeping underneath his words. The woman sang again, more forcefully, moving into a hard-charging song, then back into something slower and more meditative. The pastor prayed, and Elvis got up from his seat, brushing past others down the row until he found the aisle, then walking purposefully to the front. He was the first to throw himself on his knees in front of the stage. Soon, others joined him. Next to him, a black woman threw her full length on the floor, moaning, her arms stretched over her head. The music continued, the pastor spoke again, more people joined them. It began to be crowded.

The pastor prayed for them all, taking his time, walking down the line to lay hands on each one, tiptoeing over prone bodies. Elvis was lost in it. The music slowed and stopped. Lights came on brightly, and it was over. Elvis stayed where he was, on his knees, with his hands stretched out in front, touching the floor. Others near him were beginning to move, but he stayed put for some time. Eventually, he lifted his head and sat up, wiping his eyes with his sleeve, taking in his surroundings like a man awakening from a trance.

Next to him he found Angel, on her knees. She had joined him, and he hadn't even known. Elvis wrapped his arms around her. Her presence, even more than the service, gave him hope.

"Did you feel it?" he asked her. "Did you feel the Spirit?"

She shrugged. He felt her tension. She should melt into him, but it was like hugging a manikin.

"It was amazing," Elvis said. "Just amazing."

"Yeah," she said.

Elvis didn't know what to say during the ride home. Something had kindled inside him, but he knew he needed Angel for support. She was holding back. She wouldn't let go, wouldn't allow room for the Spirit.

Elvis threw himself into cooking a great lunch. A Thai red curry would be delicious, he decided, and made a list of ingredients. Angel was in the living room watching videos on her phone, something he had never seen her do. She looked discouraged. She also looked delectable. Elvis told her what he wanted to cook and asked if he could borrow some money to get chicken and spinach and a few other things. Angel didn't look happy, but she pointed at her purse, which he brought her.

"How much do you need?" she asked.

"Twenty should do it," he said.

Who should he encounter as he was leaving the grocery store but Jesse Hernandez, who had been in the New Life program with him. Jesse saw him first, grabbed him from behind, and gave him a big hug. He was a very friendly young guy, liked by just about everybody.

Elvis held Jesse at arm's length to look at him. "You're eating well," he said with a smile. Jesse looked a little pudgy. His cheeks puffed out like apples.

"Not like you," Jesse said. "You're really trim. You working out?"

Elvis would have liked to believe that Jesse thought he was in shape, but he knew that was baloney. The meth was killing him. He asked Jesse what he was doing.

"I've got a job working construction up in Fountaingrove," Jesse said. "Making fifteen. It's pretty good."

"Where are you living?"

"I'm sharing a trailer with a couple of the brothers," Jesse said. "Out by Forestville. You remember Junior?"

Elvis did, vaguely. Junior was a massive, slow-moving man who had come into the program at just about the time Elvis was ready to graduate. "You're sharing with him?"

"Yeah, and Melvin."

"That's great, man," Elvis said. "Say hi to those dudes."

"What about you, man? What are you up to?"

Elvis was sure that Jesse could tell what he was up to. "I'm looking for work," he said.

"You got a place to live?"

"Sort of. I'm crashing with my lady. She lets me stay as long as I cook."

"Hey, I can see if I can get you on at my job, if you want. My boss is pretty good."

Elvis thought about it momentarily. He could get a roofing job easy, and it would pay a lot better than Jesse was getting. He needed to get his life on track first. "That's okay," he said. "I need a little more time. You know, pulling it together."

Jesse nodded enthusiastically. He knew. "Hey," he said, "you want to come with me to the mission right now? Just to say hi? I'm meeting a couple of the guys who want to go for a bike ride. You could come with us."

"I don't have a bike," Elvis said.

"So come with me anyway. You can say hi to Knox."

"He there today?"

"Yeah, definitely. I have to talk to him about some computer stuff. I'm helping out some of the guys who need to do resumes for their job search."

Why not? For months he had been thinking about visiting the mission, but the shame always kept him away. Today, he had broken through and gone to church; he might as well go for two. He would feel a lot less conspicuous walking into the mission with Jesse.

Elvis was suddenly feeling optimistic. He found that strange. Usually when you quit meth, you got horribly depressed. Then it came to him that he had used less than 24 hours ago. His body didn't yet know he was quitting.

They found Knox in his office, where he was filling out a form. He had his nose so deeply buried in the paper that he didn't notice them when they came in. Elvis had to knock on the side of the door, whereupon Knox looked up, taking a moment to recognize Elvis, and then said loudly, "Mannnnnn!" He proceeded to hug Elvis. Then he thrust Elvis back at arm's length to look at him critically.

"You're struggling," he said, frowning.

Knox had a long, deeply lined black face. When he frowned, it seemed to pull the whole world down inside its sadness.

"I'm doing great now," Elvis said. "I rededicated this morning at church. I'm a new man."

"That's wonderful to hear," Knox said softly. "Sit down and tell me about it." He gestured to a chair, then realized it was stacked with packages of nutrition bars and hurried to clear it off. Elvis sat, though he wasn't sure he wanted to stay. "Where you been?" Knox asked. "We haven't seen you for the longest time."

"I was working," Elvis said. "I just never had the time to come by. The work let up a little while ago, so I remembered I wanted to come see you. Ran into Jesse at the grocery store"—Jesse was standing in the door, listening and grinning—"and he said he was coming here, so I came along. How are you doing, Knox?"

"I'm fine," he said. "Couldn't be better, to tell you the simple truth. Now what kind of work are you doing?"

"Oh, roofing; I was working for a guy named Dempster. Roofing is something I've done a lot of."

"Yeah, I believe I remember that. So, the work slowed up?"

Elvis looked closely at Knox's face to see if he was pulling his leg. It didn't seem so. He looked genuinely puzzled.

"No. Like you said, Knox, I've been struggling. You know how it is."

"I do," Knox said.

"But everything is brand new now, Knox. It's different from now on."

"Okay," Knox said. "That's good. I'm glad to hear it. Which church do you go to?"

* * *

Elvis got back to the house later than he had planned. Angel was playing a game on her phone; she looked up, flouncing her reddish hair, but didn't say anything. Elvis realized with a jolt that she probably thought he was using again. He couldn't get mad at her for that. He would have believed the same thing.

"It won't take too long," Elvis said. "Sorry, I got hung up. I met some old friends from the mission."

He applied himself in the kitchen and actually had food ready in just over half an hour. Angel came and sat down at the kitchen table. "Can I pray?" he asked her, and she said sure.

Angel took a bite and pronounced it delicious. Then she looked at him, and the way she looked at him, he knew better than to say anything. "I flushed the drugs," she said. "I smashed the pipe."

"With what?" he managed to ask.

"I used that little hammer you always complain about. The one I keep in the junk drawer and you always say it isn't big enough to hammer a tack into a bulletin board. It was big enough to break up that pipe."

He just stared at her. He knew more was coming.

"What we're doing isn't working, so now we're going to do something different," Angel said. "No drugs. Not for you, not for me. No alcohol, either. You've got a problem, and that means I have a problem."

"Is that why you went to church today?"

"No. I just realized this after we got home. I can't make you quit, but I know you did fine when you were at the mission. From now on, consider this the mission. You're going to go out and get a job. You're not going to use, like I said. You're going to go to church and you're going to go to AA. Those are the rules. If you don't follow the rules, you are out of the program."

"How are you going to know if I go to meetings? You going to go with me?"

"No, I'm not. You're going to get a signed pass. Look, I put all the NA and AA meetings on the calendar. Every time you go to one, you bring me the pass, and I put a cross on the day."

"It's like a chore chart," he said.

"A what?"

"My dad had a chore chart," Elvis said, grinning. "When you did your chore, you had to go tell him, and he would check it off."

"Did it work?"

"Yeah, it did. You didn't want to try screwing with my dad."

"You don't want to try it with me, either."

He had to go through withdrawal all over again. He slept a lot; he had stretches of paranoia and one dramatic, lunging urge for meth, but overall, it was easier than at McFriends because he had Angel. It made him feel secure, knowing that Angel had taken control. She brought order to his life.

By Thursday, he was ready to go to a meeting, which he did—all by himself. It was a good meeting. He saw a few people he recognized and stood up to tell about his recent experiences. On Friday, he started looking for a job by calling the roofers he knew. He didn't actually reach anybody, but he had started the ball rolling. A job would come. Lots of roofers had drug problems, and the bosses couldn't blackball them all or they wouldn't have any workers.

Saturday morning, he was up early while Angel slept in. An overnight wind had swept the sky clean, and now a thin, icy blue appeared through the leafless trees. He felt itchy to get out of the house, so he eased quietly out the door and walked down to Railroad Square. It was still too early for anybody to be out. The streets looked damp and deserted. In a few hours, people would be lining up on the sidewalk outside Omelet Express for their Saturday brunch.

It had been weeks since a Saturday opened up so innocently. When you're using, your days are full, what with getting the stuff and smoking it and hiding it and tweaking. He didn't know what to do with himself, but he knew he should make some kind of active plan. Otherwise he would be bored and itchy, and temptations would come along offering to fill the gap.

His thoughts went naturally to food. He could make a really fabulous dinner for Angel. That would take up most of the day. Plunking himself down on a Fourth Street bench in front of LoCoco's, he considered his favorite recipes and decided on chicken cacciatore. Just thinking of it made him salivate.

He walked straight to the grocery store to buy the makings. As he went, the sun appeared over the buildings, pale gold. Elvis had a further revelation: they would take dinner to the beach and eat it there, on the sand.

When he got back home, Angel was looking at her phone, still in her pajamas, her hair a thick mess and her eyes smudged. He didn't say anything about what he was doing. Angel never paid much attention to his cooking, so he simply began. He took his time, enjoying himself as he sautéed the mushrooms and onions and garlic and peppers. Then he cut up the chicken and carefully browned it. He added canned tomatoes and red wine. When he measured out the wine, he was tempted to taste it, but he stopped short. It actually thrilled him to say no to himself, to demonstrate some character.

When he had put everything together in one big cast-iron pot and had it bubbling snugly, he went out to the living room. Angel had not moved. He stood looking at her, taking her in. It took several minutes before she noticed him.

"How about we go to the beach today?" he asked.

She blinked. "Is it warm enough?"

"I think so. Check your phone. You'll need a sweater, of course."

"Sure," she said, and that lit him up. He never felt worthy of her.

"Let's go in about an hour," he said. "We can eat lunch out there. I'll put together some things."

They had a bottle of olives. He threw in a loaf of bread, cut up some celery, and added a chocolate bar. He took a bread knife, two bowls, cutlery, and a tablecloth to spread on the sand. Finally, he filled his water bottle. No wine. When he heard Angel get out of the shower, he began to cart things out to his truck. When he judged that she was all but ready, he tasted the chicken, corrected its flavoring, and wrapped the covered pot in a heavy towel. He wedged the bundle behind the car seat so it couldn't spill. He felt pleased with himself.

Elvis had to borrow money for gas. Life would be better, he thought, when he had some money of his own.

But then they were on the road, free. The light played over the vineyard leaves dying into brown and yellow. The old truck was running great.

"What's that smell?" Angel wanted to know, and he told her only that it was lunch. "Quite a feast," he said. "Just you wait and see."

"For some reason," Elvis told her, "this reminds me of a little guy I knew at the mission. Just a kid, really, name of Sam. I think I told you about how we got this idea of getting a car and going to North Dakota to make money from fracking. We didn't even know what fracking was. We had seen some pictures in a magazine. Sam was this little, pale guy from some small town in the central valley, and he got it in his head we should go. I decided, *What the hell*, and I went with him. Two other guys, too. We left the mission just so full of ourselves and took the bus to San Francisco, where one of the guys had a friend who would sell him a car. I think it's the bus ride that reminded me of Sam. You know, here you and I are, on a lark going to the coast, and that was a lark, too. Sam had never been to San Francisco, never seen the Golden Gate bridge. Of course, we never got to North Dakota. The whole thing fell apart. The guy who was going to buy the car met a girl, and so no car, no fracking. We were stuck. Sam ended up going back to his little town. I never saw him again."

"What happened to him?" Angel asked. "Do you know?"

He smiled, shaking his head. "He drowned. We got the message from his father that he had drowned. Of course, we assumed that was just a nice way to say he overdosed."

At that, Elvis stopped talking and pondered Sam's life and his own. You just never know how the story is going to play out. Sam had been too nice, too innocent, and too young to end so badly. The drugs, though, have their own plan. Poor Sam. It made Elvis sad to think of his little face. A sweet kid, if ever there was one. He deserved better.

At the thought of it, a powerful wave of remorse pulsed through Elvis. God, he was getting weak. He felt weepy thinking of little Sam. That kid could be alive and living a beautiful life. He had wanted to, but he just didn't get the chance.

That was true for him, too. He was twenty years older than Sam, so he had wasted even more years of beautiful life. However, one good thing: he wasn't dead.

The thought cracked a smile on Elvis's face.

"Whatcha laughing about?"

"I was thinking about Sam and it made me remember I'm not so different, except for one thing. I'm not dead. My greatest achievement: I'm not dead. You could put that in my high school reunion—you know how they have a paper that summarizes what everybody is doing? Elvis Sebastiano, not dead yet."

"Or on your tombstone," Angel said. "No, wait."

They both laughed, and then quiet descended as they thought it over and watched the truck suck down the road. They were out of the vineyards and into the frayed track of the river, where old metal bridges crossed over and back again, and stores in various stages of disarray had set up to tempt drivers to stop—everything from laundromats to tire shops to souvenir stores. They passed one of Elvis's favorite signs, hand-lettered: "TIE-DYE JERKY." At one time, Elvis had known every little muddy beach in this area, where you could park on the shoulder and wander down a footpath that made a gap in the willows or blackberries. The water was shallow in the summer, but you could always get wet. When the rains came in the winter, it was a flood zone, and every spring, the beaches emerged rearranged. Sometimes they were gone, as though they had never existed. Sometimes new beaches appeared.

"You know what's weird?" Elvis asked.

"No, what?"

"I'm not used to being sober."

"How is that weird?"

"It feels weird. Being on meth is like a dysfunctional relationship. You know, like those women who keep going back to their pimp even though he steals their money and beats them up. Everybody knows it's bad for you, but they can't leave it behind. It feels normal to be screwed up, and when you're clean and sober, you're not sure how to deal with it."

"I kinda understand, but not really," Angel said.

"When you're using, the same thing happens over and over again. You get high, you screw up, you feel guilty, you swear to change, you go back and do the same thing again. Rinse and repeat. It's so familiar, it's like a piece of your insides. When you stop, it feels like something in your life is missing. It's not normal to feel so okay."

"Is that how you're feeling now?"

He had to think. "I'm not sure how I feel. It's different, that's all I know. I want to keep it, but I don't know."

* * *

They reached the wide ocean. At Schoolhouse Beach, Elvis gave Angel the bag of supplies while he grabbed the toweled bundle of chicken-in-a-pot. The beach was a small crescent sheltered by cliffs. Once you followed the path down, you were hidden from the hills and the highway. Elvis led Angel to the farthest reaches of the crescent, where they would have more privacy.

Half a dozen people were scattered near the path, all of them busy with their own concerns. Waves smashed down just offshore and sent washes of foam up the dark sand. Nobody ever swam here; the waves were brutally cold and dangerous. But beautiful. It didn't seem reasonable that ordinary people, not to mention messed-up drug addicts, got to live here and see this.

A skim of clouds had covered the sky, so the colors were mostly brown and gray. Angel and Elvis nestled down in the sand, spread the tablecloth, and began to eat.

"God, it's good," Angel said.

"Everything tastes good at the beach."

He was gaining confidence, Elvis thought. He wanted so much to live a straight life instead of the chaos-filled carnival he had been in forever.

"It's very calming here," he said. "It's like, how can you think of messing up when you see those waves come in? They're so reliable."

"Look at the light shining through just before they break."

"I have to tell you, Angel, that I can't do this without you."

"I can't make you do it."

There was nothing to say to that, really. A little black dog came running up, skinny as a snake and with a funny habit of bending sideways, as though it was backing up on you while it came forward. Elvis held out his hand to pet it, but the dog didn't trust him and darted away.

"Look," Elvis said to Angel. "Somebody has hit that dog. See how it won't lead with its head? Half of it is coming toward you and the other half is already running away."

He plucked a small piece of chicken out of the pot and held it out on the flat of his palm. The dog saw it and sidled up to it. In the motion of grabbing the chicken, it was in such a hurry that it dropped it on the sand. An elaborate dodge was required before it could pick the chicken up and run to a safe distance.

Elvis held out a piece of bread. The dog approached with the same jittery caution, darting back several times when he imagined an assault, but finally plucking the bread off his palm and carrying it away.

Elvis didn't offer any more. After a few minutes of waiting, the dog came nearer, whining. Elvis held a piece of bread in his fist, then slowly opened it, then closed it again and got up to walk. He clucked his tongue and the dog followed, three feet behind. Soon, he had the dog heeling, following his movements as he went up and down the beach, making sudden turns. It became a game. Occasionally, the dog would leave him and approach Angel—it knew she had food—but Elvis whistled it back. He threw sticks into the waves. Blackie—that is what he had named the dog—ran after anything. It ran with a long, loose lope, as though its joints were disconnected and its limbs might fall off in any direction.

Eventually, Elvis threw himself down beside Angel again. He coaxed Blackie to come and sit beside him while he stroked its lustrous black fur.

"Somebody abandoned this dog," Elvis said. "See how skinny it is? It's a nice dog, don't you think?"

Angel preferred cats, he knew.

Elvis got up and played some more with the dog. He came back to her laughing, dragging the dog by pulling the stick it held tenaciously in its mouth.

"Can we take Blackie home with us? He's such a nice dog."

"What if somebody comes looking for him?" she asked, trying hard to show her sternest stuff.

"Look, we can post him on Facebook," he said. "If somebody is looking for him, they'll check there." Then he laughed crazily, leaped up in the air, and came down in a kung fu stance. "But I don't think anybody is looking for him! Can we take him home?"

# 7 FINDING FAMILY

Early Monday morning, about 7:00 a.m., Elvis got a call from Rizzuto Roofing, one of the companies he had called looking for a job. He picked up.

"This is Elvis." His early morning voice was full of frogs. He sounded like he was drowning.

"Ernie Rizzuto. You the one who called about a job?"

Elvis tried to clear his throat. "Yeah, that's me."

"Can you come now?"

He thought for only a moment. "Sure."

"So come to our job site. You got a pencil? Three-two-one-six Hachette. Santa Rosa. How soon can you get here?"

"Pretty soon," Elvis said. "Fifteen, twenty minutes. I gotta get dressed. Do I have time to drink some coffee?"

He could smell it brewing. Angel was already up, but Blackie had stayed by Elvis's bedside. His tail was thumping the floor as he anticipated another wonderful day. He followed Elvis as he walked toward the kitchen in his underwear. Angel was dressed and ready for work, looking at her phone as she ate a bowl of Cheerios.

"That was my new boss," Elvis said. "Ernie Rizzuto. He said to come right away."

He was surprised by her happiness. "Really?" she said with a big smile. "You got a job?"

"Looks like it. I'll have to see what it's like. The guy didn't seem like he was in a mood to talk."

"It's raining," Angel said.

Elvis had not taken that in, but now he noticed that the street was wet, and drips of water fringed the front porch gutter. "Okay!" he said. "Now I know why they want me this second."

"Why is that?" Angel asked idly, still looking at her phone.

"When it rains, people start calling about leaks." He added, "It can get a little crazy."

He didn't shower; he threw water in his face and pulled on some clothes. What took time was finding his tool belt. He went from room to room searching for it, Blackie following him every step. He bellowed at Angel, asking what she had done with it. She ignored him. He finally found it in the back of the bedroom closet.

"I'm taking the dog," he said as he went out the door.

Hachette Street was on a hillside south of the fairgrounds. The rain was coming down steadily. A white pickup truck was parked in front of the address, but otherwise, Elvis didn't see anybody. "You stay here," he told Blackie and went up the sidewalk. The house was a fake Eichler, with an overgrown front yard of live oaks and cypress bushes. He couldn't see the roof, but he was willing to bet that it was covered in leaves.

A middle-aged woman answered the door and directed him around back. He found a ladder propped up against the house and climbed it. A man crouched behind the stovepipe chimney got up when Elvis called, coming over to the edge of the roof. When they both had identified themselves, he said, "I want you to find the leak on this roof and patch it."

"Okay," Elvis said. He hadn't come expecting to work. He didn't even have a jacket. "You got supplies?"

"It's all over there," Ernie said, waving a hand toward the chimney. "You get it fixed and then call me."

"Where are you going?" Elvis asked.

"I got five jobs to look at. I can't hold your hand. You said you know roofing."

"Okay," Elvis said. "That should be fine. You found where it comes from?"

"Might be that pipe. I'm not sure."

Ernie was already on his way down the ladder when Elvis remembered to ask some questions. "Hey, how much are you paying me?"

Ernie stopped halfway and looked up into the raindrops. "Fifteen," he said.

"No way," Elvis said. "I can get that at McDonald's."

"Twenty," Ernie said.

"Twenty-eight," Elvis said. "That's what I was getting at the last place."

"Where you got fired."

"They didn't fire me. I quit. I had some problems I needed to work out."

Ernie stared at him. "Twenty-five," he said.

"Deal."

It wasn't the stovepipe. Elvis found a seam that had lifted, but he got thoroughly soaked looking for it. He needed to patch the seam and caulk it, a multiple-stage process. After cutting the patch and smearing it with caulking, he went down the ladder to check on Blackie. Being just a pup, the dog might pee in the truck. Blackie greeted him like a long-lost savior, whining and pawing. Elvis had a length of rope that he tied to the dog's collar before lifting it onto the ground. Blackie headed immediately for a tree, where he released a long-lasting, vigorous stream of urine. Then he whined and pawed at Elvis's leg.

Elvis tied Blackie to a tree in the backyard, near enough to the house that the dog could get under the eaves. But when he went up the ladder, Blackie whined and barked. He let him do it for a while, hoping he would settle down, but eventually he took Blackie back to the truck.

Elvis finished off the patch—he was really wet and cold by this time—and got back in his truck, starting the engine to get the heater going. Blackie writhed in his lap, trying to make maximum contact. When Elvis had stopped shaking, he called his boss.

"I'm done here," he said when Ernie answered. "It was a seam that had lifted. I put on a new patch and it should be okay. What do you want me to do with your ladder?"

"You got a dog there?" Ernie answered. "That lady called complaining."

"What was she complaining about?"

"She said the dog was barking. Man, you can't have a dog on the job. Take your dog home and then call me."

"The dog only barked for maybe two minutes. I put him back in the truck right away."

"I don't care. We don't have dogs on site."

Elvis hung up before he was tempted to say something. He left the supplies in a neat collection near the ladder, got back in the truck, and drove home. He really wanted to hit somebody. The house was empty, of course, and he threw himself into his favorite chair. He was soggy and cold. He had started out the day full of optimism, and now it was spoiled. He couldn't leave Blackie at home all day. He didn't want to work for an asshole anyway.

The desire for a pipe came suddenly, like a north wind cutting right through him. Out of nowhere, it filled up his chest. *Just hold on*, he said, and picked up one of the women's magazines Angel read. He couldn't concentrate on it. He couldn't even see the pictures, the desire was so strong. *Just hold on*. He counted to a hundred, very slowly. The wind grew slightly less intense. He stood up and walked around the room, but that seemed to make it worse, so he sat down again. He could feel it ebbing away. He was all right. He was still clean.

He wanted to do something productive, to move and change his thoughts, so he went into the kitchen. It was still early for lunch. After staring into the refrigerator for some time, he began going through it, checking out what could be used and what could be thrown out. He found half a dozen bottles of oriental sauces—three of oyster sauce alone—and three half-empty bottles of dill pickles. It was all useable stuff, but some of the produce—withered carrots, cheese growing mold—he threw out. In the freezer, Elvis found four almost-empty ice cream containers, frozen peas and carrots, and two steaks that had embedded themselves in permafrost. He pried them out. Maybe dinner tonight. Steak and potatoes. He would need to buy some vegetables. He wasn't going to stoop so low as to serve frozen peas and carrots.

On second thought, he fished the molded cheese out of the trash, cut away the green-white edges, and sliced some of it. It was perfectly good, and he liked cheese sandwiches. He was in the process of assembling his ingredients when his phone rang. He had left it in the living room and didn't reach it until the fifth or sixth ring.

"You Elvis?"

"Yeah. Who wants to know?"

"It's Edgar at Roofover. You called last week."

A smile took over Elvis's face as they talked. It seemed unbelievable that he got two calls in a single day. He knew there were jobs out there, but still. He thought it was his Higher Power working for him. It made him optimistic. Maybe he would find the path.

Edgar wanted to hear him say how much experience he had. He didn't need to know why Elvis wasn't working. You had to assume with roofers it wasn't a good question.

"When can you start?" Edgar wanted to know.

"I can start today," Elvis said. "Right now."

"You got transportation?"

"I got my truck. It runs most of the time."

"I can pay you twenty-three," Edgar said.

"Medical?"

"No."

"I was getting twenty-eight at my last job," Elvis said.

"That's what you'll be getting in six months, if you're still working for me. I'm not going to cheat you if you know how to do the job. I pay on the books. Nothing under the table. There's usually overtime, too."

* * *

Every night, Elvis got home from work exhausted. They went out to eat a lot, because he couldn't get going on cooking. He was just out of shape, he told Angel, and in a couple of weeks he would get his spunk back. He said it without believing it. It was a complete mystery to him why he was so tired after eight hours of running up and down ladders hauling shingles. He had never felt this way before, he said, and he even talked of going to see the doctor.

"The day you go to the doctor, I'll know you're really sick," Angel told him. According to her, he was a big baby, afraid of needles and accustomed to lying to the doctors about what medications he was taking.

They didn't have a social life to speak of. The people they used to party with had all dropped off. Two of them had died in a car accident on River Road—which put a damper on the fun, as Elvis said, even after Angel told him it wasn't funny. Some had moved away. One or two were living on the streets and had no money.

Elvis didn't really mind that it was just the two of them, plus Blackie. They watched TV. They even went for walks, just around the neighborhood. Blackie went everywhere with Elvis. The new job allowed dogs on site, as long as they were tied up and didn't make a nuisance of themselves. Most of the time, Elvis left Blackie in the truck. He just had to make sure he remembered to let him out every few hours. Elvis took that responsibility very seriously.

Life was the best it had been for a long time. Elvis knew he deserved no credit for it. Everything happened because of Angel and the program she had put him on. One day, he happened on the notebook he had started when he was doing Step Four. He hadn't been going to meetings, and he hadn't called Bob, his sponsor. Angel hadn't really pushed that; she wasn't a big fan of AA. *I ought to get back into that*, he thought.

On Friday morning, Elvis got a telephone call just before he went out the door with Blackie.

It was a one-sided conversation. Elvis said "Yeah," occasionally, but mostly he was quiet. Finally, he said, "Yeah, that works."

Angel came out of the hallway after he hung up. "Who was that?" she asked casually.

"My dad," he said. He looked excited and stunned.

"What does he want?"

He looked at her like a man waking from a dream. "I don't know." He paused and gathered himself. "He wants to meet me in Garberville tonight. He didn't say what for."

Angel frowned. "Why didn't you ask him?"

Elvis shook his head. "It's hard to explain about my dad. He talks, and you don't really get a chance to ask questions."

"Are you going to go?"

He blinked as though startled by the question. "Yeah, sure."

"Then I'm going with you," Angel said.

"You are? Why? I mean, you don't have to go."

"Remember, you're in the program," she said. "You need accountability."

"But you're not watching me when I go off to work every day."

She moved her head in a barely visible *no*. "There's something weird about the way you answer to your dad," she said. "I want to keep an eye on you."

"Okay, fine," he said. "We'll have a great time. We should go as soon as we get home from work, though. I don't want to be up all night."

* * *

They made the drive north in the dark. It was raining again, and headlights reflecting on wet pavement dazzled the eye. Elvis jammed his truck into the rain-specked cone of light with confidence, winding through the curves as though on a track.

It was tough driving, but Elvis liked the privacy of the truck cab, the two of them cut off from the world, lit by the green glow of the dashboard instruments. Blackie lay on his side between them. Angel's hand rested on his stiff fur.

"Can I ask you about your dad?" Angel asked.

"Sure," Elvis answered. "Not that I know so much. I mean, he disappeared for like thirty years."

"But I've never seen you respond like that to anybody. I can hear it in your voice when you answer the phone. He calls you and you're ready to go anywhere."

A bit of hurt hesitancy came into Elvis's voice. "But he's my dad."

"Who, like you said, disappeared for thirty years. Did he ever say he was sorry?"

"No."

"If Amber calls you, you don't act like that. Or your brother. Or your mother, before she died."

He didn't answer. She couldn't see his face to tell what he was thinking.

"If you don't want to talk about it," she said.

"Hey, I do," Elvis said. "I just don't know what to say."

A memory suddenly came to him. "I remember going fishing with him when I was little." He had not thought of it in years; maybe he had never thought of it. "Not with a fishing rod. In his boat." He must have been young; the gunwales had been so high he could barely see over them to catch glimpses of the terrifying sloshing water.

"I thought you had no memories."

"No, I have a few. I think he was gone a lot."

"Fishing?"

"Maybe. I don't know. Probably something else. I guess if he was fishing, he would've come home every night."

"I still don't have any idea why you get one phone call and you're like Blackie at suppertime. You can't wait to get in the truck to go see him. I'm not complaining; I'm just curious. Do you know what he wants you for?"

"I have no idea," Elvis said. "It might be about Aunt Carol again, but he didn't say."

"And regardless, you're going to follow wherever he says."

They were both silent for some time, watching the road opening in front of them, appreciating the warmth of the heater.

"It's something about feeling lost," Elvis said. "Like he's the missing piece in the jigsaw puzzle. You know, he's my father."

"From what you've told me about him, he sounds like the worst asshole in the whole world. He treats you and everybody like shit."

"I know," Elvis said.

* * *

It was past 9:00 when they pulled off the highway into Garberville. Elvis remembered exactly how to get to the King Kwality Inn. Going into the office, however, made him a little anxious. He had left under such strange circumstances. What might his father have said and done that morning? Also, Elvis didn't have a reservation, and he didn't know whether they allowed dogs.

The lights were on in the reception, but looking through the glass door, Elvis could see nobody behind the desk. He pushed the door open, setting off a mechanical chime. "Hello?" he said.

Mrs. Patel came out from behind the paneled barrier, a slim, motherly woman with dark eyes. "Harold, come see who is here!" she called, a warm smile breaking over her face.

Her husband also appeared. "You came back!" he said, as though he were announcing an extra Christmas.

"Yeah," Elvis said, pleased though slightly nonplussed. "I brought my lady with me this time."

"Oh, please, can we meet her?" Mrs. Patel asked. "She is in your car?"

"Yeah, she's watching my dog. Oh, yeah, I have my little dog with me; I hope that's okay."

"Of course—no problem!" Mr. Patel said. "Perhaps it would like to play with our Shiva."

As if on cue, their small white dog appeared, lifting its paws to boost them against Elvis's leg. "Shiva!" Mrs. Patel reprimanded the dog.

"She's fine," Elvis said, bending down to tousle her ears.

He went outside and told Angel that they wanted to meet her. "Is there a problem?" she asked. The rain was pounding on the roof of the car. Elvis felt a sudden impulse to kiss her, and he did. "What is going on?" she asked.

"Nothing," he said. "Just come inside. They're really friendly, and they asked if they could meet you. They want to see Blackie, too."

He scooped up Blackie. Angel was right behind him, stooping as she came up the stairs, as though she could bend under the raindrops. The

Patels greeted her in a friendly, shy way, offering their hands to shake. "We are so glad to meet Elvis's friend," Mr. Patel said.

The two dogs circled each other cautiously; then Shiva launched herself at Blackie and they rolled, snarling, on the floor. Mrs. Patel was alarmed, but Elvis put out an arm to stop her. "They are just playing around," he said. "That's how dogs do it. They aren't going to hurt each other."

* * *

When they finally got settled in their room, Elvis called his father. He must have been waiting nearby, because he arrived in no time, knocking on the door and opening it in one motion. Willard had his graying hair slicked straight back, but he looked disheveled, as though he'd been sleeping and had just woken up. He nodded at Angel without looking at her, and then threw himself onto the bed. "You ready to go?" he asked Elvis.

"I guess so," Elvis said. "Where are we going?"

"Aunt Carol's," he said. "But this time we're going together."

"Isn't it a little late for that?"

"Nah. I want to get in there while she's asleep."

"Why?"

"I want those papers, dammit."

Blackie had been sniffing Willard's leg, with Willard not noticing that he existed. All of a sudden, Blackie started barking at Willard as though he were harboring a rat. Elvis tried hard to get him to stop, hushing him and even swatting him, but without effect. The barking was loud and persistent. They had never seen Blackie so dedicated. Elvis finally gathered him up and carried him outside to the truck. When he came back inside, he brushed the rain off his shirt and said, "You sure aren't popular with him."

"Dogs never like me," Willard said. "So you ready to go? We'll go in my car."

"Wait," Elvis said. "You plan to burglarize your own sister?"

"It's not burglary if it's your own house. She's the one stealing."

"Okay, but what if she's got a gun? What if she shoots us?"

"She isn't going to know we're there. I've got a plan."

"Can't we wait until the morning and just go talk to her?"

Willard shook his head. "You don't know my sister. You can't talk to her."

Angel had not said a word. She sat in the corner and watched, as though they were a TV show. When Willard got up to go, she got up, too. For the first time, Willard noticed her. "You're not going," he said.

"Of course I'm going."

"Wait," Elvis said. "What about Blackie? Somebody needs to watch him."

"He can stay in the car," Angel said. "Isn't that what he does when you're working?"

Elvis looked at his father. "How long are we going to be gone?" he asked.

"How should I know?"

"If it's more than a couple of hours, I don't know if Blackie can hold it."

"That's not my problem. You should have thought of that before you brought him."

"I'm sure he'll be fine," Angel said.

"If you get worried, you can send her back," Willard said.

It was now past midnight. The rain was still falling, though lightly now. When they got outside, Elvis saw holes in the clouds with stars staring through. Willard's big Buick was parked at an angle, blocking anybody's passage. Elvis checked on Blackie, fondling him on the muzzle. Then he opened his dad's passenger door and started to usher Angel inside.

"Hey. You get in there," Willard said sharply. "She can sit in back."

"We'll all fit in the front," Elvis said.

"No!" his father roared. After a short silence, he continued. "I said she sits in back."

Elvis was about to get his back up when Angel said unexpectedly, "Don't worry about it. I don't mind the back."

It set Elvis on edge. Why did his father get his way? The car roared to life and spun out of the parking lot. Its shocks were gone and it was riding on its springs, jouncing down and then up as they negotiated the curb.

"Why are we driving, anyway?" Elvis asked. "We could walk."

"It's raining, you fathead," his father said. "And we're going to sneak up from the backside."

He took off up a narrow, steep road, practically a driveway, that led up the hill and away from Aunt Carol's house. They must have climbed for a quarter of a mile when the road made a T with another road. Willard swung through a left without hesitation. The road meandered across and then down the hill. Elvis had lost track of where he was when Willard suddenly swerved off the road, brushing hard into bushes and low-hanging tree limbs before he stopped. "Okay, this will do," he said.

It was impossible for Elvis to get out on his side. He scooted across to the driver's door. Blackie tried to follow but he pushed him back and closed the door. Angel had already gotten out and was standing quietly. Elvis looked warily at her dark silhouette; he had never known her to let things slide. "You okay?" he asked her.

"Just following my man," she said.

"You didn't have to come."

"I know that. I'm not complaining."

It was very dark. The road was pockmarked with invisible water-filled potholes, as Elvis soon discovered by stepping in one and then another. He warned Angel; she had on running shoes, which would get soaked. He had on his stitched cowboy boots, as well as a heavy, old-fashioned yellow slicker that he was fond of. He wore a classic five-gallon cowboy hat on his head, with a huge brim to keep the rain far from him. He would stay dry. He wasn't so sure about Angel.

"Dammit!" his father exploded. "Did you bring a flashlight?"

He didn't bother answering. He pulled out his phone and turned on the flashlight feature. He couldn't see much in its dim light, however, and anyway, his father was already on the move out of his orbit.

"It's right over here," Willard said from the downhill side of the road.

"What is?"

"The goddam path. Don't worry; I could find it with my eyes sealed shut. I had a girl who lived way up past here, and I walked the path in all weather. Here it is. I found it."

One moment, Elvis could make out his father's shadow; the next, he was gone. It looked like disappearing magic, but Elvis could hear him struggling through the brush. "Come on, you assholes, stick close!" he yelled.

Elvis grabbed Angel's hand and led the way. He couldn't really see his father, but he could hear him. The pathway was overgrown and he was fighting his way through, all by feel. He put away his phone; it was useless, and he thought he might drop it. Tree branches scraped him and sprang back. One hit Angel in the face, to judge by her yell. "I'm sorry, I'm sorry!" Elvis said.

Then they came to the blackberries, and before he knew it, his hands were ripped. Something sticky was on his fingers. He tasted it and realized it was his blood. Angel was muttering, and then speaking incomprehensibly, and then cursing audibly. "This is insane!" she said. "What are we doing here?"

They stumbled steeply downhill, clawing their way, slipping and lurching. Angel fell full length into him. He helped her up and while doing so realized that he could no longer hear Willard.

"Dad?" he called softly but got no answer.

"Oh my God," Angel said. "This is insanity." Elvis wished she hadn't come, but he knew better than to say so.

Suddenly, they came into the clear. Below them stretched the town, its lights smeared from the rain. It really was not far away, only a few hundred yards. What had seemed to be primeval forest was only a patch of brambles.

"Look," he said to Angel. "We're out of the scrub. It's easy from here."

"I'm going back to the hotel. Give me the key." She sounded furious.

"You sure? I don't want you getting lost."

"How could I get lost? In a town the size of our backyard!"

"You sure?"

They descended together, still slipping in the mud, until the terrain flattened out and she could see where to go. A moon had appeared, dodging in and out of the clouds, and the rain had all but stopped. Elvis tried to say goodbye nicely, but Angel was still steaming.

It was a relief for Elvis when she was gone. He didn't worry about her; she could take care of herself. Aunt Carol's house was to his left, he thought, and he wound that way until he saw its dark bulk. There were no lights. Nor was there any fence in the back; he walked into the yard, being careful not to make a sound. He nearly stepped on his father. It scared him, and he let out a yip.

"Keep it down," Willard said loudly.

Elvis lowered his voice into a coarse whisper. "You're the noisy one."

Willard answered in a normal speaking voice. "My sister sleeps on her good ear. She can't hear a thing."

"How'd you know that?"

"She's my sister."

"Then why'd you say to keep it down?"

"Because I'm trying to think!"

They stood together in the shadows. It was a lovely night, not cold but fresh. Elvis felt giddy. The atmosphere was quite still here on Earth, but up above, the clouds were scudding quickly across the moon. The unknowns had been worrying Elvis, but what was the worst that could happen?

By now, he realized there was no point in asking Willard what he was doing. He was on a fool's errand, undoubtedly. Hey, Elvis's whole life had been like this, wandering in and out of trouble with no aim in mind. At least this didn't seem to be dangerous, assuming—it was an assumption, he realized—that Aunt Carol didn't shoot them.

He was here because his father had told him to come. He had come to be with his father. Whatever that meant.

"What are we waiting for?" Elvis asked.

"I'm trying to remember how to get in," Willard said.

"Through the door? Through a window?"

"Through the door. There's a key. I'm sure she locks it."

Elvis had never been a burglar professionally, but there had been times. "I always look under the mat or in the flowerpot."

"Yeah," his father said but didn't move. They stood still, side by side, for another thirty seconds.

"I think I know," Willard said. Quickly, before Elvis had time to react, he was on his way to the house. Elvis caught up with him on the back porch. He was on his knees, fiddling with something. Elvis couldn't see because they were in moonshade under the porch.

"How big are your hands?" Willard asked. He seemed to be working at something where the porch floor met the house siding.

"Just average."

"We used to put the key down here when we were kids. I bet it's still there. But we had kid hands."

"Let me see," Elvis said and stooped down next to him. He couldn't see, however. It was too dark. He remembered his phone and pulled it out, creating light. Lowering it down next to where his dad was wedging his hand into a hole, he saw a narrow opening in the decking.

"Let me shine this in there," Elvis said. "Maybe we can see." Sure enough, it lit up a gleaming key. You had to position yourself just right to see it, however; the hole was small. They wouldn't be able to reach it.

"Can we get under this porch?" he asked.

"It's too low," Willard said. He was right, Elvis saw. They were only a foot off the ground.

"Let me try something," Elvis said and nudged his father out of the way. Wedging one hand into the hole, he put a grip on the board and tugged. It gave a little, enough to give him hope. He pulled hard and thought he heard a small cracking sound. Now he got up on his feet, bent his knees, and pulled with his legs and his back. The board cracked, shrieked, and then broke with a sound to wake the dead. Elvis, suddenly weightless, flew backward off the porch and landed on his back.

He was all right. He wanted to laugh. Surely, though, he had made enough noise to wake even an aunt who slept on her good ear. He lay on his backside listening.

He heard the key in the lock and thought it came from the inside: that Aunt Carol was unlocking. When Elvis pushed up on his elbows, though, he saw that his father was opening the door.

He crept after Willard into a house that felt warm and empty. His father turned on a light. They were in the kitchen, a dated room with linoleum floors and open-faced cabinets. Dishes spilled out of the sink. A large, covered stockpot squatted on the stove. Willard went over to it and lifted the lid, looking inside. "Chili," he said. "You hungry?" He cackled at his own humor.

Elvis felt so nervous he could hardly think. They were acting like the house was empty: turning on lights, talking. His aunt was liable to call the cops or come out shooting. Elvis never minded a fight, but he wanted it on his own terms. This felt like setting themselves up for target practice.

"So where are these papers?" his father asked. Elvis gestured toward the living room and led Willard to the desk. The light from the kitchen door flooded into the room, but Willard snapped on an overhead light. Did his father want to be caught? Elvis said nothing, however, but began going through the stack of papers on top of the desk. It looked as though nothing had been moved since he visited his aunt weeks ago.

"Here it is," he said when he located the folder. He shuffled through the papers and came up with a will. "Look at this."

Willard glanced at it. "Just bring the whole folder," he said. "Let's get out of here."

They walked out as boldly as they had come in. Willard snapped off the lights as they went, and on the back porch he paused to lock the door and put the key back where he had found it. He picked up the broken piece of flooring and looked it over. "Too bad you went and ripped this off," he said and tossed it over the edge of the porch.

Leading the way to the front of the house, he started down the road toward town. "What about your car?" Elvis asked.

"You can drive me up there later," his father said. "It's easier to walk back to your motel."

Elvis shrugged and followed. After hustling a few steps to catch up, he said, "What I don't get is why you wanted to sneak up from behind. All that and then we made enough noise to wake up Napoleon."

"Doesn't make much sense, does it?" his father said. "Sometimes you just go by feel. It all worked out, didn't it?"

When they reached the King Kwality, Elvis knocked on the door of their room. Angel was some time in answering, and when she appeared, the room was dark. It was obvious from her face and hair that she had been asleep. "What time is it?" she asked.

Elvis pulled out his phone and was startled to learn that it was just past 2:00. Soaked, hungry, and cold, he was suddenly so tired he could fall asleep while standing. The dog, he remembered. He needed to get Blackie. Though it would serve his dad right if the dog peed all over his car.

Willard was standing just behind him. "I need to get the dog," Elvis said. "Can we drive up there now and finish whatever we need to do in the morning?"

Willard shook his head. "The dog can wait. I want to know what's up," he said.

The room had a small, round table in one corner. Willard dumped the file on it, took a chair, and motioned for Elvis to join him. Angel sat on the bed looking stunned, and then got up to fill a Styrofoam cup with water from the bathroom sink. Elvis picked out the old will and handed it to Willard, who flipped through it, skimming.

"I didn't know they had already perfected legalese way back then," he said. "This is all gobbledygook."

"Don't ask me," Elvis said. "I can't read that stuff at all." It was true that when he looked at a telephone contract, his mind went blank. Something about legal language made him freeze.

"Let me see," Angel said. She got up and leaned over the table. Almost immediately, she took charge, flipping through the pages. "So this is your father's will?" she asked Willard.

"I guess so," he said. "Willard Trevor Sebastiano. That's my name and his, too."

"But you've never seen this before."

"No. He must have done it after I left home. Otherwise, I would know."

"Here it is," Angel said, pointing to a page. "He left everything to the church."

"What?"

"Right here. 'To the Garberville Baptist Church, IFCA, all my goods and chattel.' What does IFCA mean?"

"Independent Fundamentalist Churches of America," both Willard and Elvis said in chorus, then looked at each other.

"That was our church," Willard said. "I haven't heard of it in years."

"When they say fundamentalist, they mean fundamentalist," Elvis said. "Did Aunt Carol go there?"

"She did when we were kids. We had no choice."

"Well, sorry, Dad," Elvis said cheerfully. "Sounds like you're not getting the house."

"What about the church?" Angel asked.

"That church folded years ago," Willard said. "It's long gone." Willard stood up and stretched. "Better take me to my car," he said. He evidently had lost interest already.

On his way up the hill, Elvis asked him about that. "Aren't you bummed?"

"Nah. It was a long shot."

"Does it bother you that Aunt Carol is living there, even though she doesn't own it any more than you do?"

"I don't care. Let her live there. It can fall down for all I care."

"Then why did we go to all this trouble, if you don't care?"

"I care about money, you dipshit. If I could get title to the house, I'd sell it. Who knows what you could get for it, but you'd get something."

Elvis felt the pressure building inside him until he realized that he didn't care about the house either. He was bothered because he had come all this way trying to get closer to his father, who showed all the fatherly love of an alley cat.

"I still don't get why you left us," he said. It came out unpremeditated.

"Left you? What are you talking about? I'm still here."

"Left me and Tom. Left our mother."

"Hell, kid, that was thirty years ago. You need to get over that. You're not ten anymore."

They reached the Buick, badly parked on the side of the road. Elvis pulled up alongside. "Where you going now?" he asked.

"That's for me to know and you to find out."

"You sleep in the car?"

"Hell no. I've never slept in a car in my life."

Elvis wanted to hang on to this conversation. He had a feeling that if he let go, it was for good. All he had on his father was the thin thread of his telephone number.

"Are you around tomorrow?" Elvis asked. "I came up here to see you, and we've barely had time to talk."

"What is there to talk about?"

"I have a lot of questions about you. And maybe you have some about me. Or about your granddaughter."

Willard waved that off and got out of the truck. "Maybe some other time." Blackie barked. "Hey, you remember you got your dog in my car? He better not have made a mess."

"C'mere, Blackie," Elvis called, and Blackie wriggled his way out of the car before vaulting into the truck.

Elvis drove several hundred yards down the road before he found a place to turn around. By the time he got back to where he started, the Buick was gone. Elvis was angry, he had to admit. He wanted to get out of the truck and run until his lungs stopped him. He wanted to bust something, or throw something, or yell.

# 8 NOT BLOOD

He crept into the dark motel room, not turning on a light. Angel's steady breathing was the only sound. He thought of slipping under the covers next to her. But Elvis was too wired up. No way was he ready to sleep, he thought. If he lay down beside her, he would thrash around until he got up again.

Blackie was panting; he probably was thirsty. Elvis splashed an inch of water into the tub and lifted Blackie in. The dog acted frantic to get out, his feet scrabbling on the porcelain until he escaped. Elvis put him back in once, but after the dog leaped out a second time, he decided to let the dog figure it out for himself. If he was thirsty enough, he would remember where the water could be found.

In the old days, Elvis would have gone out to find an all-night bar. He caught himself thinking about that and made himself stop. Instead, picking up the folder of papers they had taken from Aunt Carol's, he carried it back into the bathroom. He sat on the toilet and began to read.

Most of the papers were old Garberville plat maps, property deeds, or tax assessments related to the house. Elvis pulled out the will for a closer look. It was printed on heavy, yellowing paper, with verbiage so lawyered that he couldn't force himself to read. He found the section willing all goods and chattel to the Garberville Baptist Church, IFCA. That much he understood.

Elvis felt a low cloud of guilt while holding the will, since it reminded him that they had broken into Aunt Carol's house to get it. While pondering this, however, something dawned on him. His grandfather had wanted to dedicate his house to God. Aunt Carol had thrown aside his wishes. In essence, she had cheated the church, and God.

Elvis always questioned what had caused his life to veer off the road, and why his family was so shattered. Maybe his grandfather's will was a cracked foundation, a moral flaw that set everything wrong. Maybe the whole family was being punished for what Aunt Carol had done.

It was probably too late to make it right, assuming his father was correct and the church had disappeared.

Elvis was finding it uncomfortable sitting on the toilet seat, so pulled out his phone and used its light to guide him to a chair in the disheveled motel room. There he sat, his feet stretched out to the edge of the bed where Angel slept. He googled Garberville Baptist. The connection was slow, but eventually, a series of matches unfolded. Indeed, the church didn't seem to exist—at least, it didn't have a website. Hell, a church without a website might as well not exist in this day and age.

The search had turned up lots of hits for "Garberville," and even more for "Baptist." Elvis scrolled down through them, hoping to luck into something. He had half an idea that maybe some connection to the old church might turn up, somebody or something that might rightfully inherit property on behalf of the church. Maybe after all these years, they could set things right by fulfilling his grandfather's intentions.

Twenty entries down, he hit gold. It was an old news article from the *North Coast Journal* with the headline, "Churches Becoming Bars Along Redwood Highway." The piece named several churches in the area—in Eureka, in Samoa, in Leggett, and in Garberville—that had gone out of business, their buildings taken over by a bar. Not much was said about the churches and their demise. Most of the article concerned the bars and their business plans. Garberville Baptist, it said, had become Stone Junction, offering pool tournaments, Saturday night music, and Mexican food.

Elvis vaguely remembered seeing the place on Redwood Drive. Maybe, he thought, somebody there would know about the church.

He eased out the door. He had parked on a slope, so he rolled the truck into starting itself in second gear. The rain was still spitting. All down Redwood Drive, the lights were out and shadows shrouded the cheapjack buildings. Nothing was moving. Elvis had not considered that the bar might be closed.

Stone Junction still had neon beer signs in its windows, and there were cars parked in front—including a massive Buick that Elvis instantly recognized. He parked next to it and went inside.

The room was wide, with a high ceiling and a pool table in the middle. It smelled of skunky marijuana, of bean burritos, of burnt matches, and naturally, of whiskey. Down the right side was a long redwood bar with its finish worn off in patches and scores of bright bottles beaming behind. Just pausing inside the door, taking it in, set off Elvis. The idea of a drink called to him. He could go that way; he had a million times, in rooms like this one.

At the far end of the bar, his father huddled over a glass. Elvis thought to himself: *I can spot him from behind in a dark room.* Elvis slid onto a stool next to him. Willard looked up, his face a mask no more friendly than that of a stranger whose space has been violated.

"Can't stay away, can you?" Willard said.

"It's your magnetic personality," Elvis said with a grin. "Nah; actually, I had no idea you were here until I saw your chariot. I came because I found out something interesting. This used to be Garberville Baptist."

"No way," Willard said. "It was on the north edge of town, just on the highway."

The bartender overheard. "That place burned down," she said. She was a compact young woman dressed all in black with short, dark hair. "So they came here."

"I never knew that," Willard said.

"Yeah, this place used to be a movie theater."

"I remember that."

"Yeah, when the church burned down, they took it over."

"So what happened to the church?" Elvis said. "Where did they go?"

She shrugged. "I think they just quit. The pastor moved somewhere up around Weed. Not a lot of need for churches these days. The Catholics are the only ones still going, and they don't even have a regular priest."

"You know if any of those Baptists are still around?" Elvis asked.

"What are you up to?" Willard asked, looking annoyed. "Let sleeping dogs lie."

"I just thought if there were any remnants, they should know about what we found."

"You want to throw your aunt out in the street? Be my guest."

That sank Elvis. No, he did not want to evict his aunt. He was trying to be a good guy for once in his life, trying to do the virtuous thing.

"Okay," he said. "You win."

"I damn well didn't win anything. I came all this way for nothing."

Elvis didn't know what to say to that. The bartender asked what he was drinking, and he started to ask for a Coke, then changed his mind. "I just came in to ask about the church," he said. "I don't need anything. I better go get some sleep." He stood and stretched. His fatigue hit him.

"You got a place to sleep tonight?" he asked his father.

"I'm fine," Willard said without looking up. Elvis walked to the door. He turned to get a last look at his father, who was again crouched over his drink and did not look up.

Back at the motel, Elvis managed to get into bed without waking Angel. He cuddled up with her. Now he could sleep. He could catch a few hours and they could go home. Maybe he would see his father again, maybe he wouldn't. If the old man showed any interest, it would be different.

Tired as he was, he couldn't turn his mind off. He kept thinking about his father and how unfriendly he had been. The man was an alcoholic; you could see that pretty clearly. Elvis wondered how it was that the son of a minister had turned out like that. Aunt Carol, too, as far as he could see.

Elvis took in what AA said, that alcoholism is a sickness, but he didn't completely believe it. He didn't feel like he had a disease. He fully identified with the Lord's prayer where it said, "Lead me not into temptation." You weren't forced to do it; you were tempted. You had a choice. You could just as easily not. However, it remained a mystery: why did he? Why did half the people he knew? They all could swear it was the worst thing in the world. Their families begged them. They went forward at church to be prayed for. Yet time and again, they used. Why was that?

If it was a disease, he could see that he got it from his father. Maybe his preacher grandfather had been afflicted, too, but got saved. That would explain the underlinings in his Bible. He was preaching to himself.

It gripped Elvis to think of his grandfather that way, as a source of the disease but also as somebody who had conquered it. And maybe, you could say, Elvis had already begun to follow. What had just happened to him at Breathe? The prayers had changed him. It wasn't the first time, either. Every time he had been clean and sober, it had started with something like that. He definitely needed God. AA said that.

His mind began to soften, its images shifting and turning as he relaxed toward sleep. He had in mind an old black-and-white picture of his grandfather, stern and bewhiskered, lit up as a beacon, an old-fashioned lighthouse on the Ft. Bragg headlands, with waves smashing the rocks just below, waves pounding...

Elvis started from sleep. Somebody was banging on the motel room door. The room was dark, and no light came from the window. The knocking was insistent. Blackie was barking wildly, his whip-like body poised in front of the door. Elvis thought it was his father. Nobody else knew he was here. He felt Angel sit up next to him. "Who is that?" she whispered.

"I don't know," he said and recognized what she was thinking. He had been out. Given past performance, this could be a drug deal gone wrong.

"Could be my father," he said. "He's the only person I've seen."

"Hey, hold on; I'm coming," he shouted. The knocking quit as he flicked on a light and went to the door in his underpants. He grabbed the dog, unlocked the door, and opened it to find his brother, Tom.

Elvis was so surprised he needed to catch his breath. "Tom!" he panted. "What are you doing here?"

Tom looked enormous. He was dressed in jeans and a letterman's jacket with white leather sleeves. He wore heavy hiking boots. "Aunt Carol called me," he said. Always trending toward silence, he stopped there. His face had settled in a scowl, as though he had tasted something disgusting and wanted to spit.

"When? About what? How did she get your number?"

"Can I get a glass of water?" Tom said. He barged past Elvis and into the bathroom, where he threw down two Styrofoam cups of water from the bathroom sink. He then sat down in the room's only upholstered chair. Elvis took a seat on the bed. Angel, who had said nothing, sat up with the covers wrapped around her up to her neck. Blackie, who had calmed down, went over to sniff Tom.

"I stay in touch," Tom said. "Unlike you."

"Okay," Elvis said, trying to gather his senses. "So she called you."

"Yeah. She knew you were sneaking around town with Dad."

"Wait, you didn't believe me when I told you I saw Dad. Remember?"

"Yeah, well, Carol told me."

"You believed her when you didn't believe me?"

"I'd never believe you."

"So what did she say about me?"

"She said you and Dad were up to something. She had this idea that you were going to rob her."

"I don't steal." He said it with conviction, even though he had, in fact, stolen to get drugs. That wasn't him. His true, sober self didn't steal.

"So why are you here, then?"

Elvis was full of his own innocence, and his tone of voice lifted higher. "I came because Dad wanted me to. He has this obsession about Aunt Carol's house, that it was willed to him by their father. He thought Carol stole it, and he wanted me to help him find out."

"And how are you going to do that?"

"You know, she won't talk to him. So he wanted me to go see what I could learn."

"And you did."

"I didn't see any harm in it."

"And how did you do that?"

"Well, I went to see her, and when I got a chance, I looked around."

Tom shifted in his seat. "Did you find anything?" Despite himself, Tom was interested.

"Tom, I did. I found our grandfather's will. It turns out he didn't leave the house to either of them; he left it to a church."

"Then why does Aunt Carol live there?"

Elvis hesitated before admitting his ignorance. "I don't know; I just found out about the house tonight. I think when our grandfather died, nobody did anything about the will, and she just stayed on. Dad says the house is still in our grandpa's name." He felt pleased to know something his brother didn't know.

You could almost see Tom's brain cells clogging up as he tried to think. "Wait," he said. "How did you find this out?"

"I got the will. You want to see it?" Elvis bounced off the bed.

"Wait," Tom said again. "How'd you get it? Does Aunt Carol know you have it?"

The realization stopped him: his brother would not like this.

Tom noticed. "Wait," he said. "Did you steal it from her?"

"It's not stealing," Elvis said. "It belongs to all of us. It's Grandpa's will."

"How'd you get it? Aunt Carol didn't hand it to you. You must have stolen it."

Elvis saw he would have to come clean—sort of. Tom frightened him in ways that went beyond his physical size. "Dad knew where she hid the key to the house. We just went in, and I showed him where she kept her papers, and he decided we should take it."

"When? In the middle of the night?"

"Yeah," Elvis admitted.

"You snuck into her house, went through her papers, and snuck out with them. I can't believe it. I knew you were low, but not that low."

Fortunately, Angel came to Elvis's defense. "C'mon, man; lighten up," she said to Tom. "You want to get all worked up, get worked up about your aunt stealing a house from the church. What did your brother do? He borrowed some papers that didn't belong to his aunt in the first place."

"Borrowed," Tom said.

"Well, I wasn't going to keep them," Elvis said defensively. "I planned to give them back."

"When?"

"Today. As soon as we had a chance to read them."

It wasn't strictly true that Elvis had planned to give the papers back—he hadn't thought that far ahead—but immediately he seized on the idea. He would give the papers back to Carol and offer to fix her porch. He could put this whole episode behind him.

"Let's do it now," Elvis said. "I bet she doesn't even know they're missing." The idea raised his spirits. He always believed in action.

"It's the middle of the night," Tom said.

"That didn't stop you from waking us up," Angel said.

Elvis got up from the bed and began to pull on his pants. "Cmon, Tom, we'll just go over there and see. If she doesn't wake up, we can put the papers back where they were."

Tom didn't say anything, so Elvis kept on dressing. Then Angel got out of bed and went into the bathroom. Elvis assumed she needed to pee, but it wasn't long before she came out fully clothed. "You want to come too?" Elvis asked.

"I'm not letting you go off by yourself," she said.

When they got outside, Elvis saw there was actually a hint of light at the top of the trees.

* * *

Tom and Angel were like a dog and a cat nudged up next to each other in the truck. Somehow it struck Elvis's funny bone. He received a manic energy from their agitation. They had been at each other for years; it was familiar territory and felt weirdly comforting.

He wasn't sure what they would do once they got to the house. Break in again? He didn't have long to worry about it. As they came up the dirt drive, it looked like all the lights in the house were on.

"You all coming in?" he asked after he avoided a huge mud puddle and pulled up in front of the house. Nobody answered, so he got out, clutching the green folder. Tom and Angel exited too. They all walked silently to the front door, and Elvis knocked. He didn't bang the door; he kept his knock polite. Nobody answered, but he thought he heard something faintly from inside. He knocked again, and this time said, "It's me, Elvis."

"I said come in!" This time he heard Aunt Carol clearly.

She had her hair in a towel, and the rest of her was wrapped in a massive crocheted shawl. She was seated in the burgundy corduroy recliner just as before but bundled like a caterpillar. Only her face showed.

"Hey," Elvis said.

"Hey," Carol replied. "Who's this?"

She knew perfectly well who it was, but Elvis went along. "This is Angel. And you know Tom."

She looked them over coldly. "Where's your goddam father? I heard you were following him around."

"Last I saw him, he was in a bar."

"Which one?"

"The Stone Inn?"

"You mean the Stone Junction."

"Yeah."

They stood awkwardly in silence while Aunt Carol glared. Elvis wondered whether she was trying to intimidate them or just didn't know what to say.

He finally broke the silence. "I brought back your papers," he said, holding out the green folder. Carol didn't even look at it. He set it on a table.

"We tried to find out about the church," Elvis added. "Looks like it's gone out of business."

"I should have shot you," Carol said.

"When?"

"When you broke in. You think I didn't know what was going on? I just didn't want to get out of bed. I knew my brother was up to no good. I could have shot him and you both and nobody would have had a thing to say about it."

Elvis's face broke into a smile. "You knew we were here? Really?"

"Of course I did. I don't sleep. And you, Angel darling, where were you? You could have come out to help them. God, you're looking old. You used to be so pretty."

Elvis waited for fireworks, but Angel, taken by surprise, stayed calm. "You've never seen me a day in my life," she said.

"I've seen your picture," Aunt Carol responded. "Tommy Boy there showed me. He told me all about you." She sniffed with satisfaction.

"What, were you just snoozing while your men were breaking in?" Aunt Carol added. "God knows you need your beauty sleep.

"And little Tommy, how are you? Where did you find them? Did you see your dad?"

"Nah," he said. "Not yet."

"You want to see him?"

Tom hesitated. "Yeah, sometime. I want to hear him explain himself."

"Look, sit down," Carol said, casting her hand broadly about. Elvis quickly grabbed a chair, but Tom and Angel took their time before deciding that they might as well join him. They were seated well apart from each other. It was simply a matter of where the chairs had been, but Elvis couldn't help noticing that they could hardly be farther apart and still be in the same room.

"You want me to explain this whole thing to you?" Aunt Carol asked. "Do you? It's about time somebody told you.

"Look, this has got nothing to do with my daddy's will or the church. He didn't even like that church; it was Baptist, not Foursquare. Oil and water, as far as he was concerned. He put the church in his will to make himself look good, but the church didn't want it. They didn't have money for repairs or back taxes, which were probably more than the old place was worth. He hadn't paid his taxes in years. That was after timber crashed and before marijuana boomed, and that church was barely hanging on. So I kept it. Nothing important there. That's just an excuse for Willard to go messing around in your lives.

"He has spent his whole life avoiding you, and at the same time he can't let you alone. If you think that's a strange combination, you're right, but it's not just because Willard is a sick bastard. It's because you boys were adopted. That's the piece they never told you. Willard and Mavis knew this doctor up in Angel Camp, and I guess sometimes there would be a teenage girl who didn't want to have an abortion. This doctor didn't give them any choice; if they wanted his help, they would have to give the baby away. He would call up Willard and say, 'If you want a baby, come get it.' See, Mavis and Willard couldn't have any children."

After a stunned silence, Tom said, "Mom had a bunch of kids with Ray."

"That's what I heard. So your dad must be a gelding. Maybe that's why he acts so macho. He's trying to grow some testosterone."

"Good God," Angel said, as though in wonder. "That explains so much."

"It does, don't it?" Carol said. After a pause, she added, "Maybe you should explain it to these slow ones. I don't think they get it."

That was true of Elvis. He was stunned by the news, but it didn't explain anything to him; it only added more questions.

Aunt Carol gave a cackling laugh. "See," she said. "Look at their faces. They don't get it. You better explain it to them."

"What?" Elvis said. "Explain what?"

Angel spoke slowly, as though to a child. "It explains why you two brothers don't get along. You aren't blood related. You couldn't be more different."

That was true, Elvis admitted to himself. Tom had always been an alien to him. He admired him—or at least he was jealous of him—but they never clicked.

"That's not all," Angel said. "Why do you think your dad took off when you were kids? Why didn't your mom show any interest in you? Why didn't you show any interest in her? You're not blood."

Tom had his forehead knotted up. "Look," he said, "maybe Mom didn't show any interest in him. He was drugged out and in trouble all the time."

"But she was okay with you," Angel said. "Is that what you're saying? You're the normal one? She loved you? Yeah, but you were the football star. I bet the whole town loved you. She didn't need to have you in her gene pool to feel that way."

"Dammit!" Tom exploded, jumping out of his chair. "She was my mother. You can't talk crap about her."

Elvis prepared to get between Tom and Angel, but Angel was cool. "You've got no reason to blow up, Tom. It's Elvis who should be mad. I never could understand why his mother just had no contact. Now it makes sense, sorta. But I guess she was okay with you. Lucky you. No reason for you to be angry. If you want to get mad, get mad at your father. He's the one who walked off from you both."

It put a cold finger on Elvis as the implications became clear to him: he didn't have a brother. He didn't have parents. They had been strangers to him all his life. No wonder he had screwed up so much. He had every reason to feel sorry for himself.

But he wasn't going to do that. He was too stubborn. Elvis had come on this wild goose chase hoping his father would provide a key to his life, and he wasn't ready to quit. Not yet.

"You still want to meet him?" Elvis said to his brother. "I bet we could find him."

* * *

A dim dawn had taken over Garberville. The puddles were the brightest source of light; they reflected a dark sky in their irregular mirrors. Rain had quit, but everything dripped.

Just as Elvis thought, they found the big Buick still parked outside Stone Junction. Willard was sleeping in the driver's seat with the backrest reclining. He did not wake up when Elvis tapped gently on the window. Elvis tried the door; it was locked. He knocked again, more loudly, and said, "Willard, wake up." The body stirred. It was difficult to see whether his eyes were open, because the window was fogged with moisture. He must be freezing, Elvis thought; the morning was cold.

Elvis knocked again and said, "Dad, Dad." He could dimly see Willard turn his head. "It's Elvis," he said. "I've got Tom."

From somewhere, Willard pulled out a handkerchief and wiped the window. He peered out like somebody examining a Christmas storefront, giving Elvis a half-hearted smile but making no move to open up.

"C'mon, open up," Elvis said. "I've got Tom and Angel here. They want to see you. We can go have some breakfast."

Willard managed to slowly crank down the window. "Who's paying?" he asked.

"Not you," Elvis said. He reached inside the open window and unlatched the door from the inside. "C'mon out. Can you stand up?"

He had seen plenty of drunks in his day. Watching his father slowly navigate the car door and ease himself into a standing position brought out a tenderness that surprised him. He didn't love the man, but he pitied him. They were twice unrelated—once by genes, and once by abandonment. And yet he still couldn't help thinking that this man could untangle the mystery of his life; that he was, in short, still his father.

Tom, he imagined, saw an old drunk, a decrepit wreck. Tom wasn't soft. Tom wasn't sentimental.

Tom stood ten feet away, looking.

"Hey, Dad," Elvis said, "meet Tom."

Willard stuck out his hand and looked up into the face of his son, grown into a man. "I know you. I watched every game you ever played."

It was the wrong thing to say. "Fuck you," Tom said with energy. "You think I care what you watched on TV? You fucking disappeared. You think that's being a father? You fucking disappeared."

Willard dropped his hand. "Well, fuck you, too. You don't know a thing about me."

"And whose fault is that?" Tom shouted.

Elvis treated it like it was funny. "Okay, you two; give each other a big kiss. Let's go get some grub. Tom's paying." When Tom turned on him, he nudged him. "Just kidding, man. Pulling your chain. We'll figure it out. Breakfast is cheap."

They all walked up the street to Ginger's Café, a little place with red-and-white-checked curtains in the window. The lights were on, but they found the place deserted when they went inside. Elvis peeked over the counter and saw that coffee was brewing. The waitress must be in the back, he figured. "No problem," he said to Tom and Willard and Angel, who hadn't advanced beyond the door. "Take a seat." He found the mugs and poured two cups of coffee, then took them to the table. When his dad reached for one, he slapped his hand. "I'll get you one," he said.

He got two more cups and took a seat. "Now, where were we?" he asked. "Dad, I think you were explaining why you left us when I was ten."

Willard looked at both him and Tom, slowly oscillating from one to the other. "I didn't leave you; I left your mother."

"What the hell," Tom said and looked away.

"That doesn't explain why you never came back to see them," Angel said, leaning over the table and drumming the air with the spoon she had used to stir creamer into her coffee. "Or why you made up this big hairy story about being lost at sea."

"I told your man," Willard growled. "That was his mother's idea, not mine."

"What was the deal with that?" Elvis asked. "I mean, it had to be a production. For what?"

"She thought it would be easier on you boys. That you wouldn't take it so hard. That you wouldn't feel rejected."

Elvis happened to glimpse Tom's face. It was a look that Elvis remembered from football. His eyes shrank darker and smaller. It came just instants before Tom came busting forward to crash an opponent to the ground.

"Old man," Tom said. "Quit the game. You've been hiding like a spook for thirty years. Watching me on TV, but never turning up. It's sick, you know? Even now you're hiding.

"Aunt Carol told us, you know. She said we were adopted, and it makes sense. There was never anything real there. It's like grabbing a piece of air."

Willard looked at Tom like a man sizing up a piece of land. Then he looked at Elvis with the same expression. "What do you want to know?"

"Who are you?" Elvis asked.

# 9 SECOND FAMILY

They took all three vehicles, not knowing where they were going, only that Willard had promised to show them something. Wherever they were going, none of them wanted to get stranded. Willard's big Buick led Elvis's rattling truck, followed by Tom's monstrous glistening pickup.

Elvis had to concentrate to keep up with Willard, who drove too fast. If you wanted to get the old truck going on a long straightaway, you had to floor it at the beginning, not wait until you saw that you were falling behind. The road curved along the Eel River, which was full and in flood from all the rain. On long, swinging arcs the river would appear, a ragged tableau of gray rock and water, canyoned by 300-foot trees. The forest smelled of rain and humus.

"Keep your eyes open for a Bigfoot," Elvis said to Angel. Anything might appear, it seemed: any form of life, any form of death. He got goose bumps from this country.

"Where do you think he's taking us?" Angel asked. "For that matter, where are we?"

"They call this the Avenue of the Giants," he said. "Because of the monster trees."

"Are there any towns up here?" Angel had never been this far north.

Elvis shrugged. "Eureka is the only one of any size. And it's not very big."

"That's on the ocean."

"Yeah. Right where the Eel comes out."

"The what?"

"This river. The Eel."

She was quiet after that, and Elvis's happiness dribbled away. When she kept quiet, his doubts filled up the space.

“Why are we doing this?” she asked. “Do you really hope to get anything?”

Elvis needed a moment to track what she was asking. “You mean why are we following my dad right now? You heard what he said.”

“I mean, why do you even care about him? He treats you like crap.”

He had to think. “I don’t know.”

“Were you close to him when you were a kid?”

He shook his head vehemently. “No. I don’t think so. I can hardly remember him. I think he was always out on the boat. I was just a little kid. But still, after he died and my mom was crying all the time, I was a lost pup.

“Now he’s come back to life, and somehow I have this feeling that if I know who he is, I’ll know who I am. I know that sounds crazy.”

She shook her head. “Nobody can tell you who you are.”

“I don’t mean he would tell me,” Elvis said. “I would have a foundation. Otherwise, I’m a small boat in big waves.”

“I think that’s just what life is like,” Angel said.

He glanced over at her and saw a dead-sober expression. “You’re not like that,” Elvis said. “It’s me. What was it, two weeks ago I was out of my mind? Now I’m sane. Go figure.”

“It’s not that complicated,” Angel said. “You just can’t use. Quit using and you’ll be fine.”

“Okay,” he answered bitterly. “Just quit using. I know what I need to do, but I can’t. I screw up time and again.”

“I don’t see how Willard is going to help,” Angel said.

“But why do I act just like him?” Elvis wanted to know. “Think about it. I’m not even related. He adopted me.”

“You don’t act like him,” Angel said. “He’s a rude drunk. You’re a dumb meth addict. Nothing like him at all.”

They rode in silence after that. The canyon opened up to broad, green fields and open ridges. Dark skies started to spit on them. When they came up on a little traffic, Willard’s Buick began to pass, and to keep up, Elvis had to push the accelerator and pass cars when he couldn’t see. After a close call with a minivan, he realized that his teeth were clamped tightly. “Screw it,” he said. “It’s not worth it if we’re dead.”

“Got that right,” Angel said.

Then, suddenly, they slowed into the outskirts of Eureka. Elvis had not been there in years. Shiny boxes in bright colors lined the road, new stores that looked more like strip malls in SoCal than anything in the north coast. Elvis began to think that Eureka had transformed, but then they entered the old section, and the city calmed down into its aging, gray self. They climbed a slight hill and shot out into the country again.

"Where are we going?" Angel asked with a note of impatience.

"It's a scavenger hunt," Elvis answered.

"What are we scavenging?"

"Me."

The highway ran right alongside the border of the bay, almost at water level. To their right, open pasturelands swept up to low, forested hills. "God, it's beautiful here," Angel said, amazed. It warmed Elvis to hear her say it.

"Wait a minute; where did Eureka go?" Angel asked.

"We passed it. It's not a big town."

"Then what comes next?"

"Arcata is just ahead. After that, you have to go a bit before you get to Crescent City. After that comes Oregon."

"Geez, are we going to Oregon?"

Elvis laughed. "I don't know."

At the second Arcata exit, Willard got off the highway. Turning right, they passed by some apartment buildings and a mobile home park. The Buick went left onto a lane flanked by a horse pasture and then a Christmas tree farm. They turned right again and climbed a narrow road, its pavement cratered and split, with young redwoods planted in a row on either side. Then, bouncing violently in deep, rain-filled potholes, they came into the open and saw that the road led directly into a farm. The main house was a single story painted blue with white trim. A small barn and several outbuildings spread across the hillside. Elvis swung in to park beside the Buick, and Tom's big pickup came next to him.

Blackie was the first one out of the truck; he ran over to the fence to pee. When Elvis got out, he stretched and looked down the hill. A wide expanse of trees and fields led softly to the line of the Pacific. Left down the slope was a shining slab of water, the bay, but directly ahead was a straight white line drawn across the horizon and then the deep blue-black of the Pacific, extending forever. He could not stop looking at it.

His father was looking in the opposite direction, to the house. He made a broad gesture toward it for Elvis's benefit. "This is it, the big secret," he called out in a booming voice that seemed to mock and rejoice in it. "Come on—I'll introduce you to Lorraine. I don't know if any of the kids are around; we'll see who is here."

"What about the dog?" Elvis asked. Blackie was racing across the hillside, a sleek black missile.

"He's not going to bother anybody," Willard said. "Let him have some fun."

They followed Willard in the front door. He stood bellowing, "Lorraine! Lorraine!" She appeared, a stout, graying woman wearing a frown and dressed in jeans and a green sweater. Her sweater was stretched out, hanging limply like a frayed sack. She stood in the entry looking them over with mild curiosity. Willard didn't greet her, nor did she approach him for a kiss.

"Lorraine," Willard said, "meet my kids from Ft. Bragg. This is Tom"—he pointed with his index finger—"Elvis, and Elvis's—what are you, are you married?—Elvis's girlfriend. Sorry, I forget your name."

"Angel."

"Angel. They were bugging me about keeping secrets, so I brought them up here to let them get a grip on the great mysteries of life. You being the chief one, Lorraine, how you've put up with me all these years."

Lorraine didn't say she was glad to meet them, and she certainly didn't ask any questions. She just looked at them as though she had work to do that had been interrupted and she could barely wait to be released so she could go back to it.

"So what's going on?" Willard asked. "Any of the kids around?"

"Liz and Alan are here somewhere."

"Probably in their rooms?"

She shrugged. "Are you staying for lunch?" she asked.

Tom looked at Elvis, and they both looked at Angel. She asked Willard, "Are we staying for lunch?"

"Of course!" he said. "What time?" he asked Lorraine.

She shrugged again. "I had no idea you were coming. I can make mac and cheese. It will take about an hour."

"Sounds great. I'll give them a tour, introduce them to the kids, we can talk a bit. By that time it'll be ready." He thought for a moment, as though going through a mental checklist. "Okay. Let's go."

He led them back out the door and toward the barn. Before they got there, Elvis stopped him. "Wait. Dad. Explain. Is Lorraine your wife?"

The corners of Willard's mouth trimmed upward. "Not legally. We couldn't get married without getting divorced first. Or maybe we could, but it seemed risky. Why borrow trouble?"

"And the kids?" Tom asked. "Are they your kids?"

"Yes."

"How many are there?" Elvis wanted to know.

"Four," Willard said. "Liz and Alan, plus Betsy who is going to college and Suzanne who has a job in town."

"They all live here?" Elvis asked.

"Betsy lives at college. The rest are here."

"So this is your second family," Tom said. To Elvis it seemed a needless statement.

"Wait," Elvis said. "Aunt Carol told us we were adopted. That you got us from some doctor up in Weed because you couldn't have children of your own. Is that true? But Mom went on and had kids with Ray, and you had kids with Lorraine, right? I don't get it. Something is off here."

Again, Willard's mouth edged into a smile. "No, you get it. That's right."

"You couldn't have kids, and then you could. That doesn't make sense."

"You think it doesn't make sense because you're assuming that we wanted to have kids. Your mom and I decided we didn't want to reproduce more of what we had come from. It would be better to play with the roulette wheel and start from scratch."

"Wait," Elvis said as Willard turned away and started toward the barn again. "Are these kids adopted?"

Willard beamed. "Nope. Natural born. Local stock."

"Then why...? What changed your mind?"

"You!" He laughed. "Turned out that you two were worse than anything I could imagine. God, you were a headache. I figured we couldn't do worse than that."

Willard, Tom, and Angel went on toward the barn while Elvis stopped to look at the view again, thinking about what it must have been like to raise him. His brother had been good at everything. Bigger and stronger than Elvis, he would torment him and then laugh at his frustration. Nobody did anything about it. Tom was golden. Elvis remembered this from middle school, but it might have started much earlier.

Elvis went along to the barn. It was an old wood building, dim and full of animal smells. He could hear chickens cackling somewhere. His fatigue hit; he had hardly slept, and now he was almost dizzy when he stopped.

"Here he is," his father was saying to two kids, one of whom—a boy—was holding a saddled horse by its bridle. "This is Elvis. Elvis, meet your brother and sister, Liz and Alan."

Elvis stepped forward to shake Alan's hand, and he nodded at Liz. Alan was slight and had straight, light-brown hair. Something about his eyes reminded you of Willard, but he might have been any high school kid. Liz was as tall as Alan, with long, black, straight hair that fell down her back. Her face was wide and flat, and she stood up straight like a volleyball player. Neither one of the two seemed particularly surprised or pleased to meet family. Elvis wondered if they had known any more about it than he had. Had they been told all along that they had half-brothers somewhere? More likely, they were just used to surprises.

"You going out riding?" Elvis asked Alan. "I bet there are some great trails out here."

Alan didn't respond. He just stared, looking as though he would give anything to be gone.

"Alan is a great rider," Willard said. "Prize winning. He's won every show in northern California. You should see all the trophies. What was that thing you won last week?"

"There's no competition up here," Alan said, deadpan.

"Alan, Tom here played football in the NFL. Didn't you? He was an All-American at USC. Did you ever go to the Pro Bowl?"

Tom shook his head, as deadpan as Alan. Elvis thought that when you have a father like Willard, you learn to wear camouflage. At the same time, he could feel his own jealousy, wishing for praise he wasn't going to get.

Willard led them around the rest of the farm so they could see where they kept chickens, where berries were grown. It wasn't a real farm.

"How'd you get this place?" Elvis asked.

"Oh, this is Lorraine's. She inherited it from her parents. I don't know how they got it. It might have been homesteaded."

"So she was already here when you left Mom?" Tom asked. They had stopped to take in the berries; they stood in a line at a weedgrown fence.

"Look, that was a mutual decision," Willard said. "I didn't just leave her. She wanted me out."

"She sure cried a lot after you were gone," Elvis said. "That's all I remember."

"She didn't know what she wanted," Willard said. "I couldn't win with her."

"Hey, Willard," Elvis asked, "why was Grandpa buried in Ft. Bragg? Didn't he die in Garberville?"

"Nah, he lived with us. He couldn't take care of himself. That's when my sister got the house."

"When was that?"

"When Tom was a baby. He died before you were born."

"Did you know that Mom took me to put flowers on Grandpa's grave to make me think it was yours?"

Willard shook his head. "Your mom could get some crazy ideas. Can you believe she stuck with that story for thirty years? The idea was, we didn't want you two to be thinking all the time about bringing us back together. We'd seen that kids do that—they never accept that their parents are better off split. You would be wanting to come see me, and I really wasn't into all that. I'm not a nurturer, you know? It's better to just cut it off and sew up the wound."

There wasn't much to say to that, so they walked back to the main house. Blackie came running up and paced alongside Elvis.

* * *

Tom took up his father's offer of a beer, and the two of them sat in the living room, talking and mostly not talking. Elvis said no to the drink.

"You're not drinking?" his father asked him. "What is this? You weren't drinking the last time I saw you."

"Right, Dad. I'm an alcoholic." (He resisted the temptation to say, "Just like you.") "I can't drink."

"You can, but you're pulling that holy roller stuff on me."

Elvis shrugged, and—after a suitable interval—followed the sound of Angel's voice into the kitchen, where Lorraine was busy cooking.

She acted just like her kids. She didn't pretend she was glad to see him; she just took him in with a level gaze. Angel was sitting on a stool next to the counter, and Elvis grabbed another.

"So forgive me if I'm getting personal," Elvis said, "but did you know about me? Did my dad tell you about me from the beginning?"

Lorraine was stirring a pot of pasta, and she glanced over her shoulder at the two of them. "I knew Trev had a family. When we first met, I think he showed me a picture of you boys. But he never wanted to talk about that old life, and I wasn't that interested. After he moved up here, he put that behind him, which was fine with me. We had enough to sort out without dredging up the past."

It was a hurtful comment, however realistic. Elvis thought he deserved better than to be buried with the past.

"We thought he was dead, you know," Elvis said. "That was the story my mom gave out. I never knew anything different until he showed up at Mom's funeral."

Lorraine shook her head. "I didn't know that. I just knew that Trev didn't have any contact with you, at least not that he ever talked about. He did keep up on your football games. I knew because he took the paper from Ft. Bragg."

"Yeah, he told us about that. We never had any idea."

The conversation paused there, stopped by Elvis's unwillingness to probe more deeply. He had come hoping to untangle his own existence, only to discover that his father really had nothing to do with him; he was a part of another family.

"Did you know he was an alcoholic?" Angel asked. Elvis was amazed that she would ask that. It was fine to say it at AA, but not so much in polite company.

Lorraine didn't blink. She was stirring up some kind of cheese sauce on the stove, but she looked up and smiled. "I don't think that Trev will admit he's an alcoholic. He says he just likes to drink." She gave a little laugh. "When we first met, he didn't even drink that much. It's more recently that he drinks all the time."

"I'm an alcoholic," Elvis said. "And an addict. I don't know if you were aware."

"No."

"Part of the reason I came up here was hoping to understand where I got it from. They say it's a disease that runs in families. And when I met Willard at my mom's service, I could see he had a problem. But then I come to find out he's not even really my father. Not my blood father."

Lorraine raised her eyebrows, as though in question.

"I'm adopted. I just found out. So is Tom. My Aunt Carol told me."

Lorraine just wore her mild, blank expression. Elvis thought you had to admire her restraint. She wasn't about to go digging in the woodpile, where you might find black widows.

"So I didn't get it from Willard. Or from my grandfather. I thought it might be him because Aunt Carol gave me his old Bible, and it's got these verses about strong drink underlined and outlined like he wanted to light them up with floods. Maybe he was a drunk, or maybe he was in recovery, or maybe he was white-knuckling it, because I don't think they had AA then, did they? Anyway, it doesn't matter because I don't have his genes. Unfortunately, I don't have Tom's genes either. He's never had a problem, to my knowledge."

"Why does it matter where you got it from?" Angel asked in an all-business tone. "What I want to know is, who's going to help you get rid of it?"

That made Lorraine laugh. "I'm pretty sure that's not Trev," she said.

"How do you put up with him?" Angel asked. "Pardon my French, but from what I've seen, he's a complete asshole."

That seemed to tickle Lorraine no end. She chortled, and then stopped, then chortled again. "He's the father of my children," she said when she achieved a straight face. "He's not around all that much. He goes off a lot, so I don't have to put up with him all the time. We coexist. I stay out of his way, and I make sure he stays out of mine. It's not very inspiring, I know, but I think it's good for the kids to know their father. What would you say, Elvis? You know more about growing up without a father than I do."

He had to think. "Yeah, I agree. I wish I had known him growing up. As long as he's not acting ugly."

"He's not," Lorraine said. "I don't know that he's really that interested."

"Another thing I can't figure out," Elvis said, "is why he was so determined to get the old Garberville house back from Aunt Carol. Do you know how that came down?" He told Lorraine the story of breaking into the house and stealing the papers. "And then, suddenly, he just wasn't interested in it. At all. I mean, I don't know about all the legal stuff, but it seems to me that if his father willed it to a church that doesn't exist, maybe he and Carol could get the title and split the money. They're the only living heirs."

"They'd have to pay lawyers," Angel said. She was amazing; she understood this kind of stuff. "It might not be worth it."

"I think it was more pride than money," Lorraine said. It struck Elvis that she had moved off neutral and was actually enjoying this conversation. It was a subtle difference; something in her body language indicated she had moved in. "He couldn't believe his father would skip him and give the house to his sister. A girl. That just offended him, and he was obsessed with proving it wrong. He was adopted too, you know."

Elvis stared at her. "No, I didn't."

It was almost too much for him to take in. He had thought of the family as a web, connected through the generations, but it appeared those connections were imaginary. His family was just a made-up thing.

"He says he never got on with his father," Lorraine added. "He was always trying to be good enough. His father was a jerk. Trev hated him. I think he wanted to prove that his father really loved him. Which, naturally, he would show by putting him in his will."

"So what he found," Angel said, "was that he loved the church more."

"Yeah," Lorraine said. "Guess so."

* * *

The mac and cheese was good. Lorraine had shredded vegetables into it, so it was actually sort of healthy. That didn't take away from the solid cheesy flavor, or the heft of the pasta glued together. Elvis ate a lot. He had not realized how hungry he was. It had been a long day—a long day and night and day again, he thought. He was almost staggering with fatigue, the way you feel after an all-night haul.

As he ate, Elvis thought about his conversation with Lorraine. Somehow, she helped put his mind at rest. He might never see these people again, but he looked around the long dining-room table with warm feelings for them. Lorraine and the two kids could have acted like jerks when he barged into their family, and they didn't.

Willard was in form. He held forth on a number of subjects, including the county inspectors who were giving him grief about his sewage system. "I told them, 'What are you so squeamish about? The same stuff comes out of your orifices. It's practically you. How can it be dangerous?'" He also held strong opinions about the salmon run and the dams on the Eel that diverted water to the grape farmers in Sonoma—"That's you, Big Boy," he almost shouted at Elvis. "You're stealing my water." He didn't listen to anybody else; he just talked.

Willard told them to stay the night, but Tom said he would get on home, and Elvis said the same. When he got up from the dining room table to say goodbye to Lorraine, he felt a sudden impulse to lean forward and buss her on the cheek. Her close proximity, with the scent of soap, made him think of his mother.

Willard escorted them out of the house. The kids had disappeared to wherever kids go, so it was just the four of them. A wind had kicked up off the water, whipping through the bushes lining the fence. It was cold, and none of them was dressed for it.

Willard offered his hand. "You happy now?" he asked.

"I don't know about happy," Elvis said. "At least now I know the facts."

"Facts!" Willard said, throwing an arm across the arc of the sky. "Facts!" Elvis had no idea what he meant by that. After shaking hands with his brother, who didn't even look him in the eye, Elvis called Blackie and then got into the truck with Angel to head home.

# 10 TWELVE STEPS

Elvis had every intention of driving all the way home, but he soon realized he wasn't going to make it. He was wobbly from lack of sleep. "What do you say to stopping in Garberville?" he asked Angel.

"For the night?" she asked.

"If we keep going, I'll be driving in the dark," he said. "I don't think I'm up to it."

So they had a nice meal and checked in to the King Kwality. Mrs. Patel was surprised and pleased to see them again. "We are getting to know you quite well," she said.

Elvis showered and got in bed, but when he lay down, his mind started working, going over the extraordinary day, traveling backward until he found himself reliving the fire.

* * *

"I need help," the woman said weakly, fretfully. She was just a shadow in her wheelchair, wrapped in the darkness of the house. "I can't get in the car by myself. Can you help me?"

"Yeah, sure," Elvis said. "We need to get you out of here. Have you got your phone? Your wallet?"

"I have my purse right here," she said. He heard—rather than saw—that she patted something leathery. "Can you drive?"

"Sure," he said. "Let's go."

Elvis put his hands on the wheelchair handles and began to push forward. He had to rock the chair to get it over the threshold and onto the small concrete porch. "Where's your car?" he asked.

"It's in the garage."

"I'll need the keys, then."

Grabbing her flashlight, he went back into the house, through the living room and the kitchen until he found the door to the garage. He located the garage door switch and pushed it. No action. He pushed again, and then realized that of course, there was no power.

Elvis shone his light around the inside of the garage. It was pristine. Shelves displayed cardboard boxes lined up as though on display. A handful of tools hung neatly on pegboard. The car, a blue Nissan, was centered on the spotless garage floor.

He spotted the cord hanging down from the chain mechanism of the garage door opener. Piece of cake. When he pulled on it, however, it did not give; and when he jerked harder, the cord broke. In disgust, Elvis threw the red wooden handle across the room. He shone the flashlight on a tiny nubbin of rope left behind on the mechanism. Maybe he could get it loose with a pair of pliers, assuming he could find a pair of pliers. He began shining the flashlight around the walls, looking for pliers, but then had a better idea. This was taking too long. They could go in his truck.

Elvis hustled back through the kitchen and living room and through the front door. For a split second, he did not see the lady in her wheelchair, and his heart went into his throat. She had only moved to one side, however. Her glasses reflected the red-and-gold light. Flames crackled around the roofline of a house opposite them, driven by a ferocious wind. Farther down the street, toward his cul-de-sac, another house had fire slipping up one side, like a reversed waterfall.

"Time to go," Elvis said. "We'll take my truck." Grabbing the wheelchair, he eased it down a single step onto the sidewalk. The air was doubly hot now, and the wind so strong it pushed back against the wheelchair. They reached the corner to turn into the cul-de-sac and found it all on fire. A violent explosion shook them like a bomb, sending a shock wave through the visible flames. A hot basket exploded like a mad orange tulip on the street in front of Elvis's SLE. It was his truck, completely engulfed in fire. Elvis could not even see the truck body, only the flames.

He needed to think, but he was distracted by the gorgeous, blooming inferno. Blazing firelight gave no depth. Everything seemed to be right up to his face. Turning the corner, the step-down on the curb fooled him; he sprawled forward and cracked his knee on the pavement.

He could feel such heat off the buildings that he knew he had to leave or die. Where could they go? He could not think of a safe route out:

Coffey Park was one dense maze of two-story houses, set on small lots. The whole subdivision was ablaze.

"What's your name?" he asked. He had gotten up from the pavement and was pushing the wheelchair down the dead center of the street. No telling whether he was headed the right way or wrong, but he had to go somewhere. He had begun to pray, just your ordinary "God, help" kind of prayer.

"Wilma," she said.

"Wilma what?"

"Wilma McTavish."

"I'm Elvis."

"How old are you, Elvis?"

He laughed. "Too old!"

"I'm eighty-two," Wilma said and broke into a cough. It took her several alarming minutes to bring it under control. "I shouldn't be coughing like that," she said.

"The smoke is bad. Here," he said, and peeled the T-shirt off his back. "Put this over your head. It's clean." He grinned at the absurdity, worrying about cleanliness when they were probably going to die. He didn't think he should say that to Wilma.

To his surprise, Wilma began to laugh, a high, herky-jerk falsetto laugh. "What's so funny?" he asked her.

"Don't you think this is funny?"

He looked down to see by the dimmest shadow that Wilma had put his T-shirt over her head, so that only her head of hair, permanented into a helmet of fluff, stuck out the top.

"Yeah, I do." He had pushed the chair a block down the street, to a place where only one house was on fire. Looking ahead through thick gusts of smoke, he could see more infernos. That light made the obscurity deeper where they stood, as though they were strolling in a vat of ink. The darkness was scariest, but the fire would kill them.

"Does that shirt help with the smoke?" he asked.

"I think so," she said. "But I can't see anything. I hope you know where you're going."

"I don't," he confessed. "But I'm going to try. We can't stay here."

"What about the park?" Wilma asked.

He hadn't thought about the park, though for the last two weeks, he had driven past it every day. It was a small space, just a few acres, with small trees and a playground. At least there, they might put a little distance between themselves and the burning houses. Elvis headed for it as fast as he could push the wheelchair. It took no more than ten minutes, but by the time they arrived, the full raging firestorm was on, blasting like an angry furnace.

All the buildings were on fire—every one. Sparks and embers whipped through the air, biting Elvis's bare chest. The oxygen had been sucked out of the air and out of his lungs. He choked and coughed and sucked at the hot gases. Twice he glanced down at Wilma in the flat, ginger-red light and saw her clothing had caught fire. He frantically swatted it out, burning his hand. At first, Wilma talked to him, but her responses slowed and then stopped completely. Dear God, was she dead? He didn't want to know. He was tethered to that chair: it gave him purpose. What would he do with a wheelchair carrying a dead lady? He stood between her and the furnace, brushing off embers.

He might die himself. If he was going to die, he wished he could see Amber first. Angel was his love, but Amber was his regret. After years of missing his own father and blaming his mother for her neglect, he had disappeared just as thoroughly from Amber.

Everything burned, but it didn't all burn at once. When one street was blasting flames into the air, another crashed into cinders. Elvis moved around the park, pushing Wilma ahead of him, trying to escape the worst. He had no idea of time.

His legs grew heavy and weak, trembling with the load. The sky changed: no longer red, now a dull gray. Elvis could see by a thin gruel of light that seemed to rise up out of the ground like fog. The park took on form and depth. Fires still burned in every direction he turned, but the wind had died and the flames no longer arced and tangled in the air. They fluttered now, finishing their job, consuming every last stick.

Not a single house stood. He saw hulks of burned metal that had been cars in their garages: the garages gone, they seemed to have been parked in the open air. Blackened and melted on their iron rims, they were the tallest objects in the landscape. Everything was gone, right to the dirt, for as far as he could see in any direction.

"Wilma," Elvis said and shook her shoulder. She groaned, and the sound released some hope in him.

"Wilma, I think we made it."

* * *

Snug in the Garberville motel, molded to Angel's warmth, Elvis had fallen asleep. When he awoke, the fire memories stayed with him, like the shredded remnants of a dream.

He had survived, and Wilma had survived. People congratulated him for not abandoning Wilma, but really? He didn't think of himself as a hero. It wasn't as though he had anywhere better to go or anything better to do.

It was perfectly dark in the room, and he felt Angel's breathing. Gratefulness covered him. Then he thought of the lady with the cat and the men in the SLE, whom he had warned but who had disappeared in the dark. Somebody might say that he had abandoned them, not understanding what it is like in that panic state.

He thought again of his father. Willard *had* abandoned him. Think of that, just going off and leaving a ten-year-old boy. You had to wonder how he could do that. For thirty years to never even send a note. At least Amber had always known how to find him.

During the fire, when he thought he might be dying, she had been on his mind. He would have to tell her that when he saw her.

Suddenly he was crying, not knowing why. He started sobbing and couldn't stop, deep, wracking sobs that stole all the oxygen from his lungs. Angel woke up; she tried to hold him, asking, "What's wrong? What's wrong, baby?" It was several minutes before he could control himself enough to answer her.

He explained about Amber and about his father's abandoning him when he was a little boy. He was still shaken, but not sobbing. He tried to calm himself.

"You're all right, baby," Angel said, holding him.

"I just feel so sorry for myself," he said. "Ten years old! My father walked off and abandoned me!"

"He's an asshole," she said.

"I've never gotten over it," he said. "I'm an abandoned child."

"Not to me," she said. "Not yet, anyway."

He smiled despite himself. "Okay, you haven't abandoned me. Everybody else."

"Not everybody else. Lots of people have hung in there with you."

"Like who?"

“Your church. The mission.”

“That’s different. They have to put up with me.”

“No, they don’t. But really, baby, I don’t think anybody has abandoned you. It’s the other way around. You usually ditch them.”

“Because I’m an abandoned child.”

“Even your brother.”

“Tom?”

“You have to admit he’s tried, in his own horrible way.”

“He’s tried? How?”

“He came all the way down to Santa Rosa and talked to you that time, remember?”

“Yeah, like trash.”

“Yeah, but he was trying. That’s a long drive. And he took care of Amber for years.”

“And threw away all her meds. And made her hate him.”

“That was stupid, baby, but he didn’t know any better. Where would he learn?”

Elvis didn’t know how to answer that. Tom probably thought he was doing the right thing. Even coming to Garberville and breaking in on them in the middle of the night.

* * *

In the morning, they were well on their way south, almost to Willits, when it came to Elvis that he wanted to see his daughter.

“Don’t you want to get home?” Angel asked when he told her.

“It won’t take long,” he said.

That made no sense to Angel. “Doesn’t she work on Sundays? We’ll get like ten minutes, max.”

“I just want to see her.”

He didn’t really know the logic of it, but the impulse was very strong. He could see that it had been poking its head up through the snow for some time. In the last year, he had called Amber several times, usually when he was loaded. There was that one time he had even stopped to see her and slept over at her apartment. They hadn’t really talked then.

She wasn’t even twenty yet. There was still plenty of time. A lot could change for the better. Look at what had happened to him, just yesterday.

That reminded him. "You haven't told me what you think of Willard," he said to Angel. "Now that you've gotten to know him."

She had her shoes off and her feet up on the dash. "I still think the term is 'asshole.' It must be a relief to know that you're adopted."

He didn't respond.

"C'mon," Angel said. "You don't actually like him, do you?"

It made him feel vexed and perplexed. "He's different," Elvis said. "But I'm different. I don't want to judge him. He's my father, after all."

She clucked her tongue. "How is he your father? A dog who finds a bitch in heat is more a father than him. Excuse me."

It was hard to answer that. Elvis wasn't good at arguments. Nevertheless, he tried. "He raised me until I was ten. That's something."

"Yeah, right. And deserted you when you were ten. What kind of father is that?"

Elvis was stumped. "I guess you're right," he said glumly. "But to tell you the truth, I feel better after seeing him and finding out where he lives. Good or bad, I know who he is."

Angel looked out the window at the trees flying by. They were still in dense forest, with dark green boughs feathering each other. "To tell you the truth, I'd rather not know."

"That's because you've always known your parents. You didn't grow up with the mystery."

"Mystery?"

He tried to tamp down his emotions. "The mystery of who you are. I wasn't looking for him; I was looking for me."

"Is that why you want to see your daughter?"

He couldn't see the connection. "Do I have to have a reason? She's my daughter."

"You think."

That caught him off guard. He was about to fire something back and then realized she was right. His brother wasn't his brother. His father wasn't his father, his mother wasn't his mother. All he knew about Amber was what her mother had said. How did she know who was the father? He doubted she kept careful track. She didn't know what day it was half the time.

"You really think she's not my daughter?" he asked.

Angel laughed. "She's your daughter, all right. I mean, you could do a paternity test, but what difference would it make?

"And while we're on that subject, your father was terrible, but he's still your father. Which is what I'm telling you about Amber. You have done the best you knew how, and sooner or later, she's going to need to get that."

"I think she does," Elvis said, "but she's just a kid and she has a lot of other things on her mind. I've been AWOL a lot. That's why I want to go see her today."

* * *

Elvis couldn't quite remember where on State Street the restaurant was, so he got off at the first exit and followed the road all the way down. The streets and buildings were dark with rain. Elvis thought he might have passed the place, which made him drive a little faster than he should, because he was nervous. Just when he was ready to double back, he saw Rosie's pink sign.

"This won't be long," he said to Angel as he parked. "You want to come in?"

"Of course I'll come in," she said. "It's cold out here."

The skies were clearing and the wind rising as they crossed the street and walked into the warm noise of the bar. Elvis scanned the waitresses, looking for Amber, and realized he hadn't warned Angel about the costumes.

"I forgot to tell you," he said while he continued looking. "This place is like Hooters."

Angel laughed. "Is that her?" she said.

Amber was standing on one leg, taking an order from one of the back booths. The way she was turned, Elvis couldn't really see her expression. When she walked their direction, the overhead lights caught her face. To his eyes, she looked fierce and unhappy, but he remembered that she had worn that look since she was in second grade. It was where her face went when she wasn't thinking about it.

Then she saw him. He gave a little wave and watched as her face made recognition and then took on a tight little smile. She came directly their way, gave him a short politeness hug, and air-kissed with Angel. "What are you doing here?" she asked, her head swiveling between them.

"You aren't going to believe it," Elvis said. "We've been up north, visiting your grandfather and your great-aunt and your uncle. Trying to make some sense out of this crazy family of ours."

"Sounds interesting," she said in a way that indicated it wasn't.

"I need to tell you about it," he said. "We found a whole new set of family members we didn't even know existed."

"Huh," she said.

She was young, and as such, not interested in family trees. She was barely interested in him and Angel. He had been the same at her age. He wanted, nevertheless, to tell her about it. He wanted to tell her what he had gone through, to spin out the story. She was his only real purchase on family, and he wanted to draw her in. He wanted to sit with her in a warm place and talk.

"Can you get a break?" he asked. "I know you're busy, but can we get fifteen minutes?"

She hesitated but said they could. "Just wait here for a minute," she said and walked off in a little take-charge strut. Elvis wondered what the hesitation was about. He asked Angel.

"Maybe her boyfriend is coming by," Angel said. "Maybe he's already here and is waiting for her to take her break with him."

After a wait, Amber led them over to a table in the back. It was set for lunch, but she scraped off the napkin-wrapped cutlery and sat down across from them both. "Do you want anything?" she asked, but they waved that off.

As Elvis told her about his father, Amber's curiosity kicked in. She wanted to know what all these people were to her: cousins, or aunts, or uncles, what was their exact relationship? Great-aunt? Second cousin? Stepbrother? Elvis wasn't good at that kind of terminology, but he floundered into it, trying his best because he thought he ought to master it. Amber was looking at him, and her hazel eyes were bright and focused. Through most of their years, she had looked away, wearing a scowl.

"You know what?" Elvis said. "You should quit this job and come back to Santa Rosa. There's plenty of restaurants where you could work. You could live with us if you wanted." The idea had come to him spontaneously, and he didn't need anybody to tell him that it was brilliant. Even so, he glanced at Angel. Her expression was perfectly blank.

Amber seemed to take him seriously. "When?" she asked.

"Now! Today! You can come with us today and we'll come back to clean out your apartment later."

She gave him a crooked little smile. "I guess I'll have to think about that," she said.

"Why not now?"

She gave her head a little shake. "Dad, that's pretty sudden. I need to think about it."

"What is there to think about?"

Angel put out a hand and touched his arm. "Elvis," she said.

"What?"

"Give her some space."

* * *

During the last leg of the journey home, down the steep section following the river, Elvis asked Angel if they would go to church tonight.

"I don't know why you even ask," she said.

That threw him. He was unsure of her meaning. "Well, I'm pretty tired. It would be nice to stay put."

She didn't respond right away, and he wondered whether she was smiling. He hoped so. Even after all their years together, she intimidated him a little. He was a screwup, and she was the adult supervision.

It seemed like minutes ticked off the clock before she spoke. "Look, Elvis, you're in my program. Now tell me what the rules are."

He thought she had to be kidding, but he went along with it. "Go to church, go to meetings, no alcohol, no drugs."

"No exceptions."

"No exceptions, no fun, no screwing around, no partying, no wild living. From now on, we are seventy years old and we use our walkers to get to the bathroom."

"You got it."

"We go to church tonight," he said.

"We go to church tonight. Look, it's not for me."

"Right."

For a moment, he thought she was going to cry, which frightened him. There were no sounds except for the truck's rattling. They were climbing in the last hilly section, just before Geyserville. Out to the left, across two lanes of highway, Elvis could see down into the valley, a dead gray. All the grass was gone and the trees were stripped for winter.

# 11 THE FOURTH STEP

Elvis felt like his head had been in a pinball machine the whole weekend, with bells and lights exploding. He found it hard to settle down after all that stimulation. At work, the hours dragged.

He wanted Angel to go over everything with him: Aunt Carol, Lorraine, her kids, the stories his dad had told, and above all, motives. Why had Willard done what he had done? What had made him desert his family way back when Elvis was just a helpless kid? Angel was polite about it, but she wouldn't pile into his analysis. She wouldn't speculate. The skin around her mouth showed a hint of impatience.

"If you don't want me to talk about it, I won't," Elvis said.

"It's up to you," she answered. She wouldn't even give him the benefit of an argument.

On Tuesday, he called Bill to get a ride to AA. Elvis felt strange and jittery making the call. Bill would give him hell, he knew, because he had disappeared just when they were getting started on the steps. Any time in his past, he would have dodged Bill, choosing another meeting to avoid him. He couldn't do that anymore. He needed a sponsor. Angel didn't even have to tell him to call.

Elvis was right: Bill would hardly speak to him. Elvis kept running his mouth. He was afraid Bill would hang up.

"Let me ask you this," Bill finally said in his gravelly voice. "Did you ever do any of that Step Four stuff we talked about?"

"I did some. I don't want to lie to you—I got messed up for a while. Now I'm really back. I'm serious. Angel is working with me this time, and that makes all the difference. I know I need to work the steps. That's why I need your help."

"How much did you do?"

Elvis told himself to slow down. He was so nervous, it was hard to talk in a way that made any sense. "I did some." At that, he ran out of things to say. He felt stupid telling Bill how eager to work he was.

"Okay," Bill said. "I'll come and get you at six thirty. Did you say you're at Angel's place now?"

Originally, the house had been his place, but he didn't need to say that. "Yeah. Thank you, Bill. I appreciate it."

"You bring the notebook," Bill said. "Try to get some more of it done."

* * *

The meeting was hard to get through. The last time Elvis had been there, he had two years sober, and now he barely had two weeks. He felt he had a sign on his back that said, "I relapsed." They all remembered him, he thought, and not in a good way.

It wasn't in his nature to keep quiet. He stood. "I'm Elvis, and I'm an alcoholic."

"Hi, Elvis."

He knew he needed to spill himself, to break the ice and get on the other side of this awkwardness. "I'm not going to lie to you," he began, "it's been pretty rough for me since the last time I was here. I totally relapsed. I was arrested and thrown in jail; I went through detox at McFriends; it was pretty bad. I guess I don't have to tell you about it; a lot of you know what I'm talking about. Anyway, that's in the past. A new beginning is always available, every minute of every day, and I'm on it. My lady, Angel—she really is an angel, but that's her name—is doing it with me, and she's helping me. She is one tough lady. I mean strong. We are totally committed together, and I'm feeling it. I've got my sponsor, Bill, working with me—thank you, Bill—and I've got my church. I know Jesus Christ is on my side; he's forgiven me and cleansed me. I just wanted to give credit to my Lord and to AA and to Bill and to Angel and everybody who's helped me get to this point. I'm thankful I'm alive, and I'm feeling very positive for the first time in a long, long time."

He sat down to a smattering of applause. After the meeting, several people came up, shook hands, and said welcome back. It was always a good sign to hear from somebody who picked himself up and started over, they said.

When he and Bill settled down over coffee at Peets, he started to fill Bill in on his father and his aunt and all that had transpired over the weekend. Bill cut him off. “You got your step work?” he asked.

“Sure,” he said. “But don’t you want to know what’s happened?”

“I guess,” Bill said, “but let’s get on the step work first. If we have time, you can tell me about what’s been going on.”

Elvis pulled out his notebook. He really hadn’t done much since they’d last met. Bill flipped through the few pages. “Do you understand this?” he asked. “Do you know what you need to do?”

“Yeah, I think so. Like I told you, I’ve been pretty messed up. I’m ready to get on this stuff now. By next week, I’ll have it done.”

“You understand it has to be thorough. You need to list everything. Once you’ve done that, there’s a lot more to analyze. The Big Book has all kinds of detail that you need to study and respond to. This is not easy. You can’t just toss this off in an afternoon.”

“I know that,” Elvis said. “I’m ready to do this.”

They started with resentments. Tom was number one. Elvis began to explain the history to Bill, but he stopped him. “You do one column at a time,” he said. “Just list all your resentments. Anybody who makes you angry. Or anything. Put ‘em all down.”

Bill had a printed list of prompts, and when Elvis got stuck, he would read from it. It took a lot of prying and pushing to come up with this:

1. Tom
2. Willard
3. Ray
4. Mavis
5. Mr. Johnson (high school baseball coach)
6. The law
7. Lilly (Amber’s mother)
8. Rizzuto Roofing
9. Hernandez (probation officer)
10. Eddie Costas (first beer)
11. May Lindecott (first meth)
12. Mr. Costello (high school principal)
13. Vietnam
14. Dr. Baylis (dentist)

"That's all you got?" Bill asked when he stalled after reaching the dentist.

"I'll probably come up with more when I think about it."

"That's okay; you can add them. It's normal. You understand, this isn't a one-and-done. It's the work of a lifetime. You start here because these are the things that make you use. You can't deal with them until you identify them and understand how they're working you."

Bill went on to the next column: what made him resentful. He watched as Elvis filled in each slot. For some of them, like Tom, he had more than one reason. He could devote a whole page to reasons he resented Tom.

Once he got past Tom and Willard and Ray, it went more quickly. When he got to the bottom, he felt like he had been grinding for a week.

"Tired?" Bill asked.

"I can keep going," Elvis said.

Bill gave a rare smile, showing the hole in his teeth. "I think that's enough for tonight. We'll take on the rest next week. Okay?"

Elvis wanted to know what they still had to do with resentments.

"You have to say how each person or thing affects you. We'll use some categories from the Big Book for that. It's a little complicated, so we need to go over it together. The last column is probably the hardest: what did you do to create that problem? Not what somebody else did, what you did. How are you responsible?"

Elvis couldn't help thinking back to the weekend. He had not made any sense of it; it remained a bright swirl. He didn't even know how to feel about it. He had certainly felt excitement, stuffing a year's living into three days and nights. If he was going to take responsibility for what happened, he didn't know how to do that.

"We'll work on that next week," Bill said. "In the meantime, you can start a new page listing your fears."

Bill heaved himself up out of his seat, ready to go, but Elvis tried to get him to sit down and talk. The weekend begged for discussion.

"Hey, man, you said we could talk about my weekend after we got through the Step Four work."

Bill paused but did not sit back down. "If we had time, I said."

"Don't we have time?"

Bill's face naturally fell into a scowl, and he was scowling down on Elvis now. "Look, I think that's all a distraction for you. You need to focus on your step work."

"But you said yourself that if we don't understand how things are working on us, we can't get control of them."

"Yeah, the step work helps you break it down. If we just go talking about everything that happens, we'll never get any of it to make sense. Those are just stories. I know, you like to go into all that stuff, but I don't see it being helpful to you. Go home and talk about it with your wife. You and me should stick to the steps."

"She's not my wife."

"Huh?"

"We're not married."

Bill looked pained. "What difference does that make?"

* * *

Angel was waiting up when Bill dropped him off. She had put on red flannel pajamas, ready for bed, but she came into the living room looking pale and beautiful. She gently kissed him. He was feeling frustrated, even though the meeting had been good and he was glad for launching into Step Four. He still wanted to talk through the weekend. He was sure that he could find buried treasure if he followed all its questions to the end. So much had happened, he couldn't keep it straight in his own mind, but he had a strong feeling that if he went through it with Bill, the tangled ends would appear.

"What's the matter?" Angel asked. With just a glance at his face, she knew he was upset.

Throwing himself on the sofa, he told her he was still trying to find his way to sobriety.

"You want a cup of tea?" she asked.

Elvis recognized it as an offer to sit and talk, but he hadn't adjusted to the new regime: he didn't like sipping tea. If he couldn't have a beer, he didn't want anything. He said no.

She stayed put and asked him whether he had been frustrated by AA. Elvis shrugged. "Not really," he said. "Bill is taking me through Step Four, and I've got a lot of homework to do."

"What kind of homework?"

"Like making lists of all the people and things that make me mad. I never realized how involved it is. I'll be doing it for weeks."

"What is that supposed to do for you?"

"I think the idea is to really understand what makes the old clock tick. Like why I do what I do. I'm trying my best, but I don't see why I need all this psychoanalyzing. It's pretty simple, really. When everything is normal, I don't even think about using. And then, it's like a little switch is flipped and I turn into a drug-seeking zombie. I'm fine, and then I'm not. I don't see what that little switch has to do with my resentments."

"I think the idea is that you use to short-circuit the pain."

"Yeah, okay, then why isn't the switch on all the time? I resent Tom all the time. But most of the time, I'm just fine. Then, boom."

He looked at her suspiciously, as though she were hiding something. "Do you have a switch like that?"

"No," she said. "With me, it's different. With you, it's like you lose self-control."

"Exactly," he said.

"I don't know what to tell you, except that people do get clean through twelve-step programs. You've seen it, I've seen it."

"But it doesn't work for me."

She puckered her mouth. "You've never really tried."

"I have," he said, clinging to his sense of integrity. "I've tried, but I never succeeded."

She put a hand on the back of his neck, pulled him to her, and kissed him. "Keep on trying," she said.

* * *

He needed a long time to get to sleep. Angel was acting very strong, but who could say what she would do if he lost it again? Lying on his back in bed, staring into the dark, he tried to remember how many times she had come back to him. How many times she had been waiting when he got out of detox or jail or a program.

It didn't matter so much about his father, or all the other family he had encountered for the first time. Angel was his foundation.

He flashed back to Bill, who had assumed they were married. That had annoyed him, and his annoyance had aggravated Bill, who wanted to know what difference it made. It did make a difference. He had always said he liked his freedom, but now he was staring in the face of being left solo. They should get married. He didn't know what Angel would say, but in the morning, he would ask her. He didn't have a ring, but he would get down on his knees and make a proposal. Maybe he could pick some flowers from the garden. He would be sweet, and she would smile and try to make a joke out of it, but he would persist.

Elvis fell asleep thinking of that, but in the morning, he had forgotten all about it. Only after he had started to work, Blackie riding next to him, did he remember his plans. Always a screwup. He felt bad. There really wasn't time in the morning, though; they both were moving, getting ready for work. Maybe he could do it tonight, he thought. Or on the weekend. The urgency had faded, unfortunately.

During the day's work, his memory kept getting sucked back to that airy view from his dad's farm, overlooking the blue Pacific. Something about that wide space made him feel good; it had relaxed his soul, all that room. He wondered why Willard had taken them there. He was revealing his secrets, of course, just the way they had insisted he do—his secret family; his other children; Lorraine, who had replaced his mom. At the same time, he kept a bunch of secrets, like what he did for money and where he went. It didn't sound like he spent so much time on the farm. Who was Willard, really? Where did he keep his boat, assuming he was telling the truth and still had a boat? Was he just pretending to have no feelings, or was that him?

When Elvis had worked himself through all that, he thought about his brother. He couldn't believe that Angel wanted him to see some good in Tom. That he had tried to help Amber and had even wanted to be helpful when he came to Santa Rosa to deliver a lecture.

And Aunt Carol. Plenty of mysteries there. The house. The will. His grandfather. Where was his grandmother? Nobody ever said anything about her.

Elvis would never get to the bottom of these questions. He would need to spend a thousand hours with his dad if he had any hope of getting straight information. It wasn't possible. Inevitably, he would keep bumbling along, bumping into objects in the dark.

Elvis thought back to his last, gloomy conversation with Angel about that little switch in his brain. Even in his times of sanity, he knew that without warning his cravings could appear, like spooks coming out of the shadows to present the insane possibility of smoking meth and all that went with it. Certainly, he could never say no to those cravings. He never had. The best he knew was to keep them on the edge of consciousness, forcing them into the distance, ignoring them whenever he caught them in a sidelong glance. That wasn't the clean and sober he longed for. He wanted it sweet and clean and without effort. He wanted those cravings to get lost and stay lost.

* * *

His phone rang while he was in the shower. He heard it and thought about answering. After he dried off, he checked and saw an unfamiliar number.

His spirits improved with the shower, possibly because constitutionally, Elvis was incapable of staying depressed for long. Dressing with care, he put on orange jeans, a red plaid shirt with yellow suspenders, and a black leather vest made in a western style, with fringes. It took him some time to locate his fancy hat, a black fedora with a belt of silver shields circling the crown.

While he admired himself in the mirror, the phone rang again. It was the same number. When he answered, a soft and unassuming female voice asked if he was Elvis Sebastiano.

"Yeah, who's calling?"

"Elvis, this is Lorraine. Trev's wife."

It took Elvis a moment to realize that Trev was Willard. "Yeah," he said, "how are you? Is everybody okay?"

"Yes, we're all okay. I have something to tell you. It's kind of a secret. Your father doesn't know I'm telling you."

"Okay."

"I'm your real mother."

He knew he had heard Lorraine correctly, but he had no idea what to say. For at least half a minute, he was mute, and so was Lorraine.

"Okay, Mom, glad to meet you," he said, trying to break the ice with humor. She didn't laugh. Elvis felt his nervousness build to the brim. "Look, Lorraine, you better explain. I have no idea what you're talking about."

He heard an audible sigh. "It's all so long ago, and I don't even know why I need to tell you, but I do. Your father and I got involved when I was in high school. He would come up to Arcata with his boat, and we just met. I didn't know he was married and had a kid, and the first thing you know, I was pregnant. Trev knew this doctor who would help, but I would have to give the baby up for adoption. So I did. I never got to hold you. I was all doped up, and by the time I was with it again, you were gone. I knew you were a boy, and that was all. Trev disappeared and I went ahead with my life, until eight or nine years later when I ran into Trev again. The short version is that my parents had passed, and I was trying to keep the property together, and Trev moved in. I knew he had a family in Ft. Bragg, but I never learned much about you. You know how Trev is."

"So you think I am your baby?"

"Yeah."

"What makes you think so?"

She sighed again. "You look so much like Trev."

"I do?"

"Yeah. And you look like me. My own kids said that. When you said as how you were adopted, I got suspicious and asked Angel what your birthday was. Perfect match."

"Wait a minute. You're saying that while my dad was married to my mom, he got you pregnant up in Arcata and arranged to have you adopted by him and my mom."

"I think so."

"But never told you."

"Not in all those years."

"I guess he thought you would want to contact me."

"Which I would. I'm doing it right now."

After another silence, Elvis said, "I need some time to take this all in."

"Yeah, you're not the only one. I never expected to see you, ever." From the sounds traveling through the telephone, Elvis thought she was beginning to weep.

"What am I supposed to do with this information?"

She cleared her throat. He could hear a lot of emotion in her voice, though she spoke calmly. "I think it would be nice if you could come up here for a visit. I'd like to get to know you."

"How are your kids going to feel about this?"

"They already know. I think they're fine."

"And my dad?"

"He doesn't know I know. He'll just have to deal with it. Which he will, in his way."

Another silence. "I need to talk to Angel."

"Okay."

A thought came to him. "What about Tom? He's not yours?"

"No. I don't know where Tom came from."

* * *

When Angel came in the door twenty minutes later, she found Elvis splayed out on the sofa, his hat riding on his belly. He was staring up at the ceiling and didn't even look over to see her.

"I just had the weirdest conversation of my life," he said.

"That's a statement," she said. "You're covering some ground there."

"I know. Hey, when we were up north, did Lorraine ask what my birthday is?"

After a moment's reflection, Angel said, "Yeah, I think she did."

He nodded to himself. "Did you think that was weird?"

"A little, I guess. I can't say I thought about it."

"She just called me and told me she is my mother."

"What?" Angel sat down.

"She said she got suspicious when she saw me. She thinks I look like her, and like Willard. That's why she wanted to know my birthday. She says Willard got her pregnant when she was in high school, and she gave up the baby sight unseen. Later on—like years later on—Willard came back into her life. She knew he had another family, but she had no idea I was part of the picture."

"Oh my goodness."

"Yeah."

"No wonder your father wanted to keep clear of you."

"You think that's why?"

She raised her eyebrows. "Your father doesn't like complicated relationships, in case you haven't noticed. That's a pretty complicated deal."

"Yeah, it is."

"Let me get changed," she said, standing, "and then we'll talk some more."

As he felt around in himself, Elvis found happiness. When Angel came out of the bedroom, he told her.

"What are you happy about?" she asked.

"Maybe it's just that hope springs eternal. I don't know. I keep looking for something to explain why I'm so screwed up."

"She's not going to explain anything. She only just found out you exist."

"No, but if she really is my mother, don't you think that's big? I haven't had a mother since I was a kid. Maybe Lorraine is what I've been looking for. A home base, so to speak."

Angel wore her blank, skeptical face. Her lips began to form words, then stopped. "Well, she did call you. I'll give her that much."

* * *

It disappointed Elvis that Angel was skeptical. She made the point that Lorraine hadn't spent a single day with Elvis. So what if they shared some genes? She didn't really know anything about him.

"You don't think that a mother feels something special for her son?"

"I'm sure she does. But how is that going to make any difference?"

"What are you worried about?" Elvis wanted to know.

"It's probably another goose chase. Just a distraction."

"A distraction from what?"

That annoyed her. "From the program you're on. Remember that? Remember the rules? Aren't you supposed to be working on Step Four?"

"I'm working it!"

"No, you aren't. You're talking about Lorraine."

"I can talk about my mother and still work the steps."

"Sure, you can, but will you? It's a distraction, and you're good at distractions."

Elvis had to admit that was true. He appreciated that Angel cared enough to argue with him. Backing away from a fight, he got up and began to cook dinner, something he always enjoyed doing. It gave him time to think. When dinner was on the table, he sat down and said a prayer, then asked Angel if they could talk some more.

"I'd like to go see her," he said. "I want to take Amber with me, if she'll go. It's her grandma. I get what you're saying about distractions. Only thing I can think to do is tell you I'm in your complete control. You make a list of what I need to do every day, and hold me to it. I appreciate that you know what's best for me. But I would really like to see my mother. I'm just burning up with curiosity."

* * *

They drove north on Friday night, picking up Amber on the way. She got somebody to trade shifts with her, but she said she had to be back by Saturday at 5:00. Elvis said that was okay because he had to be home for church on Sunday. The boss said so.

"What are you talking about?" Amber wanted to know.

"Angel," he said. "I promised her I would do whatever she said if she would help me stay sober."

"And she's telling you to go to church?"

"Yeah. Among other things."

They arrived late. Elvis got confused driving up the hill in the dark and ended up in somebody else's driveway. When they finally found the right address, Lorraine came out of the house to welcome them. She looked at Elvis under the cold blue arc lights flooding the front of the house, held out her arms, and kissed him on the cheek. Then she kissed Amber and gave Angel a hug, too. She had cooked dinner. They sat down—just the four of them, the kids had gone out—and gradually got over the awkwardness of wondering what to say. A lot of their talk was Elvis explaining to Lorraine what he'd been doing all these years.

He tried to skip over some of the rougher patches, but she wanted to hear everything. Angel interrupted to remind him of a few things, like his going to prison for stealing a cement truck just because the motor was running. She thought it was funny, but he tried to tell it straight because Lorraine seemed to want that. She listened with her big blue eyes looking straight at him. She wasn't looking for humor.

He also got Amber to tell about her life. That was interesting to hear. She was surprisingly positive about Ft. Bragg, even life with Tom.

Lorraine had less to tell. She said she'd been on the farm, raising kids and trying to keep everybody alive and fed. They asked about Willard, but she didn't add very much to what she had said before. If she had any regrets for her life with him, she disguised them well, though it did seem that he was mainly an absentee partner.

The conversation ran down after dinner, so they cleared the table together and did the dishes. Lorraine seemed happy to put her focus on that. She showed them their rooms.

"How long are you going to stay?" she asked.

"We have to get back tomorrow afternoon," Angel said. "Amber has a five o'clock shift."

"Well, then, we'll talk more in the morning," Lorraine answered.

"Any chance we'll see Willard?" Elvis asked as she was disappearing down the hall.

She turned clear around to look at him. "I don't know," she said.

Angel fell asleep immediately, but Elvis couldn't. His mind was twisting and turning with half-formed questions. Eventually, he got up and felt his way down the hall, through the heavy, dark shadows of the living room and to the front door. It wasn't locked.

The moment he stepped outside, he smelled burning tobacco. He saw a shadow and thought he saw the bright tip of a cigarette. "Hello?" he said.

"Hello." He recognized the voice as Lorraine's: soft, slightly rusty.

"I didn't know you smoked," he said.

She let out an audible sigh. "My little secret. I can't quit."

There was nothing he could say to that. It did set off alarm bells in him, though. Practically everybody in AA smoked, but the mission didn't allow smoking. It was treated as just one more addiction, and if you tested positive for nicotine, you had to leave the program. Nowadays, it made him nervous to be around smokers. He hadn't imagined his mother in that category.

"It's tough," he said. "I know."

"But you aren't a smoker," Lorraine said.

"Not now," he said. "I was. But now I'm on this program."

"I thought your problem was meth."

"It is, but this program is strict, and you can't smoke. You have to go to church, and AA, and work the steps with your sponsor, and...it's strict."

"Is this part of the mission?"

He laughed into the dark. "It was, but I've been out of the mission for a long time. This is under the supervision of Dr. Angel."

He wished he could see Lorraine's face to judge what she was thinking. Eventually, she spoke. "So that's why she came along."

"Yeah," he said. "She's my accountability."

"And what does she think about me? Does she think I'm going to be a good influence?"

He couldn't tell if she was serious; he thought she probably wore a smile, but he couldn't be sure.

"She's skeptical," Elvis said.

"Skeptical of what? Of me?"

"No." He paused to think: what was Angel skeptical of? "She's skeptical of me. I get distracted, and she thinks this could be another distraction." Elvis paused, realizing he needed to explain more. "I keep thinking that if I had a family, if I knew where I came from, I'd be different. That's why I kept following Willard around. I thought it would help. And now it's you."

"By 'different,' you mean you could stay off the drugs," Lorraine said.

"Of course."

She took a drag on her cigarette; he saw the lighted tip flare. "I don't know," she said. "It's an experiment, isn't it? I don't know what it's like to have you in my life, and you don't know what it's like to have me in your life. We don't really know each other, do we? But for me, it's a pretty powerful thing. Once I started thinking about it, I knew I had to try to see you."

"I guess it's the same with me."

"Then we'll see where it takes us," Lorraine said. "Otherwise, I would always wonder."

"Does Willard know now?"

"No; I've barely seen him. I don't know if he would care."

"He was taking a chance when he brought me here," Elvis said. "Maybe he wanted you to figure it out."

* * *

Elvis woke up when the morning light flared around the bedroom curtains. Angel still slept. Hearing no stirrings in the rest of the house, he went outside to take the view. There wasn't one. A misty rain had come in off the Pacific, isolating the house in a gauzy gray blanket. He saw what had been invisible in the night: a sagging green sofa that dominated the narrow front porch. Flopping down on it, he tried to register how he felt about the coming day. Jumpy, he decided. Why so? Willard might come, which was plenty of reason. His father kept everybody off balance. Also, and maybe more important, there was a letdown. Lorraine had done her best to welcome them, and when she first kissed him on the cheek, it had been like melting into butter. Just what you want from your mother. However, as the evening went on and they talked, it grew less so. And standing on the porch in the middle of the night, he had encountered somebody wary, keeping her distance like a dog that has been kicked. He hadn't thought of her like that. He hadn't thought of her awake in the night. He hadn't thought of her smoking. He kept repeating to himself that she was his mother, truly: she must be. The idea of a mother was strong, but the idea was thin. He wondered if he had already squeezed everything good out of it in a single evening.

He wanted to run. He knew he couldn't. No way he could tell Angel and Amber that they were leaving before breakfast. Women didn't see the logic of acting on impulse; they would say that they had come all this way. Thinking of it made Elvis feel squeezed.

Stupid, he knew. This was the feeling, though. Thank God there was no dope here.

He heard a vehicle racing up the hill. The sound could be very far off; the mist distorted. For a moment, the sound all but disappeared and he turned his attention away; the next moment, it snarled as though just down the lane. He tried to track it through the fog. He turned his head to follow its trace. The sound almost disappeared again.

Then he glimpsed a gray projectile turn the corner and disappear into a screen of trees. It emerged on the drive, moving too fast. A dark blue Lincoln Continental, its springs gone, bouncing like a carnival ride, almost airborne on the upside. Elvis flinched as it raced into the yard and slid, fishtailing to a stop.

He knew who it was before he saw the door open and the head emerge.

Willard looked a mess. He stood beside the car, taking the view. When he glimpsed Elvis sitting on the porch, he broke into a crooked smile.

"You been up all night?" Elvis asked as he came down the stairs to shake his hand.

"I'm an early riser. What brings you up here?"

"You don't know?" He said it with a smile, just teasing.

"You need to call before you come. I don't want you just showing up." He walked past him into the house.

"Lorraine!!!" He stood in the hallway, bellowing.

"Dad!" Elvis said.

"Lorraine!"

"Dad, sit down. Let's talk."

"Lorraine! Get in here!"

"Dad, Amber is here."

"Who?"

"Your granddaughter."

He made an impatient gesture with his hand. "Lorraine!"

She appeared in the kitchen doorway, already dressed in a light-green housedress. Her face was quiet, showing no sign of impatience. She said nothing, just waited for Willard's attention.

Willard stopped shouting in mid-breath and visibly scrambled for something to say. "There you are. Is the coffee made?"

Watching Lorraine's quiet courtesy, Elvis's heart fell into love. She turned around, back into the kitchen.

"Have you had breakfast?" Elvis asked his father. "'Cause I'm starving."

Lorraine made pancakes while Elvis and Willard sat drinking coffee at the kitchen table. "You got time to do some work for me?" Willard asked.

"What kind of work?"

"Work work. The kind where you get your fingernails dirty. You know how to work?"

"Yeah, I do. I'm a roofer."

Willard didn't say anything to that. He was stuffing pancake into his mouth.

"Hey," Elvis said. "You got a new car. What happened to the Buick?"

Willard barely raised his eyes. "I got rid of it. I like to change things around." He stuck another wedge of pancake in his mouth, then asked, "So what brings you here?"

"Mom told me," Elvis said. "She gave me the history. I wanted to get acquainted with her."

"Well, now you know. You started life wrong and it goes to show."

"Goes to show what?"

"You can't make a silk purse out of a cow's ear."

"Trev!" Lorraine said, giving him a playful swat with her spatula. "What a thing to say."

"I was putting it nicely," Willard said. "Whaddya think that makes me?"

Lorraine gave a sudden screech. "Oh, you scared me!" Amber had arrived silently, barefoot in her purple pajamas, her hair in tangles. "Sit down, honey, and have some pancakes. You want some coffee?"

Amber did not move; she was half asleep. "Trev," Lorraine said, "this is your granddaughter, Amber. You haven't met, have you?"

Willard looked up from his plate, surveyed Amber up and down, and said, "You're quite a looker. Pleased to meet you."

Elvis saw what his father had noticed. Amber was, indeed, quite beautiful. She didn't need makeup. "I'm trying to talk Amber into moving down to Santa Rosa," he said.

"From where?" Willard asked without looking up. He had gone back to his breakfast.

"She's in Ukiah," Elvis said. "She's got a good job, but I think she could do better in Santa Rosa."

His father merely grunted.

The others came in: Liz and Alan, still in their pajamas, and Angel, bright from a shower, her hair in a towel, but otherwise dressed. Everybody got introduced, and they took some time establishing that Liz and Alan were Amber's aunt and uncle. Amber found this hard to understand, since she was older than they. *She has never had any family*, Elvis thought.

Willard didn't say much to anybody while he ate. Elvis watched him, wondering if he was about to explode. Leaving his plate on the table, Willard got up and sashayed out of the room. Elvis followed him.

"You taking off?" he asked when he got to the front door and saw where Willard was heading.

"What does it look like?" Willard was already opening the door to his car.

Elvis pulled back just before he said something he would regret. He held his peace as Willard backed out, then spun his wheels on the gravel. A feeling of sadness enveloped Elvis. Still, he had held his tongue. That had to be the first time, ever. It was not much, but it was something.

* * *

The ride home was quiet. They sat in a row, Amber on the passenger window. She had opted for togetherness rather than taking the back seat, which was full of Elvis's junk. Angel acted really nice to Amber, asking her what she had thought of her new family. What had she noticed about Liz and Alan and Lorraine: did she think they were nice? About Willard, she didn't ask, which jumped out to Elvis.

Just as they passed the Bigfoot Trading Post, north of Garberville, Amber sat up straight and asked Elvis if she could ask him a question.

"Dad," she said, "you think you are ever going to be able to stop using?"

Panic flooded him. He glanced over at her; she had her head turned away.

"What do you mean?" he said to buy time. She didn't even bother answering.

"Go ahead," Angel said. "I want to hear this myself."

"All right," he said. "If I have to be perfectly honest, I'll have to say, I don't know. I've made a lot of resolutions in my life. Sooner or later, though, the stuff has always defeated me. So I don't honestly know.

"I do want to quit, with all my heart. I can tell you that. I want to. The stuff has defeated me, but it hasn't pinned me. I've fallen, but I've always been able to get back up again." He choked unexpectedly. It surprised him how emotional he felt. "With a lot of help. Let me say that. With a lot of help from Angel. I don't know if I would be alive without her. And you know, she is committed to helping me. I'm in her program now.

"I've had a lot of help, from her, and from AA, and from the mission, and sometimes from random strangers who took pity on me. From my church, too. They're definitely not random strangers to me; they are my family."

"Not family like us," Amber said.

"No, not like you. But more than some of my blood family. More than most of my blood family. As you saw today, I think."

"I'm curious," Angel asked, "how you felt about seeing your mother. You were acting like that would be magic for you."

The question made him sad. They rattled down the highway. He wanted to think before answering, for once in his life.

"It wasn't really magic," he said. "I think she's a nice woman. Pretty down-to-earth. Patient. She has to be patient, living with Willard. She's been ground down, I think. She really wanted to see me, maybe as much as I wanted to see her. But there's no magic."

He thought some more. "She smokes, you know. That kinda surprised me."

"Everybody smokes," Amber said.

"I don't," he said. "Not anymore."

Without realizing it, Elvis had slowed down, distracted from the gas pedal by his emotions. Now he speeded up again and watched the forest trees stream past.

"So how are you going to do it?" Amber said. "What's going to work for you?"

"You sound like you know something about this stuff," Elvis said.

"It's something you come across," Amber answered. "If you live in Ukiah."

"If you live anywhere is more like it," he said. "I bet there's more addicts than you will ever know, hiding. Truthfully, that's the biggest thing I can say about my recovery. I'm not hiding. Step One. 'We admitted we were powerless, and that our lives have become unmanageable.' I'm signed on to that. I'm pretty sure I have got that one down. Now I have to keep moving. I'm working on Step Four. Do you know what that is?"

She said yeah, she did.

"You really have learned some of this stuff, then. It's a hard step. I've never done it. I'm going to, though. I have to trust God that somehow if I commit myself, I can succeed. I've never done that, but I'm going to do it."

"With a little help from your friends," Angel said.

"Yeah," he said. "I need all the help I can get."

## ACKNOWLEDGEMENTS

I relied on friends and family to read drafts of this novel and give me feedback. I want to thank my wife, Popie, and my children, Katie, Chase and Silas, as well as my daughter-in-law Helen. They all took time to read unfinished work in unfinished formats, which most people don't find to be that much fun. They were very helpful, as were my sister Kathy Sutherland and my friends Dean Anderson, Jill Bolinder, Joyce Denham, Robert Digitale, Joy Fargo, Mike Fargo, Paul Gullixson, Peter Lundstrom, and Haron Wachira. It is wonderful to have such generous and insightful people in my life.

I also want to thank the Redwood Gospel Mission, where as a volunteer I encounter drug addiction every week, and where I have made great friends with men struggling against it. I deeply appreciate the staff at the mission, who are dedicated to those men (and women, in another program), and who support me in my volunteering even though it means having a writer in their midst.

Made in the USA
Monee, IL
16 November 2021